His grin faded ... stand close an... ...er gut instinct ye... ...ot to leave. He should leave, though.

"I should go."

"Yes."

Neither one of them moved.

Lucy breathed a wry, awkward laugh. He reacted with more heat going into his eyes. The awkwardness fell away and suddenly it became incredibly important to her to explore where this would lead.

He took a single step toward her. She lifted her head, his face close to hers. Her skin flushed and a shaky breath eased out of her. His face lowered, maybe an inch. His gaze fluttered from her mouth to her eyes, where it stayed. And then as quickly as the heat had rushed upon them, he withdrew and stepped back.

"Good night," he said, and walked out the door.

Lucy went there and turned the dead bolt, resting her forehead against the wood until her heart calmed and the excitement of Thad kissing her reduced to a warm memory.

Dear Reader,

Continuities are one of my favorite types of books to write. There's always something titillating going on, and the stories span more than one book. In this second installation of The Adair Legacy, I am fortunate to have Thad Winston as my hero. He's a crime scene investigator who's in the thick of an assassination attempt and a struggle with his feelings for Lucy Sinclair.

Other than weaving the tale of Thad and Lucy's love, one of my favorite parts of writing this book was tossing a character like Sophie into the mix. She challenges Thad's ideals and enriches his relationship with Lucy. See if you agree!

Jennifer Morey

EXECUTIVE PROTECTION

—

Jennifer Morey

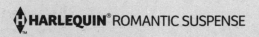
HARLEQUIN® ROMANTIC SUSPENSE

Special thanks and acknowledgment are given to
Jennifer Morey for her contribution to
The Adair Legacy miniseries.

Recycling programs
for this product may
not exist in your area.

ISBN-13: 978-0-373-27870-1

EXECUTIVE PROTECTION

Copyright © 2014 by Harlequin Books S.A.

Printed in U.S.A.

JENNIFER MOREY

Two-time 2009 RITA® Award nominee and a Golden Quill win-ner for Best First Book for *The Secret Soldier,* Jennifer Morey writes contemporary romance and romantic suspense. Project manager *par jour,* she works for the space systems segment of a satellite imagery and information company. She lives in sunny Denver, Colorado. She can be reached through her website, www.jennifermorey.com, and on Facebook.

To Susan LeDoux and Laura Leonard
for their ever dependable proofing.

Chapter 1

Thadius Winston left the muggy, late-February air and stepped into the Raleigh, North Carolina, police department. Bright fluorescent lights shone over the reception area, closed off to the rest of the station. Gladys saw him from her post behind the desk straight ahead and gave him her customary once-over. She'd been after him for a couple of months now. And though he never encouraged her, she hadn't gotten the hint he wasn't interested, and he wouldn't hurt her by telling her.

"Mornin', Thad," she greeted, flirting again. Maybe it was her nature. Maybe she flirted with all the cops.

She wore a lot of makeup. Blue eye shadow, heavy mascara, caked-on foundation that embedded in the wrinkles forming around her eyes and mouth. She dyed her hair blond and used too much hairspray. Hurricane force wind wouldn't ruin her style for the day.

He'd heard her husband had left her for someone younger. She was about twenty years older than Thad. If it made her feel good to flirt with younger men, what harm did that do? It sometimes made his stomach turn, but he could tolerate a few moments of discomfort every now and then.

"Good morning, Gladys. Is Darcy Jenkins in yet?" He always kept their interaction to business.

"Yes, he is, handsome. He's waiting for you in the first conference room."

Slipping the lanyard holding his badge over his neck, he nodded his thanks and strode to the double glass doors. Entering through those, he followed a sterile white hall to the conference room at the end. The door was open.

Darcy's five-eleven frame leaned over some photos. He always wore a dress shirt and tie with slacks. Never a jacket. He looked up when Thad entered, his thick black hair cut short and dark eyes intuitive and a little haunted, but not from all he'd seen as a special victims unit detective.

Straightening, he moved around the table. "Hey." He gave Thad's back a firm pat.

"Does Gladys flirt with you?" Thad asked.

"She flirts with everybody. Don't let it go to your head."

Thad grunted a laugh, not offended by his friend's sarcasm. They'd met at the police academy and had been friends ever since. There wasn't anyone Thad trusted more than Darcy. Thad had trained for crime scene investigation. Darcy had grown up aspiring to become a detective. Thad wasn't sure if it was catching killers that had drawn him as a kid, more likely it was the heroism. Reality had overruled. Darcy did the most good in Homicide, the closest to a superhero he'd ever get. Thad was more interested in the science behind solving crimes. Superheroes had never enchanted him. Maybe that was due to the fact that there had never been anyone in his childhood who'd fooled him into believing in them. As with Darcy, reality had overruled.

He looked down at the photos Darcy had studied more than once and picked up the images of the conference room where Thad's mother had been shot.

"How's your mom?" Darcy asked.

As one of his closest friends, Darcy knew how much these photos bothered him. "Out of ICU." Finally. Things had been touch and go for a week. "Doctors are going to keep her a few more days."

"That's good news."

There was nothing good about his mother being shot. Thad should have seen it coming. He should have been able to protect her. There had been a lot of hype about the possibility that she'd run for president. A well-liked former vice president, she was a viable candidate. That also made her an open target for anyone against her views, anyone who wasn't sane. He should have been more vigilant, should have been aware of the danger. Had his lukewarm sentiments toward politics made him too lax?

Thad didn't relate to his mother's thirst for politics. It consumed too much of her time and energy for one thing, and made her skirt direct answers. His mother was a good politician. While he wasn't fond of her chosen profession, he knew her in a way the public never would. She was his mother. He loved her with all his heart. If she'd have died, the grief would have crushed him. And he'd have never been able to get over the feeling that he hadn't done enough to save her.

He dropped the photos onto the table and turned to Darcy. "Anything new?"

"The SAC passed along some preliminary results from the forensics lab," Darcy answered. "Still waiting on some cytology reports they promised, but thought you'd want to see this."

The SAC was the special agent in charge of the Washington field office of the U.S. Secret Service. In a conversation Thad had had with him, he'd indicated the government was being secretive with their investigation. They claimed to be working with the USSS and local police, but as far as Thad could see, they were only putting up a good impression. And Thad wouldn't put it past the SAC to know more than he admitted.

Thad took a report Darcy handed him.

"The bullet is a .308 caliber from an LWRC manufactured SABR," Darcy narrated while Thad read. "Sniper assault battle rifle. Popular for its versatility and grain. A shooter gets accuracy along with a little weight. Not overly expensive. Portable."

"Yeah, and if a guy wanted to find one, he wouldn't have a tough time," Thad said.

"He gets distance, too."

His mother had been holding a fund-raiser at a historic hotel. The twelfth-floor ballroom had two walls of windows, and there was an office building across the street. Darcy had to wait for search warrants to get into the vacant unit that Thad was pretty sure the shooter had used. Thad didn't have to hear Darcy tell him the government had beaten them to it. "Anything on the location?"

"Yeah, and you aren't going to like this part. I'm getting pushback from Chief Thomas," Darcy answered. "He knows we're doing some looking around. Said the government is taking over the investigation. I think this is the last we'll see from them."

"The SAC may know more than he's letting on." Thad verbalized his earlier thought.

"Why would they cut us out of the investigation?"

That's what Thad would like to find out. As a crime scene investigator, he had been involved in gathering all the evidence. Federal agents from the USSS and FBI had been there, of course, and hadn't put up too much resistance. Now they were clamping down, no longer sharing what they found. Why? The assassination attempt of the former vice president of the United States and possible presidential candidate did warrant taking care and being discreet, but Thad was Kate Winston's son. He was also a good investigator. So was Darcy. They could help.

"I suppose I shouldn't be surprised," he said. "It all comes down to politics." Politics drove how the government would reveal progress of the investigation to the public. Local police made for too many hands in the fingerprint powder.

"I'm not keen on politics, either." Darcy gathered the photos and put them in a neat stack. "But the fact is our hands are tied. We can't work on your mother's case anymore…not overtly."

Thad caught Darcy's unspoken reassurance. He'd continue to help him. Thad would carry on without him if he had to, but between the two of them, they'd make a solid team. Darcy had connections Thad didn't, and Thad had the mind to unravel details from evidence.

His mother's gunman was still running free, free to take another shot at her. Thad hadn't been able to protect her. The Secret Service hadn't been able to protect her. The gunman had shot Kate and tried to shoot her again when the first bullet didn't kill her. Agent Dan Henderson had put himself in the line of fire and saved her life. After getting off a couple more misses, the killer had gotten away. Thad vowed to find that person.

Why had someone tried to kill Kate Winston? And who? What reason did they have? Was it just some crazy person with extreme political views or was there another reason? The clampdown on information relating to the case made Thad suspicious.

"I can understand the need for secrecy, but…" Darcy left the sentence unfinished.

"Something about this isn't right," Thad said for him.

"Yeah. Why is it so important to keep it quiet? The chief isn't happy, either. He got into an argument with the SAC of the USSS."

At least he'd fought for them. Thad put the report down on top of the stack of photos.

"He's probably going to talk to you, too," Darcy added. "He's been talking to everyone who was involved in the investigation."

"Always runs downhill, doesn't it?" The chief had received his beating and would make sure he wasn't alone in the suffering.

Darcy answered with a dry grin and then asked, "What do you want to do next? Anything you need me to do?"

"What you do best." Thad gave his friend a pat on the back of his shoulder.

"I'll let you know if anything comes up."

"Thanks, Darcy." Thad turned for the door.

"Hey, you still coming over to watch the hockey game tonight?" Darcy asked as Thad reached the door.

"Wouldn't miss it." His friend was having a hard time dealing with the finalization of his divorce. Darcy was too much of a man to admit he needed a friend right now, but he did need one, and Thad would do what he could to support him.

Thad was halfway to the exit when Chief Thomas appeared ahead of him.

"Winston," Wade Thomas said. "In my office."

Boy, when Darcy was right, he was right. Thad followed the average-height man of a considerable girth. Fifty-three years old, he had thick, gray hair and wore glasses.

The chief walked around his cluttered desk and sat his heavy frame down. The lighting in here was dim. Everyone joked about how Chief Thomas was a vampire. He claimed his eyes were sensitive to light and that was why he only had one floor lamp on in his office and kept the blinds shut over windows that faced the sea of cubicles where all the detectives worked.

"How's your mother doing?" he asked.

"She's going to recover. Thanks for asking."

He dropped a newspaper on top of a stack of folders, the headline reading something about the attempt on the former vice president.

"Kate Winston may be your mother, but she's also a prominent political figure. The media is going to stay on this story until the shooter is captured."

"I'm good at avoiding the media," Thad said, trying to keep the sarcasm out of his tone. But then he said, "Darcy told me you're getting some pressure from the feds." Wade didn't take orders from outside his jurisdiction well.

"They're going to handle the case," Wade said, his voice dripping with resentment.

"I know." He took pity on the man. His hands were tied just like Thad's and Darcy's.

"I'm concerned that you'll try and solve it on your own," Wade said.

The pressure must be heavy for him to push this so hard. "Why so much security?"

"The shooter isn't caught. That's embarrassing for the Secret Service. They told me hands off or else, and I believe them…as should you."

"The Secret Service told you that?" Thad would try to fish for information. "I thought it was the FBI investigators who were keeping things tight."

Frustration made Chief Thomas shake his head. "The rumor mill around here is like a bad virus. I'm sure they're working together."

"But excluding us."

"Don't get any ideas," Chief Thomas said.

"I just—"

"I know you, Winston." Chief Thomas cut him off. "You don't lack initiative and that sometimes gets you into trouble."

He'd taken initiative to catch the man who'd tried to kill his mother. "It's my mother."

"You can take all the time you need helping her recover. I hear it may take her a few weeks before she's 100 percent. Beyond that, leave it up to the feds."

Thad stopped himself from arguing. Chief Thomas was following orders.

"Are we clear?" Chief Thomas asked.

"We're clear." Clear that Wade Thomas could not find out what he and Darcy did to investigate the shooting.

Wade stared at him for several seconds, not believing. If Thad's poker face wasn't working, he couldn't tell.

"If that's all, I'd like to go see my mother," he said to get out of there.

"That's all for now."

Thad nodded once and turned, vowing to be extra careful not to clue Wade into anything. He'd fallen short in that duty once. He'd be damned if he'd fall short again.

Lucy Sinclair looked forward to coming to work every day. She loved being on her feet at Duke University Hospital, helping patients recover from whatever had put them there. Talking to them, getting to know a little about their lives. Except when they died, of course. No nurse she'd ever met enjoyed that part of the job. Today was a good day because nobody was going to die.

Her smartphone vibrated. Stopping on her way to Kate Winston's room, she removed the phone from her uniform pocket and leaned against the hallway wall to get out of the way of a gurney being rolled toward an operating room. Lifting one white New Balance walking shoe, she propped it up on the wall behind her and navigated to the new message on her phone, smiling when she recognized the name. Cameo Harmon. Or Cam as he called himself, the new man she'd met online who had exciting potential. She'd gone on two dates with him this week. He called and texted her every day. A man who gave a girl that much attention had to be interested. That put him on the top of her list of eligible bachelors.

A sales director for a data management company, her first impression of him was that he was a hard worker with a vibrant personality. She supposed he got that from being a salesman. Her mother had cautioned her about that. She said salesmen couldn't be trusted because they were like actors. They acted their lives out instead of living in reality. But Cam was nice and successful—and not bad-looking.

How's my new girl today? his text said.

"It must be good if it puts a smile like that on your face."

Lucy looked up to see Thad Winston standing before her in the hallway, handsome in dark slacks, black leather shoes and a black leather jacket over a lavender dress shirt. The first thing that struck her was how much better looking he was than Cam. Taller. Four inches taller than her five-nine, to be precise. His hazel eyes had a powerful certainty to them. His light brown hair was stylishly messy. And then she recovered. Why had those thoughts run through her head? Why the comparison to Cam? Especially with Thad. Her first meeting with him had been nearly intolerable. He'd barked orders and snapped at her.

"I'm glad I ran into you today," Thad said. "About when we met…"

Closing the text, she tucked her phone away and pushed off the wall. "Irritability is a symptom of the snake flu, you know." She started walking down the hall.

"Snake flu?" He fell into step beside her.

"Swine, bird. Snake. It's the latest strand. Haven't you heard? It's been in the news."

"No."

"Aside from irritability, infected victims get a low-grade fever that they don't always notice, and that develops into a body rash and blisters. Vomiting. Dehydration. And then blood vessels weaken and rupture. Eventually, you bleed internally and die."

"Sounds pleasant."

"I treated a patient who had it. The poor man was so

sick. Barking orders at everyone the whole time. He was the first fatality in North Carolina."

"You're joking."

She sent him a straight face that flattened his near-grin.

Before he could question her further, they reached his mother's room. Two Secret Service agents were posted outside the door. Not everyone was the son of a former United States vice president.

The agent closest to them gave them a nod and stepped aside so they could enter.

"I didn't know it was your father who operated on my mother," Thad said as they entered the room, the door swinging shut behind them.

Before tending to Kate, Lucy turned to Thad. "You think I'm kidding about the flu?"

"I don't know what to think about something called snake flu. I'm trying to apologize."

Seeing his humble face, with smart, sexy eyes looking right at her, a sense of humor lurking somewhere in there, she resisted the softening coming over her. "Why does it matter who my father is? Would knowing that have changed your attitude?"

His gaze traveled down her body and back up, as though he was trying to gauge *her* attitude. "I was worried about my mother. I'm sorry for the way I behaved."

She folded her arms, tolerating him and trying hard not to be affected by his handsomeness and the macho part of his ego that he'd tamed in order to apologize.

"I read about him," he continued. "Your dad. He's a good doctor. Well respected. No wonder you're such a good nurse."

"I'm a good nurse because of who my father is?"

He missed her rising temper. "He must have been a great role model. Is he the reason you're here?"

She scoffed. "Yes. Yes, that's it exactly. I'm a good nurse because I'm Dr. Sinclair's daughter. There's no other reason for it. How would I have gotten this job if it weren't for my father?"

He eyed her peculiarly. "I'm detecting a note of sarcasm."

"If you like my dad so much, why don't you go and tell him yourself?" With that, she turned and saw Kate Winston watching them.

She had been moved from the intensive care unit yesterday and would be held in recovery for a few more days, possibly a week. She was lucky to be recovering from a gunshot wound to her abdomen. She was still weak, but alert and observant. Lucy would rather she didn't observe her with Thad.

"You aren't close to your father?" Thad asked.

"I'm very close to my father." She checked her vitals and IV fluids. The oversized blue hospital gown didn't suit such a dynamo. She had short brown hair with a hint of graying at the temples, wasn't tall at five-five and had a petite frame. It was a miracle the bullet hadn't killed her.

"How are you feeling today, Ms. Winston?" Lucy asked.

Her clever, light sapphire eyes turned from her son, who'd moved to the other side of the bed. "Better than I was the day I was rolled in here. Call me Kate."

Lucy had to look at Kate again to make sure she'd heard right. The potential presidential candidate was asking her to call her by her first name?

"Lucy is a fine nurse, Thad. That has nothing to do

with who her father is, although I believe I do owe him my life." She struggled to sit up more. Lucy helped her.

"I didn't mean to imply—" Thad started.

"Do you need anything?" Lucy asked Kate, going to the clipboard on the built-in desk to jot down some notes.

"Yes. I need my son to find a girl like you."

Lucy turned in her surprise. "You must be feeling better," she quipped. "I don't think your son can handle a woman like me."

Thad's brow rose as they spoke as though he weren't there.

"Au contraire, my dear. He needs someone who isn't afraid to call him to task when he's being politically incorrect."

What if she was the one who was incorrect? She glanced at him standing there so comfortable in his skin while enduring what she and his mother were saying.

She did get defensive when people implied that bragging rights belonged to her father when it came to her abilities. It was the only complaint she had about her father—her whole family for that matter.

"Most women are all too eager for a chance to marry Kate Winston's son. Little do they know he's altar-shy."

"Mother…"

Kate laughed softly and then coughed with a wince.

Thad went to her side and held her hand. "Take it easy. Don't try to talk too much."

Lucy watched the care he had for his mother. Altarshy, huh? Too bad. She studied his strong hands and from there his arms and face, profiled with chiseled features. Nose. Jaw. Eyes. Everything about him was sexy. But he wasn't what she was looking for.

Why was she even considering that? Flustered over

her reaction, she put down the clipboard. "Press the button if you need me. I'm here until three today."

"Thank you, Lucy," Kate said. "Don't give up on Thad, okay?"

Give up on Thad? She glanced back over her shoulder and saw Kate's wily smile. Even in her weakened state she was shrewd and perceptive. How had she picked up on the undercurrents between her and Thad? They were subtle, especially to Lucy. Sure, he was great to look at, but not a dating option.

He stood by the bed, watching her. Or was he waiting for a reply to Kate's comment?

This was too much. Leaving the room, she heard footsteps hurrying to catch up to her.

"Lucy."

Lucy kept walking and he caught up to her.

"I… Look, we got off on the wrong foot before, and…" He struggled for what to say. What did he mean to say? Why had he come after her?

She stopped and faced him. "Are you here to see your mother or me?"

"My mother, but that could be about to change." He grinned.

Was he flirting with her? When unexpected heat flashed in response, a welcoming response, she couldn't gather her wits. She took in his hazel eyes that now held a little mischief, and a mouth she suddenly found kissable.

What on earth was going on?

"Would you like to go out for a drink later?" he asked.

A date? With Mr. Altar-shy? While her heart urged her to say yes, her much smarter defenses rose up to protect her. As sexy as he was, he would be a waste of time.

Her cell phone vibrated in her pocket, offering a diversion. She saw Cam had sent her another text, this one asking her what she was doing later.

Lucy showed him her phone. "I have a boyfriend."

Thad looked at her phone and then those clever eyes shifted back to her. "Is it serious? 'How's my new girl' doesn't sound serious."

Lucy replied to Cam, agreeing to dinner tonight. "Not yet, but it could get to that point." Finished with the text, she noticed Thad's amusement. Far from intimidated, he was about to pursue her. She sensed it.

"How long have you known him?" he asked.

He had to know it wasn't long. But she played along. "Almost a week."

"I just broke up with someone I saw for that long."

She tucked her phone back into her pocket. "What happened? Did she start talking about marriage and babies?"

"Don't listen to my mother."

"Is it true?"

"That I'm altar-shy?" He cocked his head. "I wouldn't say 'shy,' but I do question the ideology of marriage."

"You don't believe in it?"

"Let's just say I've seen too many people fooled by the illusion."

"Have you ever been married?"

"No."

Then how could he know if marriage was an illusion? What made him view it so negatively? She couldn't afford to care.

She leaned so that her face was close to his. "I joined an online dating site so that I could find a man to marry and have babies with."

The way his head moved back a bit, she thought he may have flinched.

"I'm twenty-nine," she said. "I want babies by the time I'm thirty-two or thirty-three." If that didn't scare him away, nothing would. This attraction they seemed to have stirred up made her uneasy. His idea of love and family was the opposite of hers.

"You have it all figured out."

"It's called plans. I have *plans* for my future." What kind of plans did he have? None? He'd romance women his entire life?

Why did going out with him tempt her still? It had to be the masculine aura about him, the inner strength and confidence. And, of course, those green-gold hazel eyes and hard, strong body.

"Aren't you thirty-two?" She had to put an end to this crazy attraction that made no sense.

"Yes. How did you know my age?"

"Do you ever plan on settling down?" she asked instead of answering.

"Did some reading on me, huh?" he said, dodging her question.

Caught, she didn't respond. She'd been curious enough to look him up online. Why would she do that if she wasn't interested enough to go out on a date with him?

"Nothing is private with a mother like mine," he said with a hint of teasing.

"That bothers you?" *Stop trying to get to know him,* she inwardly chided herself.

"Immensely."

His tone sounded full of humor but she could tell he was being honest. He obviously loved his mother despite the shortcomings of her being a notable politician. He'd been fiercely protective of her when she'd first arrived at the hospital. And helpless. He'd feared for his mother's life and could do nothing to save her. He'd had to leave her in the hands of doctors. Were it not for seeing that, she'd have thought he was a complete jerk.

He must be capable of love, and maybe that was what prevented her from easily rejecting him. For a moment she imagined taking a chance on him. His eyes darkened as he noticed the change in her.

Snapping herself out of that daydream, she cleared her throat and stepped back, tucking a few strands of dark hair that had escaped her ponytail behind her ear.

"I should get back to work," she said.

They both turned their heads toward some movement outside Kate's hospital room door. A black-haired man wearing a hat walked down the hall and stopped, looking at the agents and the open door. He was shorter than Thad, but taller than Lucy. One of the Secret Service agents had noticed, too, and was walking toward the man.

The man spotted him and started down the hall toward the exit. He passed Lucy and Thad. Thad started after him. The Secret Service agent put up his hand.

"I've got this."

Thad followed him to a stairwell. Lucy trailed behind. Down three flights of stairs to the lobby, she stopped beside Thad and watched the Secret Service agent run outside.

The man was gone.

Chapter 2

"Can you believe that she cheated on me?"

Feet up on an ottoman, bowl of popcorn on his lap and a beer on the side table, Thad munched as he watched the hockey player ram into the wall as he tried to take the puck.

"Did you hear me?" Darcy asked.

"Yes." But Darcy had mentioned his ex-wife's many trysts several times now. And Thad was distracted by thoughts of Lucy. He couldn't get her out of his mind. Lucy with her long, auburn hair in a ponytail, thick and swaying and begging for someone to free it from its grip. Clear, light green eyes so full of life and humor. She was infectious. And she had a body that was impossible to ignore, tall and slim, well-proportioned breasts that pushed out her uniform top every once in a while.

"You're normally more enthusiastic about sports.

Didn't you see that hit?" Darcy paused in his self-pity long enough to comment. His divorce was final today and this was his way of celebrating; invite his best friend over for the hockey game, drink beer and whine about how he had discovered his wife was a cheater.

She'd bought out his half of the house and Darcy had bought this one, a smaller bachelor pad with a pool table in the dining room and two of the three bedrooms empty. There was nothing on the walls in the living room and most of the decorating money went into the leather furniture and big-screen TV.

"I feel like such a fool," Darcy said.

"How could you have known?" Thad asked, trying to be a good friend but wishing Darcy would hurry up and get past it.

"Wasn't I…you know…enough for her?" The black leather of the sofa squeaked as Darcy leaned over for his beer.

"Some people are just that way. They look for other people and don't care about how the one they're with will feel." He hoped Darcy wasn't going to need reassurance that he wasn't bad in bed.

"Yeah, but why'd she marry me if she wasn't sure she wanted me?"

"She probably didn't know what she wanted. She still probably doesn't."

Darcy took a swig of beer. The hockey game went to commercial.

"I should have listened to you," Darcy said, sipping some beer again.

"Are you going to get drunk?" Should he be concerned?

Darcy put the beer down. "You warned me this would happen."

"All I said was half of all marriages fail and that I didn't want to contribute to that statistic."

"And now I am. I'm never getting married again. Everybody I know is divorced. That statistic is probably wrong. It's probably more than half that fail."

Thad looked over at his friend and wondered if he really meant he'd never marry again. He was sure marriage wasn't for him, but it might be for Darcy.

"Just because your first one didn't last doesn't mean your next one won't." He didn't want to taint Darcy's outlook on love. He had to make up his own mind about what suited him and his life. He couldn't go by Thad's opinion.

Darcy grunted. "I thought my now-ex-wife was the love of my life until she dropped the bomb on me over hamburgers and French fries. It was one of my rare nights off. I thought we were on our way to a romantic evening. A little dinner. A little wine. Go to bed early. You know? And then she hits me with 'I have a new lover. Move out.'"

"Yeah, that's rough." The hockey game came back on.

"What's with you changing your tune on marriage?" Darcy asked.

"I haven't changed my tune."

"You just encouraged me to try again."

Thad took a handful of popcorn and passed the buttery bowl to Darcy. Women cried and ate chocolate. Men watched sports, drank beer and ate popcorn.

"What's up with that?" Darcy pressed. "You meet a girl?"

"No," he answered defensively, and Darcy noticed.

"Who is she?" Darcy grinned. "I have to meet the woman who made you start softening up on marriage."

"I haven't softened. I'm never getting married or having kids. That hasn't changed." Lucy wanted both. Marriage and kids. She'd be dangerous to get involved with.

Darcy eyed him as he munched on a handful of popcorn, not believing him. Had meeting Lucy made him fantasize that marriage wasn't as harmful as he originally thought?

No. He barely knew Lucy. She was sexy and opinionated and determined to procreate, but she hadn't affected him that much. He'd just have to be careful that she never did.

"You'll have to keep me posted on that, Thad. Let me know if you start dating this mystery woman."

"I didn't meet anyone I want to date."

"That nurse is pretty hot. You notice her?"

Thad looked over at him, amazed at how intuitive he was. It must be the detective in him.

"Aha. It's the nurse!"

"I'm glad that's working to get your mind off your ex."

Darcy chuckled and put the bowl aside. "How's your mom doing?" Darcy asked.

Thank God. He'd stopped talking about Lucy. "Much better. I need to make plans for when she comes home. She's got a long recovery ahead of her."

"After being shot like that I'm not surprised."

Darcy had come to visit her a couple of times when she was in the ICU. He'd joined in on a lot of family functions over the years.

"There was a man at the hospital today," Thad said. "He left when the Secret Service agents saw him and tried to talk to him. I think he ran out of the hospital."

"Really?" Darcy looked concerned. "Did the agents chase him?"

"Only to the front lobby. He was gone by then."

Darcy took a while to respond, thinking it all through. "Do you think he was trying to get close to your mother?"

"That's what it looked like."

"That's strange. Why go out in the open like that?"

Why, indeed.

Lucy had fun getting ready for her date. She showered and took her time making herself pretty, drinking a glass of wine with some upbeat music playing. She'd told Cam she'd meet him at the restaurant. Safety first. She didn't know him and wouldn't risk being trapped in his car. He'd tried to get her to change her mind, but she had steadfast rules on dating. She wasn't ready to let him pick her up at her house. On their first date they'd met for coffee. On the second date, they'd met for lunch. Now it was dinner. The serious date.

Her stomach was full of butterflies all the way to the restaurant, an upscale seafood place that had excellent reviews. She'd only been here once before with her family.

Cam was waiting for her outside. She loved that he did that rather than get a table.

He smiled when he saw her, appreciating her little black dress with his brown eyes. He was a little taller than her and had short blond hair. Handsome in a clean, businessman way. It made her feel funny. Thad's face popped into her head at that moment.

Why would she think of Thad now? He drove her insane. And he was a bad choice for her.

"You look beautiful," Cam said, stepping forward and offering his arm.

She looped hers with his, her butterflies becoming listless. Why was she having this unexcited reaction to him?

Inside the restaurant, they were led to a table that he already had waiting for them.

"You plan ahead." That normally would have thrilled her. Why didn't it now?

He smiled as he held the chair for her and scooted it in when she sat.

Was she having some sort of bad-boy episode? The bad boy attracted her more than the sure, stable type? Did her heart crave a challenge?

"Are you going to let me pick you up next time?" he asked.

"Maybe," she answered in a light, teasing tone.

His eyes showed annoyance, just a little, before he caught her teasing and smiled.

"I was thinking we could go to a movie tomorrow night," he said after a bit.

Tomorrow? So soon? She didn't like how fast he was moving this. Calling every day showed his interest but so many dates in one week might be too much. Luckily, she had plans.

"I'm going to my parents' house for dinner tomorrow night."

He looked disappointed. "What about the next night?"

"I work until nine."

"And the night after that?" He wasn't going to give up.

"I volunteer at the Westside Literacy Group. Sorry."

More disappointment intensified his expression. "Do you have to go to your parents' tomorrow night?" He removed the silverware from the napkin on the table.

"No, I don't *have* to." She tried to keep this light. "I *want* to." She wasn't kidding when she'd told Thad she was close to her father. She was close to everyone in her family.

His hand curled around the knife as the waitress appeared and took their drink order.

When the waitress left, he said, "Why don't you meet your parents another time? Go out with me. Besides, if you're tied up the next three nights, that means I won't see you for almost a week."

"I can't reschedule. If I reschedule that means I won't see my family for almost a week."

He didn't like that answer. She saw it in his eyes. They went hard and he didn't say anything, just fidgeted with the knife, which gave her an uneasy feeling.

She was beginning to change her mind about this one. Was he a control freak?

"Your family is very important to you," he finally said, the intensity softening from his eyes.

"Very. I love them. We do things together all the time."

The waitress dropped off their drinks and took their food order.

"Do you want kids?" Cam asked after she left.

She didn't hide her enthusiasm. "Do I ever. Three."

He smiled and the Cam she'd first met returned. "Me, too. I don't care about the number, but I want a family."

"And one wife?" she joked.

He laughed. "Yes. I'm a faithful man."

"Then you're perfect."

He seemed to take that to heart. The way he looked at her, his brown eyes warming to almost a creepy degree, unnerved her.

"What about work?" he asked.

"I would still work." Aside from liking her job, she needed to prove to herself and everyone else that she was capable without her father's influence. She respected him and his well deserved reputation, but she'd work for her own, on her own.

"Wouldn't you rather stay at home with the kids?"

"And be worthless if my husband ever left me for another woman?" She laughed at her own teasing, which he didn't find funny. "I like my job," she verbalized her thoughts.

"I want my wife to stay at home. I want to provide for her and my kids."

His kids?

"I would stay home after delivery. Maybe for about six months or a year, but after that I would be itching to get back to work. I like to stay busy."

"You don't think kids would keep you busy?"

"Oh, I'm sure they would. But I need adult busy. Brain challenge. Catch my meaning?"

His smile faded and his eyes got that offended look again.

"Why do you want your wife to stay at home?" To control her and everything in the household?

"It's just my idea of an ideal family. I make a lot of money. My wife shouldn't have to work. And I don't want my kids being raised by strangers."

"That's understandable. My nursing job could be flexible. I wouldn't have to work full-time." And maybe she wouldn't want to. She didn't know yet.

When she realized it felt as though she were arguing with Cam and that he'd push the issue if he were ever in a position to have a say on the matter, all-out dread brewed in her.

This was not going to work.

Their food arrived, and Lucy was no longer hungry or excited about this evening.

"Part-time would be all right with me," he made it worse by saying.

"It wouldn't be up to you," she said.

This time he covered his dislike. And he did dislike her response. She could feel it in the energy between them, in the way his eyes shifted from his food to her.

"You wouldn't take your husband's wishes into consideration?" he finally asked.

"Would you take your wife's into yours?" She was not putting up with this.

He surprised her by smiling and then laughing it all off. "You sure are a spitfire."

"An independent one." He better believe it, too.

"I like a little fight in my women."

He still smiled, but what he said could be construed as a taste for violence. What kind of fight did he like in his women? The kind that "made" him start swinging punches if his woman didn't act according to his warped script? Or was she reading too much into this, into him? Maybe he was only trying to get a feel for her boundaries. His ego would love to have a woman he kept at home, but that wasn't as much of a priority as love and family. That would be the normal way of thinking in a secure man. Abnormal would be he'd resort to domestic abuse to have it his way.

Eating their dinner was awkward and she was glad when it was over and she had her own car there.

Cam tried to lighten up the conversation by talking about other things like barbecues and sporting events. He liked going to festivals, too. She didn't reveal anything else about herself. She wasn't sure if she was going to see him again.

He walked her to her Subaru and when he leaned in for a kiss, she allowed a brief one.

"Thank you for dinner," she said. "It was delicious." And it had been.

"You're welcome." He smiled, liking that she'd thanked him. "I'll call you."

She faced her car.

"I'd like to take you to a movie when you're free. How about next Wednesday night?"

"Maybe. I'll talk to you soon."

"'Maybe'? Did something upset you tonight?"

She sat in her car, shut the door and started the engine before rolling the window down a few inches.

He looked concerned. "All that talk about working and having a family didn't upset you, did it? I'm sorry if it was too soon to start talking about something so serious."

"It's okay. I do like to take things slow." She meant to keep things neutral for now.

"I can see that. Otherwise you'd let me pick you up at your house for these dates."

"Thanks again." She pulled out of the parking space and drove away, seeing in her rearview mirror that he stood there watching her. It gave her an uncomfortable feeling. There was something about him that didn't ring true. In fact, it rang like a warning bell, one of those outdoor warning sirens cities used to signal evacuation during dangerous storms.

Just before noon the next day, Lucy walked into Kate's room to find her sitting up on the bed. Her eyes were much clearer today and her brown hair neatly combed.

"Feeling better today?" Lucy deposited a tray of food on the bedside table and moved it over to her so she could reach it easily.

"Much better. The doctor thinks I should be able to go home in a day or two."

"That's wonderful." She checked the IV fluids and found their levels right where they needed to be.

Kate picked up a spoon and investigated the bowl of chicken noodle soup. "But he says I have a long recovery ahead of me. I'll need some home care and physical therapy."

"That's to be expected after being shot and nearly killed." Had she imagined the leading tone in Kate's voice? She went about her usual routine.

"Yes, I do suppose that's true."

There were more flowers and a bag of cards that the Secret Service had filtered before bringing into the room.

"It smells like a flower shop in here," Lucy commented, adjusting a few of the vases that were too close to the edge of the deep window frame.

"That's not even the half of it. I've had to donate a good portion of the deliveries." Kate sampled a spoonful of soup. All of her meals were specially made due to tightened security.

"It's good to know you're loved."

"Beats being shot."

Lucy laughed a little. "At least your sense of humor is returning." Kate had been shot in the abdomen. She'd undergone major surgery to repair her intestines. The bullet had narrowly missed her right kidney and a major artery. She was incredibly lucky. "Have they caught the man who shot you?"

Kate put the spoon back in the bowl, her hand a little

unsteady but managing the job. The topic appeared to bring down her mood and ruin her appetite. "Not yet. How is Daniel Henderson doing?"

Lucy had checked on him before coming to the room, predicting that Kate would ask about the Secret Service agent who'd taken a bullet that would likely have finished her off. The gunman had fired four times from a building across the street from her fund-raiser. One had injured her, another had nearly killed Daniel Henderson, and the last two had hit a wall.

"He's still in critical condition in ICU," Lucy reluctantly said. Kate seemed to be attached to the agent.

Her worried blue eyes met Lucy's. "Is he going to be all right?"

"I don't know. He isn't improving yet." She kept her tone neutral.

Kate turned away with a weak sigh. She may have the outward appearance of healing but she still had a long way to go.

"He's in good hands," Lucy reassured her. "The best doctors at Duke are taking care of him."

"Your father?"

Lucy adored her father and he deserved all of the attention he received. Someday she hoped to earn the same level of respect. "He's one of them."

"You're a very good nurse, Lucy." Kate grimaced as she moved too quickly to pick up the spoon again.

Lucy helped her, handing her the spoon. Why had she said that?

"Thank you." She stirred the soup. "I can see you enjoy what you do. And you take the time to do everything right. You don't miss a thing. You care for your patients."

She did care for them. That was what she loved about the literacy program where she volunteered. Helping others gave her a sense of achievement and self-worth. And she met a lot of people. Lucy loved talking to people, the social side of it. She wasn't one who liked being alone. She lived alone now, and frequently talked to herself. Maybe a dog or a cat was in order so she could at least talk to something with a beating heart instead of her empty home.

"If it wasn't your father who inspired you to become a nurse, what did?"

Realizing she hadn't responded to Kate's compliments, and that she had strategically done so, Lucy felt as though she should explain. "It was my father who inspired me. I loved listening to the stories he'd tell. The lives he thought he couldn't save but did, who the people were. He believes in what he does. He believes he's making a difference and he appreciates having the talent and the brains to help others." Lucy smiled fondly. "My father is doing what he was meant to do. He doesn't do it for the status. He does it because he loves it. And that's why he's so good at it."

Kate smiled with her. "And you're the same way."

Appreciating that Kate recognized that about her, she said, "You're being awfully kind."

"Kindness has nothing to do with it. My son could learn a thing or two from you." Kate grimaced again as she tried to sit up straighter.

"Thad?" Lucy went to help her, adjusting the pillows behind her and the angle of the bed. What could Thad possibly learn from her?

Kate breathed contentedly, more comfortable now. "Thad is a very good crime scene investigator. Smart.

Tenacious. But he's also bullheaded when it comes to his personal life."

Lucy wasn't sure she wanted to continue this conversation. "I doubt I can help him with that." Not his personal life.

"You love and respect your father. Enough to want to be like him."

Lucy didn't reply, not quite knowing what to say to this or why Kate had broached the subject.

"It's not the same for Thad," Kate continued. "And I feel that I'm partly to blame."

Lucy opened the blinds a bit more, letting more cheery light into the sterile room. The busywork didn't keep her curiosity at bay. She turned from the window. "Why do you say that?"

Kate sipped some iced tea. "I was home with the boys when they were young, but then I started working more in politics. Buck had always aspired to go into politics, ever since he was a teenager. He was a senator when he died."

"I don't see how Thad's bullheadedness relates to that." So his parents had both been busy. That didn't mean they didn't love their kids or could be blamed for how they'd turned out.

"I wasn't around much. I was vice president and then U.S. ambassador to France. And Buck…"

Her voice trailed off as she fell into memory.

"What happened?" Lucy had to ask. She was drawn in now. She'd read some news reports, but to have it come right from Kate's mouth was sensational.

When she turned sad eyes to her, Lucy felt contrite. This was a living, breathing person. As famous as she might be, her relationship with Buck and his infidelity had hurt her.

"Buck was a fantastic senator who unfortunately had a taste for extramarital affairs," Kate said.

"I've heard a little about that," she said gently. "I'm sorry."

Kate waved her hand, letting it fall to the hospital bed, a testament to how weak she still was. "I'm over it."

"Why are you telling me all of this?" Lucy had to ask. There had to be a point. Kate seemed to be delivering it quite deliberately.

"If Thad seems bullheaded about marriage, it's because he endured the fallout from his father's bad behavior," Kate answered. "The press had a field day when Buck's body was found in his mistress's bed. It wasn't his first affair. He had many and I knew about them. I didn't do anything because I did love him and I was having a hard time working through the fact that he didn't love me the same way. The boys were aware of his infidelity, too. Thad saw what it did to our marriage. To me. I gave Buck my heart, unfettered. It was difficult to overcome his betrayal. It broke me for a while. The press was merciless. They found out about all of the other affairs and that I had done nothing about them. I stayed with him. It was awful that his body was found where it was, but it was worse with the string of other affairs splashed everywhere in the media. I was humiliated. Thad resented his father for that. And after Buck died, he couldn't mourn the way he should have. He lost his father, but he was robbed of mourning the loss of a father. He lost his cheating father, not the man he grew up idolizing."

Lucy could see how that would mar a person's outlook on marriage. "You still haven't told me why you're sharing this with me." She was a true politician, skirting direct answers.

Apparently coming to the same conclusion, Kate said, "I see the way you look at each other. And at the same time, I hear the things Thad says. I know my son, Lucy. He's attracted to you."

Lucy held up her hands. "Whoa." She waved them in protest. "Whoa. Thad is easy on my eyes, but I am not interested in him."

"Because he's opposed to marriage and a family? You want a husband and kids and you don't think he's capable, isn't that right?"

Wow, how had she gleaned all of that? She'd heard some of their conversation, but…to confront her with it? "I'm not even remotely entertaining any such possibility with your son."

"Yes, I know. And I'm not trying to force you. I'm only trying to help you understand that Thad needs to adjust his thinking when it comes to women, and it will take a special woman to make him do that."

Adjust his thinking? Did Kate consider Lucy the kind of woman who could do that? A special woman…

"Thad is all hot air when he talks about marriage and kids," Kate continued. "When he falls in love, he will see how wrong he is. He'll want marriage and children because he'll finally realize that it will be different than it was for me. He uses me as the basis for his judgments, and that's a mistake."

"He also may never fall in love." He could spend the rest of his life believing marriage wasn't for him. He may never get married, may never have children. He may live with someone, even for the rest of his life, but there would always be that part of him that he withheld.

Lucy did not want a man who'd cut himself off to the full potential of love, a man who expected any and all relationships to fail. She was a firm believer that thoughts manifested themselves. If he believed and expected marriage and family to fall apart, they would.

"I'm not asking you to start dating my son," Kate said. "All I'm asking is that you keep in mind the cause of his wrong thinking when you're with him."

Lucy didn't respond. What could she say? If she agreed to do that, she'd agree to spending time with Thad on romantic terms. Kate may claim to not coerce her, but she definitely supported something along those lines.

Chapter 3

Lucy arrived home from her parents' house. Her mom had made her favorite brisket recipe, and her dad had rented a funny movie. Her older brother had been there with his wife and young boy. They were expecting another baby. He was a lawyer and practiced in Raleigh. He'd stayed close to family the way Lucy wanted to. Family nights were the best. She felt rejuvenated. Happy. Content.

What made the night awkward was how many times Cam had text messaged her. Everyone had noticed. She'd tried to keep up with answering them and then finally gave up. Cam wouldn't quit. He knew she was with her parents and he kept interrupting her.

Removing her shoes, she checked her phone. There were six more messages, each one a desperate attempt to get her attention. The last one said, Why are you ignoring me?

"That's it," she said aloud. Not only would she not reply to any of his messages, she would never see him again. Thank God she never gave him her address.

Maniac.

Her cell rang. Seeing it was Cam, she subdued a rush of alarm and quieted the ringing. Going to her front window, she peered outside into the darkness. No cars were parked on the street and nothing seemed amiss. She went through her 1930s era two-story Victorian house and made sure all the windows and doors were locked. Then she went up to bed. Her phone rang again fifteen minutes later.

Another text message chimed five minutes after that. When he called yet again another fifteen minutes later, she gave up trying to fall asleep and grabbed up her phone, mad as hell.

She answered. "Why do you keep calling me?"

"Lucy," he answered, sounding relieved. "I got worried when you didn't answer."

Worried? What was he? A freak? "Look, Cam. I think you're a nice guy and all, but I don't want to see you anymore."

"What?"

"I told you I was going to my parents' tonight."

"I know."

"You kept text messaging me and calling. You've texted and called me about thirty times tonight."

"Not thirty." He snorted a laugh.

"I don't want to see you again. Please stop calling and texting."

He was silent for several seconds. "Are you serious?"

"Yes." God. *Just get lost,* she thought. She normally

wasn't a mean person but he was about to turn her into one if he didn't listen.

"I don't understand. I thought we hit it off great."

"We barely know each other."

"Then why not give it a chance? Aren't you being a little rash?"

Lucy sighed. "I'm not interested anymore. I'm sorry."

"Why not?"

"I need to be able to live my own life without being interrupted every fifteen minutes. I can't watch my phone and constantly text you. I have a life I'm living here."

"I won't text you, then. Come on. Don't give up yet. Let's get to know each other. I'm sorry I texted you so much tonight. I'm just…I don't know…excited to have met you. I didn't mean to freak you out." He laughed at himself. "I can see why you don't want to see me anymore. I'm sorry. Really."

She hesitated. "All right. It's late. I need to get some sleep."

"So, you aren't breaking up with me?"

"Breaking up with you? We aren't in a relationship yet."

He was silent on the other end.

"Look, why don't you let me call you next time, okay? I'm going to be busy over the next few days." Then she'd call him and tell him she didn't want to see him. For now, she just wanted him to leave her alone.

Several seconds passed before he said sadly, "All right. I understand."

"Thank you."

"Bye for now."

She disconnected, not liking the way he said "bye for now."

* * *

Thad thumbed through a magazine, sitting in a chair waiting for the doctor to come and tell them when his mother could go home. His mother stirred, waking from sleep.

"Ah." He put the magazine back on the table.

"You're still here." She blinked past her drug-induced grogginess, growing more and more alert. Not even drugs could douse the fire in his mother. No wonder she was such a good politician. She kept going and going.

"We need to make arrangements for when you come home," he said.

"That's easy. Hire Lucy."

When she tried to sit up on her own and grunted in pain, he went to her. Stacking her pillows, he helped her sit up and lean against them.

"Lucy has a job." And he didn't need her that close to him while he searched for his mother's shooter. "I'll call a home care company."

"I want Lucy." His mother moved toward the side table where a container of water sat.

Thad reached over and put it in her hand. She held it by the handle and sipped through the plastic straw.

"Why do you want Lucy?"

"Offer her the job, Thad."

His mother could be stubborn, and he could see she was going to be regarding this. "Me?"

"Yes, you. Please, do this for me."

"Why Lucy?" he repeated.

"You yourself mentioned how good you thought she is. I agree. There is no better nurse for me. Offer her the job."

"What about after you're better? You won't need a home care nurse after you heal. She's not going to give up her permanent job just because you want her for a month or two."

"Offer her twice what she makes here. And talk to her boss and see that he gives her a leave of absence so she can have her job back when I'm no longer in need of her. If she wants it."

What was his mother up to? "What do you mean, 'if she wants it'? Why wouldn't she?" At Duke University Hospital. She had a great job there.

"Who wants what?" Another female voice joined in.

Thad inwardly cringed as he recognized Lucy's voice. Facing her, he took in her trim shape in the white uniform and her long, auburn hair up in a ponytail. And those green eyes. He could stare at them for an hour.

"Just the person we need to talk to," his mother said. Her energy was returning with each passing day.

"Mother…"

"This is my decision, Thadius H. Winston." She leaned to put the water container on the table.

Thad took it from her and did it for her. If he didn't suspect she was playing matchmaker, he wouldn't care who she chose for a home care nurse. But Lucy…?

"What's going on?" Lucy went about her usual routine in the room.

"My mother is going to need a home care nurse and she's decided that should be you," Thad said. If he didn't say it, his mother would. She was in one of her I-will-have-my-way modes.

Lucy stopped what she was doing over by the IV lines and shot a look at him, and then Kate. "What?"

"I'll make all the necessary arrangements." Thad explained the terms on salary and that he'd make arrangements with her boss. "All you have to do is move in with my mother until she can take care of herself."

"Is that all?"

Hearing a note of sarcasm, he pressed ahead regardless. "Yes. I'll take care of everything."

"You'll take care of everything." More of that sarcasm came into her tone.

"You won't have to do a thing. Other than...take care of my mother." He studied her eyes, those green windows that revealed nothing but patient contemplation, yet he sensed there was more burning behind them.

She folded her arms. "Last I recall, this was my life and I made all the decisions regarding it."

She was offended. He hadn't meant to offend her. Why was she so hard for him to predict? With most women he saw what was coming ahead of time. With Lucy, he never knew what he'd get.

"I wasn't trying to control you. I..." Jeez. What the hell? She'd reduced him to a blithering idiot. Maybe it was that uniform and ponytail.

"What Thad meant to do is *ask* if you'd be willing," Kate said, stepping in. "It was my idea. I'm the one who requested you."

Lucy's eyes shifted to her and her stance eased. She lowered her arms, uncertain now. Would she agree? Thad almost hoped she wouldn't.

He was near panic over the idea of having her so close to him, because he'd already planned to stay with his mother after she was released from the hospital. He wasn't taking the chance that the gunman would try again...and succeed. There was no one else available, no one he'd trust anyway.

His middle brother, Sam, was still recovering from

being held captive for three months in a foreign prison while on duty with his army special forces unit. His physical wounds had healed in the six months he'd been back. It was the mental wounds that needed more time. His oldest brother, Trey, was busy running the family business, Adair Enterprises. He was also grooming for a senatorial run and getting ready for his wedding. That left Thad to step up and take care of his mother. His brothers stopped by as often as they could to visit her, but couldn't be there around the clock.

And now Lucy would be part of that equation, if she agreed.

"That's a very generous offer," Lucy finally said, "but I don't need anyone to talk to my boss, much less take care of everything."

"Does that mean you'll do it?" *Say no. Say no. Say no.*

Dating her was much different from having her living under the same roof, even though it was a big roof.

"Thad isn't the best at diplomacy," Kate intervened again. "A politician he is not." She reached for Lucy. "Come here."

Reluctantly, Lucy stepped over to the bed.

Kate took her hand. "Please, Lucy. I mean it when I say I think very highly of you. You're the best nurse I've seen at this hospital. I need someone I can trust while I heal. You'd be doing me and your country a great service if you agree to be my home care nurse."

"But…"

Thad heard the wavering in her tone and refrained from clenching his fist.

"You'll have your own private room with a bathroom and a balcony," his mother continued. "You can come and go as you please, as long as you take care of me."

How could anyone refuse that plea? Thad had to hand it to his mother. When she wanted her way, she could be very persuasive. But she did have two valid points. She did need someone she could trust until she was well enough to take care of herself, and Lucy would be serving her country by helping her.

Lucy slid her gaze to Thad. "Are you sure about this?"

Not in the least, but he kept that to himself. "If twice your salary isn't enough, just tell me what you require and I'll see that you get it."

"No…" Lucy hesitated again. "That sum is…quite adequate."

"Good." Kate let go of Lucy's hand. "Then it's settled. All we need now is the doctor to tell us when I can go home."

Lucy stammered without saying anything. Shell-shocked, she stared at Kate, whose exuberance was clear. She wanted Lucy as her nurse, and not just to set her up with Thad. She recognized Lucy's skill, and Lucy could see that.

She didn't refuse. She hadn't agreed, either, but Thad would make sure that she did.

Her cell phone vibrated. Thad heard it going off in her pocket. She took it out and read the message. Her brow lowered and her mouth pressed subtly tighter. She also stared at the message longer than normal and then didn't respond to it.

At last, Lucy looked at Kate. "We'll talk about the home care work later."

"I'm so happy it will be you taking care of me." Kate ignored what she'd said. "I feel like I'll be in such capable hands."

Lucy smiled awkwardly, but Kate's genuine praise

softened her. Kate did want Lucy, not only for Thad, but because she did truly believe she was the best choice.

Without further comment, Lucy finished up in the room and said goodbye to them both. Thad heard her cell vibrate again. She stopped in the hall and read it, another frown clouding her profile. Who had just tried to contact her? Was it the same man who'd text messaged her before? She didn't appear to welcome it.

He followed her out into the hallway. She saw him but barely acknowledged him, her attention returning to the phone and her brow creasing deeper.

"Someone you'd rather not hear from?" he asked.

She merely looked up at him.

"Who is it?" he asked, holding out his hand.

"Cam. The man I went out with."

"Do you mind if I take a look?" When she didn't move to hand him the phone, he said, "It's the cop in me. I can tell when something isn't right."

Breathing a sigh he had to call relief, she handed him the phone. He read the first text message asking how she was. And then the second, and then the third. The fifth asked why she was ignoring him.

"How many of these does he send you?" He memorized the cell number.

"I lost count."

"Have you told him you aren't interested?"

"Yes, but he talked to me about it and I agreed to give it more time…sort of. I need to tell him in no uncertain terms that I don't want him to contact me again."

"Why haven't you?"

She looked off into the distance, down the hall. A doctor walked by and then a nurse pushing a wheelchair.

Someone was paged over the intercom. Lucy was oblivious to all of it. She was concerned over this Cam person.

"Are you afraid of his reaction?" he asked.

She turned back to him. "No. Well…I…"

"Would you like me to tell him?"

Now she laughed. "No."

"Not used to anyone doing things for you, are you?" She had a fierce independent streak, something he found attractive.

"It's not that." She waved a hand up and then let it slap against her thigh, a very slender, long thigh. "Not to the point where it feels suffocating. I'm a capable woman."

"What did Cam do to make you feel suffocated?"

"Some things he said over dinner, but then he backed off. It made me feel funny. Like he's a control freak."

And then he'd text messaged her excessively. "I don't like control freaks, either." Women who wanted to control him into marriage.

"I'll tell him tonight that I don't want to see or hear from him again."

Thad didn't get a good feeling from this. "Let me know how that goes, okay?"

She nodded. "I'll be fine. If he doesn't stop calling and texting, I'll change my number."

"You shouldn't have to do that. If he doesn't stop after you tell him to, let me know. I won't say I'll take care of it, but I can arrange to make him stop contacting you."

"I don't want it to get to that point. I'll tell him to get lost." Although she smiled, he sensed her dread. She'd rather never talk to the man again.

"You could just ignore him. Eventually he'll get the idea."

The flattening of her smile and another distant look

said she wasn't convinced. The cop in him urged to protect, even if she wasn't the type to like being protected.

Lucy left work a little after nine and headed for her Subaru. It was dark and chilly outside, having rained all afternoon. The temperature had sunk below fifty once the sun had set. She dug into her purse for her keys. Reaching her car, she unlocked it just as she heard a car door open behind her.

Someone had parked in the space beside hers. She turned and saw Cam get out of a black Honda Accord.

Alarm snapped her heart into a frantic shudder.

He held up his hand. "Before you go ballistic, let me say that I just came to talk to you."

"I was going to call you," she said, not really sure if she would have. She wasn't the type of woman who blew people off to avoid confrontation, but she may have become one temporarily because there seemed to be something peculiar about him.

"I couldn't wait. You still going to volunteer at your literacy program tomorrow night?" He took a step toward her.

Lucy moved back against her car. "Yes."

He controlled his disappointment but it flashed across his eyes for a second. "Are you free the following night?"

She was, but she wasn't going to see him again. "Cam…"

Brushing the lapels of his suit jacket aside, he put his hands on his hips, looking belligerent and on the verge of losing his temper. "What did I do to make you change your mind about me?"

"It's not something I can itemize." Not without offending him. "It's just a feeling." *That you're a jerk—a*

Dr. Jekyll, Mr. Hyde jerk. She'd stay far away from a man like that. "Sometimes it just doesn't work out between two people."

"Why isn't it working with me anymore? We hit it off when we first met."

"Yes, we did." *But then I got to know you a little.* "But then something changed. I'm not interested in you anymore." Even more so now.

"Why won't you tell me why?"

Plain English wasn't working on him. "Look, I don't have to tell you a damn thing. All you need to know is I'm not *interested.* I'm not going to *date* you. I'm not going to *talk* to you. We aren't *friends.* So, stop *calling* me. Stop *texting* me. I can't make it any *clearer* for you!" Turning, she opened her car door.

A meaty hand clamped around her upper arm and spun her around.

"Nobody talks to me like that."

She yanked her arm free and shoved him. He only stepped back a foot or so, anger storming his blond brow.

"Keep your hands off me!" she shouted, turning for her car again.

"Who do you think you are?" He yanked her around as before, scowling like a whining six-year-old who wasn't getting his way. "You pretend to like me and now you're turning on me?"

Lucy tried to wrench her arm free. His grip was painful. "I never pretended to like you. I don't even know you. The only thing I know is that I never want to see you or hear from you ever again!" If she had a shred of doubt before, she had none now.

"You are interested." He looked down at his hand on her arm as though only then realizing he held it and then let go. "We just talked about some things that should have waited. You're interested."

No didn't mean *no* to this man. "If I ever see you outside this hospital again—or anywhere near me—I'm calling the cops!" She turned to her Subaru once more.

"Don't you turn your back on me," he growled, pure evil spitting from him.

She began to get scared. This situation was beginning to feel as if it was headed toward becoming a crime. She prepared herself for a fight, ready for him to grab her again, vowing to slap or punch him, only he didn't get the chance. She heard him grunt. Looking back, she saw Thad pushing him against his car, slamming his back over the rim of the back window.

"I'm only going to say this once. If you don't leave now and stay away from her, I'll have you arrested." Thad's tone was calm but ferocious as he leaned over Cam, a good three inches taller than him.

"Who the hell are you?" Cam grabbed ahold of Thad's wrist that clamped over his throat.

"Someone you don't want to mess with," he answered.

"He's a cop," Lucy said, happy to provide that piece of information.

That got Cam's attention. He stopped struggling to be free and stared at him. Thad let him go, and Cam smoothed his suit jacket.

Then he looked at Lucy. "If we could just talk sometime…"

He kept saying that. And tonight he'd attacked her. "What makes you think I'd ever want to talk to you again?"

"You know. We really do have something special. I don't understand why you're fighting it. We just have a misunderstanding. We can get past this. I promise. You won't regret it." His sick, pleading face unnerved her.

"You're the one with the misunderstanding." Thad reached out and shoved Cam, jabbing his fingers on the man's chest. "She doesn't want to see you anymore. Didn't you hear her? She should only have to say it once. How many times has she told you now?"

"This is none of your business." Cam's lightning temper flared again. It didn't take much.

"It is now." Thad moved closer, intimidating and fearless.

"I don't have to take this from you." Cam took a swing at him.

Thad easily deflected that and slammed his fist to Cam's jaw. Then another punch drove into his sternum.

Cam gasped for air as he went down onto his knees.

"That's it. You're under arrest for assaulting an officer of the law."

Lucy put her hand on his shoulder. "No, Thad. Let him go." This was bad enough. Arresting him would only escalate things and prolong her dealings with Cam.

Leaning down, Thad pushed Cam's head back, forcing him to look up at him. "Leave her alone or I'll make you."

Cam met Thad's fierce eyes and didn't say anything— for once. Finally, he was forced to accept that he could not control this situation, that he could not control Lucy, a woman he'd imagined in his crazed mind belonged with him.

Giving Cam's head a harder shove that sent it banging back against the Honda, Thad rose and stepped back.

Cam glared at Thad as he stumbled to his feet. Thad had given him one more chance than he deserved.

Standing up, Cam walked around the front of the black

car. Over the hood of the Honda, he looked at Lucy with such resentment that it gave her a shiver.

When Cam drove away, Thad went to Lucy. "Are you all right?"

"Yes." She was now, thanks to him.

He touched her arm where Cam had grabbed her. She might be bruised. She'd never had anyone defend her the way he had tonight, never had a reason to need that from anyone. But tonight she had, and Thad had been there for her. Appreciation mushroomed into more, warmth that her undeniable attraction fueled.

"Maybe you should stick to the traditional method of meeting someone," he said.

His logical solution to her scary encounter chased the rest of her tension away. She stepped closer to him. "Okay, Officer. Traditional it is." She played with the collar of his shirt. He wasn't wearing a badge. She never saw him actually wear it. "Does this qualify as traditional?"

"We're in a parking lot, and I almost arrested someone."

Hardly traditional. Just then she realized he must have waited for her in the parking lot. "What are you doing here, anyway?"

"I'm a cop." Giving her a grin, he stepped back and then headed toward his blue Charger.

That was the reason he gave her, but Lucy was certain there was another reason he'd waited. He'd been concerned. And more than the cop in him had compelled him to stay and keep an eye on her. He liked her, and he'd protected her. And, strangely, she loved that he had. Not only because he'd saved her from whatever Cam would have done. If anything, he'd cared enough to ensure she made it home safely.

"Hey," she called.

Thad stopped at his fast car.

She was going to take a plunge headfirst. "I have to volunteer for a literacy program tomorrow night. Would you mind going with me?" She had two motives for this. One, she was afraid of what Cam would do, and two, she wanted to torture Thad with children. What better way to see just how interested he was?

There went that grin again. He had a really nice grin. "Not at all," he said. "What time?"

"I have to be there at six."

"I'll pick you up."

"But you don't know my address."

"I have your address."

Cop. He was starting to sound like Cam, except there was no comparison. Thad's reasons for hanging around and looking up her address were completely different from Cam's. They were two completely different men. Still, she couldn't let Thad's boldness go without at least a little teasing…

"You're not a stalker, are you?" she asked. "Should I be worried?"

He took her seriously. His grin went flat. "No, not you. But Cam should be real worried, because if he ever comes within ten feet of you again, he'll have to answer to me."

Sexy, handsome, protective cop…

The way her heart thumped gave her second thoughts about inviting him to one of her most cherished pastimes.

Chapter 4

Darcy wiped the coffee that had dribbled onto his lavender dress shirt with a damp napkin. "He's got a rap sheet."

Thad leaned against Darcy's desk, looking at the mug shot of Cameo Harmon that Darcy had brought up on the screen. Cam's mouth drew a defiant line, eyes gleaming hatred and reddened from the consumption of alcohol.

"Surprise, surprise," Thad murmured.

"Domestic violence. His former wife pressed charges after he beat her for the last time. Put her in the hospital." Darcy reached for the small printer on his desk and handed a few pages to Thad.

Thad took them. "Does somebody have to die before this guy gets sent to jail?"

"Yeah, he's a real dream date," Darcy said. "Two restraining orders. One DUI. Robbery when he was a juvenile." Standing up from his desk chair, Darcy pointed to the line on one of the printed pages. "Stole a camera from a Walmart."

Thad had seen sheets like this before, and many worse.

"Amazingly, he has a good job," Darcy said. "Nice house. Decent car. He puts up a good front."

"Lures them in and then the beatings begin, huh?" Thad could see how Lucy might have missed what a loser Cam was. "His online dating profile is a real smoke screen, too."

"Guys like that have to fool women into getting close to them," Darcy said. "This one's probably on his way to doing something that will land him in prison for a few years. I wouldn't be surprised if he winds up with a life sentence someday."

As in murder. That didn't sit well with Thad. Domestic violence usually escalated in men like this.

He flipped through the printed pages until he found what he was looking for and put it back in front of Thad. "Lucy met this piece of work online a little over a week ago."

"What are you onto?" Darcy asked, looking at the page. When nothing there clued him in, he met Thad's gaze. A few seconds later he caught on.

"Kate was shot around then."

"But not killed." Thad pointed to the page.

Darcy looked down and read the part about Cam having a military background. Gunnery sergeant.

"He was a sniper," Thad said. "According to this, he has an NRA membership. Gun permit. And I'll bet if we got a search warrant, we'd find all kinds of weapons in his house."

"Guys like that feel big and powerful if they own a bunch of automatic weapons and a few Rambo-style hunting knives," Darcy added. "Do you really think this could be the gunman who shot your mother?"

"I'm not saying anything, but let's not leave any stone unturned."

"He drives a Honda." Darcy chuckled cynically.

"Smoke screen."

"His favorite movie is probably some gory slasher film."

Thad nodded along with Darcy's dark humor and checked his watch.

"Going somewhere?" Darcy asked.

"I'm on my way to pick up Lucy."

"Lucy?" Darcy cued in on that. "You have a date?"

"It's not a date." Some might argue that it was…like Darcy…and his mother.

"Where are you taking her?"

"Not dinner." He headed for the door. "Thanks, Darcy."

"Where are you taking her?" Darcy called after him.

Thad just looked back with a grin. Out in the hall, he didn't escape Chief Thomas. Like the rest of them, he worked too much.

"Hey, Winston," Wade shouted from across the room of desks, wiggling his finger and not looking happy. He stood in the doorway of his office.

Thad looked back at Darcy, who'd stepped out of the conference room carrying a folder with the photos inside. "Good luck," he mouthed.

Reluctantly, Thad started toward Wade's office. Once he reached it, Wade let him in and then closed the door.

"What's with the background on Cameo Harmon?" Wade asked.

He had found out. Thad stopped before Wade's desk as the chief of police walked around to his chair. "How—"

"Don't ask me how I know." Wade sat down. "Answer the damn question."

Thad knew he'd have no choice, given the sound of his tone. He explained about Lucy and her date Cam, leaving out his hunch that Cam may be connected to his mother's shooting.

Wade scrutinized him like the hardened chief he was. "Is she your girlfriend or something?"

"No." Why did everyone keep making references to that?

"Who is she to you?"

"My mother's nurse. She's an acquaintance."

Thad suffered more scrutiny. "Why are you involving yourself in her affairs? She's an adult. Nothing's been reported yet. If she decides to report something about this man she met, she can do so on her own."

"I can't stand aside and do nothing. The man nearly assaulted her in the hospital parking lot."

"Then let her report it."

There was no reasoning with him, so Thad stopped trying.

"Taking matters into your own hands?" Wade asked.

"No, sir."

After another lengthy scrutiny, Wade pointed his finger at Thad. "I don't like how sneaky you've been lately."

"It's not intentional. It's a personal matter. My mother's been shot and her nurse was attacked. I want to protect them, that's all."

Wade seemed marginally placated by that.

"Maybe I should take a leave of absence," Thad offered. "My mother is going to be released from the hospital soon and I'd like to be home with her while she recovers."

Wade didn't believe him. He thought Thad would run his own investigation on his mother's shooter. He was, but that didn't have to be confessed.

"I need you here," Wade said.

Where he could keep an eye on him. "I need to be with my mother. She's got a long recovery ahead of her. She needs me."

He watched Wade consider it. Would he really stop him from being with his mother—especially when she was almost murdered? Employees were entitled to take time off. Wade could find a way to get rid of him for it, cover up the true reason with other documented infractions, but Thad didn't think he'd take on that fight. And fight Thad would.

"You have one month. You start snooping around on the Kate Winston investigation, I'll find out about it."

Maybe he would, maybe he wouldn't. Thad decided it didn't matter. The only thing that did matter was putting the shooter behind bars.

Thad picked Lucy up five minutes early. Punctual. Lucy liked that. She liked too many things about him, a man who didn't agree with marriage. Not that she meant to set out to marry him. He was disqualified from the start. And that's what ruined all of the fun. Cam had looked good on paper but in person he'd done nothing for her. Thad was different. He'd probably look good on paper and he definitely did something for her in person.

Thad parked in front of the Westside Library, an old, two-story building on a quiet street corner. After performing his job to make sure Cam wasn't following them, he lifted the box of children's books Lucy brought along out of the backseat of his car.

Walking beside him toward the library, she was so glad he was here. Last night, she'd been afraid Cam would find out where she lived and come to her house. She hadn't slept very well.

She opened the library door for Thad, who easily carried the box of books inside. This was her favorite part about volunteering for a literacy program. She'd gotten the books from a local festival that had gathered donations for tonight's event. Lucy was supposed to read a short story to the kids, but she had her own idea. Besides, she wanted them to do the reading. That's how they learned.

Inside, she led Thad to one of the meeting rooms. She could hear the kids already. It was playtime until her program began.

She checked on Thad, who looked ahead to where the noise was coming from, his brow low with dread.

"Kids aren't complicated," she said. "Just go with it. Be a kid again yourself if that helps."

"I'm okay."

She smiled at his false bravado and then led him into the room. It wasn't a large room. There were four round tables and a small platform where she was supposed to sit on a stool and read while they followed in their own copies.

Thad put the box down on the nearest table, and Edith noticed their arrival.

"All right, everybody," Edith said, an older, plump woman in a pink dress who was in charge of this event. She clapped her hands. "Take a seat." Parents sat talking at one of the tables in the back. Some of them dropped their kids off and picked them up after the two-hour session was over.

Edith was a retired schoolteacher who inherited a comfortable sum from her mother and who wasn't ready to stop teaching.

The yelling and running around slowly calmed. Boys and girls scurried for seats at the tables, swinging feet and fiddling with the books in front of them.

Lucy had to stop a quick laugh when she saw how Thad stiffened and watched out for small torpedoes with feet.

Lucy spotted seven-year-old Sophie charging toward her. She crouched for the impact of the girl's hug.

"Lucy! Lucy!"

Lucy's heart soared with affection. Why this youngster had taken to her so tightly, Lucy couldn't guess, but it warmed her to the nth degree.

"Hey there, Sophie." Sophie Cambridge was a special little girl. Recently orphaned after her mother was killed in a car accident and her father hadn't stepped forward to take responsibility for her, she'd been thrust into the hands of the state. Her studies in school had rapidly declined, as anyone would expect.

She ruffled the child's thick head of shoulder-length light brown hair. "How's my girl?"

"I read a book!" Her golden-brown eyes were alight with innocent pride.

"You did? Which one?" Sophie reached out for approval whenever she could.

"A red dog."

"A Clifford book? Good for you!" Sophie was behind the others in her class in reading. Lucy was sure she'd struggled with the book. "Did Rosanna help you with it?"

Sophie's face fell, and she shook her head. "She had to do dishes."

Housework was more important than a child's ability to read? Rosanna seemed like a good foster mom. Lucy searched for her in the room and didn't see her. "Where is she?"

Sophie shrugged.

Rosanna had dropped her off and hadn't stayed for the program. Something must have come up. "Well, that's okay. At least you're here. Are you ready for a story?"

The child's face beamed once again, and she nodded vigorously.

Lucy steered her to the table where Thad stood. Sophie grew shy when she saw Thad towering over her, but she sat down as Lucy guided. She'd be good for him. Nothing like a sweet seven-year-old to melt a few cubes of ice around a heart.

"Take a seat here." Lucy pointed to a chair and waited for Thad to register her command. He looked from the girl to the chair and then Lucy.

"She won't bite." Wow. Was he really this awkward with kids? The hero cop had a handicap.

He saw how Sophie eyed him uncertainly and sat down. "Hi."

Sophie glanced up at Lucy. "Thad is a police officer, Sophie. You're safe with him."

Sophie wasn't convinced, staying in her shy shell that had probably intensified since her mother had died.

Edith came over and Lucy introduced him to her and Sophie. The old woman studied the handsome man and then turned speculative eyes to Lucy. Lucy never brought anyone to her literacy volunteer job and Edith was well aware of her hunt for a husband. Helping kids read better was a deep part of her, a part that meant a lot to her. She didn't share her love of written words and belief that all children should be able to read them with just anyone. Reading was intelligence, and with intelligence, kids could make their dreams come true.

Lucy held up the book to Edith. "We aren't going to start with this. I have a story I'm going to tell first."

Edith smiled with her good-humored reproach. "In one of your moods, huh?"

Every once in a while she broke free of the expected and went with whimsy. She began to pass out the box of books, and Edith helped, announcing to the room of kids, most of whom hadn't settled down yet, "Quiet down now. It's time to start."

Lucy took a seat on the stool and waited for the buzz of children's voices to go silent.

"Before we read from the book you each have in your hands, I'm going to tell you a story," Lucy began, capturing the attention of ten young faces. Stirring their imagination was her favorite part. "It's a true story about a girl from New York. She lived a long time ago, long before any of you were born. She was an orphan who wanted to learn all she could about the world." Lucy saw Sophie listening with wide eyes, immediately connecting to the girl in Lucy's story. It's what Lucy had intended. "Imagene Evertine ran away from her mean stepmother and went to live in a library. At the library, she could read all the books she wanted and could learn about the world. She taught herself how to read, and read she did. She read and read and read."

Lucy paused and met each one of the children's faces. "Imagene lived a long and happy life. She got married and had kids of her own, who she taught to read and took to the library where she grew up. Like all people, one day Imagene became old and, at last, God said it was time for her to come to Heaven. He had a calling for her. A job. So after she passed here on Earth, she took over as Heaven's chief librarian. She's still there today, happily making sure all children have books to read." Lucy held up the one she was going to read tonight. "That's where these came from."

Murmurs spread across the tables, and some of the parents exchanged knowing smiles. Thad sat back on his chair and smirked at her.

"Did she give them to you?" one of the boys asked. He was about six.

Lucy nodded. "Yes. I know Imagene very well."

"Does she really give you books for us?" a little girl asked.

"Oh, yes." Lucy nodded.

"She was an orphan?" Sophie asked.

"Yes, except she grew up in a library, not a foster home. And no one adopted her."

Sophie mulled over that, too serious of an issue for a child.

"But she was very successful and happy her whole life," Lucy said, giving the girl more to ponder.

She didn't let her ponder too long. She began reading from the book. On words she suspected would be difficult for this crowd to read, she spent extra time pronouncing them and used a whiteboard to write them out and explain what they meant and why they were spelled the way they were before moving on in the story.

Two hours later, Lucy's mouth was dry and she sipped from a bottle of water Edith had given her. After closing the book, she looked up to see Rosanna sitting at one of the tables in the back with all the other parents. Kids dispersed, meeting up with their parent or both parents, depending on who'd brought them here. Rosanna went over to the table where Sophie sat. She hadn't gone to her foster mom.

Lucy went over there.

Rosanna smiled. "You do such a fantastic job with these kids."

"Thank you. I enjoy teaching them."

Thad stood. "I especially liked the true story."

Lucy didn't miss the way he said "true story" and smothered a smile and introduced him to Rosanna.

"What do you think, Sophie, you ready to go home?" Rosanna held out her hand to the girl.

Sophie didn't take it and stood, turning to Lucy. "I was thinking. Imagene lived in a library, why can't I live where I want?"

Rosanna looked at Lucy, perplexed. She hadn't been here when she'd told the story.

"Where do you want to live?" Lucy asked, keeping her wariness out of her tone.

"Well…" Sophie hedged. "I was thinking maybe I could live with you."

"Me?" Lucy was shocked. Where had this come from? Her story about Imagene? Lucy checked on Rosanna, who seemed hurt.

"The people who brought you to me won't let her, honey," Rosanna said. "Let's go home and make chocolate milk."

That worked to lift Sophie's spirits some.

As Rosanna met Lucy's gaze, Lucy wondered if she'd imagined the somber self-awareness in the foster mom.

Was something bothering her and had Sophie picked up on it? Sophie had never behaved this way before, as though she dreaded going home with Rosanna.

"Come on." Rosanna took Sophie's hand.

Sophie looked sullenly back at Lucy, whose heart melted with the sight.

Thad moved to stand beside her.

Lucy shook her emotions back into line and gathered her purse. "Ready?"

"Everything okay?" he asked.

"What do you mean?" Had he noticed what she had?

"Is Sophie okay? Is there something going on with her mother?"

"That's not her mother. Rosanna is a foster mom. Sophie's mother died in a car accident almost two years ago, and her father wouldn't take responsibility for her. She doesn't have any other family. Her mother had no siblings and her parents aren't alive anymore."

Lucy waved to Edith and walked with Thad out of the room.

"That's tragic," Thad finally said.

He seemed at odds with learning that news, as though it had touched him but he wasn't sure what to do with how it made him feel. Lucy suspected he needed to feel more when it came to kids and love. He probably hadn't been exposed to much of either.

"Is anyone going to adopt her?" he asked.

"I'm sure someone will come along. She's an adorable little girl."

They left the building and walked to Thad's car. He opened the passenger side for her and she got in.

"My mother is being released from the hospital on

Monday morning," he said when he sat behind the wheel and started driving.

"I heard." Why was he bringing that up now?

"It would mean a lot to her if you'd go with her," he said.

Lucy wasn't so sure that was a good idea. It wasn't in her plans. And she never liked it when people made plans for her.

"She talked to your boss."

Lucy shot a look his way. "What?" Without talking to her first?

"He supports you helping her."

She was too stunned to respond right away. Of course her boss had to agree. Kate had been the vice president of the United States!

"Your job will be waiting for you after my mother is fully recovered," he said.

"So I'm to report to your mother's house and be her home care nurse? Just like that?" she finally asked.

He glanced over at her. "No. I'm asking you. My mother spoke to your boss to help sway you to agree, that's all. She would like you to say yes."

Lucy relaxed and wondered if she'd overreacted. She had a choice. She could refuse and go on with her life. Or she could agree and go on a mini adventure.

She looked over at Thad's profile. It was too dark in the car to see his hazel eyes, but she remembered well that they had hints of gold and green. She took in the rest of him, his messy hair that wasn't really messy, his broad shoulders, his trim hips.

That's when she realized he was the only thing stopping her from saying yes. And she shouldn't allow that. So he had an unconventional outlook on marriage and family. So she was attracted to him. She wasn't afraid of falling in love with him…was she?

Regardless, she refused to let that be her deciding factor. Kate needed her. "All right. I'll do it."

As he pulled to a stop in front of her house, a sexy grin lifted his mouth, creasing the skin slightly on each side.

Mesmerized, Lucy remained seated in the vehicle while Thad walked around and opened her door. When he extended his hand, she took it, and he guided her out.

It seemed natural for that moment that he accompany her to her door. It would be old-fashioned if not for Cam's frightening behavior.

"Would you like me to take a look inside?" he asked.

She'd locked everything tight before leaving. But the assurance would be nice so she said yes.

Unlocking the door, she felt him touch her hand when she reached to turn the knob.

"Me first," he said in that deep, gravelly voice that shouldn't be doing hot things to her.

She stepped aside, and he entered. Following, she watched him check her living room, opening closets and turning on more lights than she'd left on before leaving. All of the rooms were small in her old house, but the previous owners had renovated the kitchen and opened the space. Her long and narrow kitchen was visible over the snack bar. Pendant and recessed lighting illuminated white cabinets and dark granite countertops.

Lucy waited in the living room for him to finish his search. It didn't take long. When he returned downstairs, he came to stop before her.

"Did you scare the boogeyman away for me?"

"No boogeyman. Not under your bed. Not in any closet. You're safe."

There was that sexy grin again. He liked being with her as much as she liked being with him right now. That indelible energy wouldn't cool.

His grin faded as they continued to stand close and look at each other, the consequences of allowing passion to take flight settling in. As with her, temptation made him yearn for him to stay, but leaving was the smart action.

"I should go," he said.

"Yes."

Neither one of them moved.

Lucy breathed a wry, awkward laugh. He reacted with more heat going into his eyes. The awkwardness fell away and suddenly it became incredibly important to her to explore where this would lead.

He took a single step toward her. She lifted her face so that it was just beneath his, anticipation building. Her skin flushed and a shaky breath eased out of her. His face lowered, maybe an inch. His gaze fluttered from her mouth to her eyes, where it stayed. And then as quickly as the heat had rushed upon them, he withdrew and stepped back.

"Good night," he said, and walked out the door.

Lucy went there and turned the dead bolt, resting her forehead against the wood, unanswered and unsatisfied desire churning inside of her.

Chapter 5

It was late and the bar was closing. Darcy Jenkins walked there with his partner, knowing the bartender was finishing up for the night. They'd been there earlier when it was busy and had spoken with a few regulars and waitstaff. The bartender was the last one they needed to talk to.

"Time to lock the doors, gents," the man said. He was tall and skinny with thin brown hair that would fall straight to his shoulders if it wasn't tied back in a ponytail.

Darcy and his partner, Kyle, showed him their badges, which the bartender looked at without reaction. But he stopped wiping the bar surface.

"Detective Jenkins and Detective Morrison," Darcy said.

"Yeah," the bartender said. "I heard you were here asking questions. Something about a woman who was murdered?"

Kyle took out a notepad and a pen.

"Yes," Darcy said. "She was killed two nights ago and was last seen here with a man." Kyle showed the bartender pictures of the woman. "Do you recognize her?"

The bartender shook his head. "Naw, man. I was working that night, but I serve a lot of people in here."

"We're trying to find out the name of the man she was with." Beside him, Kyle jotted a note down. Probably something like "another dead end."

"Her sister said she'd gone on a date but couldn't tell us the man's name," Kyle said. "They'd just met. Are you sure you don't recognize her?"

His partner didn't talk much, but he was getting frustrated with this investigation. Both of them feared it would wind up in the cold case files. Kyle had moved here from Detroit to get away from his ex-wife.

The bartender shook his head and resumed wiping down the bar. "Sorry, man. I wish I did. There is someone who might be able to help you, though. You haven't talked to her yet. She's a regular here and sat at the table next to the couple you're talking about. The waitress for that section told me after you questioned her. She didn't think it was important or she would have mentioned it to you. When we talked, I realized who sat at the table next to the couple."

Darcy nodded, a new glimmer of hope emerging. Maybe the woman had heard something.

Right after the bartender said the woman's name, a high-pitched scream penetrated the walls. It came from above, on the second level.

Darcy looked with the other two toward the sound. There was a doorway beyond the end of the bar that must lead to the second level.

"What's upstairs?" Darcy asked.

"Owner lives up there."

Another scream followed by something crashing to the floor propelled Darcy into motion. The door was metal and locked.

The bartender knew where the owner kept a spare key and gave it to Darcy, who unlocked it and ran up a narrow, filthy stairway that turned at a landing and ended at another door. It, too, was locked. Still holding the key ring from the other door, Darcy tried the other keys. The last of the remaining two unlocked the door.

Dropping the keys, Darcy took out his gun and followed his partner inside. The upper-level apartment was warehouse-style. A large open space accommodated all of the rooms. The kitchen was adjacent to where he and his partner entered, living room to the right. Ahead was a bedroom and a closed-off area where the bathroom must be.

"Get off me!" a woman shouted.

Near the king-sized bed covered with a leopard print comforter, the blond-haired woman struggled beneath a big man on a bearskin rug.

"Stop!" she screamed.

The man had her pinned to the floor. A lamp lay broken at their feet. There was a torn red blouse on the bed, a jean skirt next to it. The man had just removed her bra and all that remained were her underwear.

Darcy and his partner rushed inside.

"Raleigh Police," Darcy's partner yelled. "Hands in the air!"

"Get off the woman and put your hands up!" Darcy ordered.

The man stopped and turned his head, disbelief frozen on his face.

The woman still struggled beneath him, trying to break free of his heavy weight.

"Get off her!" Darcy commanded, stepping forward with his gun aimed at the man's head.

"What the…? How did you get in here?"

"Get off her," Darcy's partner repeated the command. He was just as big as the man on top of the woman.

The man moved off the woman, who scrambled to her feet, holding her hands over her breasts, beginning to cry and breathing erratically.

While his partner cuffed the man and told him his rights, Darcy went to the woman, picking up her skirt on the way. After handing it to her, he found a sweatshirt in an armoire and offered it to her. Fright still hadn't left her blue eyes. She was about five-six and in pretty good shape, enough to put up a good fight.

"I'm Detective Darcy Jenkins and that's my partner, Kyle Morrison."

Trembling, she meekly thanked him and donned the sweatshirt first, then slipped into the skirt. While she dressed, he went into the kitchen and found a cloth, which he dampened with cold water.

Darcy handed her a pair of shoes he'd found on the floor, three-inch red pumps. She took them but didn't put them on. Guiding her to the living-room area, he sat next to her on a black leather sofa and handed her the cloth.

"What's your name?" he gently asked, taking out a small notebook and pen from his front pants pocket. Both he and his partner carried them.

"Avery Fletcher," she said, dabbing her swelling lip where blood oozed a little.

She was an attractive woman. He could see that through her runny mascara and injuries. A bruise was beginning to form on her arm.

"Are you hurt anywhere else?"

Shaking her head, more earnest sobs released from her. Her hands still trembled.

He looked around for some tissues. Getting up, he left his notebook on the sofa and went into the bathroom and retrieved some toilet paper when he couldn't find any.

Darcy went back to Avery and handed her the tissue, sitting beside her again. "You're safe now."

She held the wad of tissue to her face as she cried.

More police arrived as he returned to the sofa, along with paramedics. The warehouse apartment filled with uniformed people. Darcy watched Kyle hand over the would-be rapist to some other officers. He was taken away.

Three paramedics came over to Avery. Darcy waited while they briefly examined her.

"I'm okay," she told them, and then turned to Darcy. "Thanks to him and his partner."

Keeping the warmth her appreciation instilled at bay, he said, "I need to ask you some questions. Is that all right?"

Normally when he arrived at a crime scene, it was to a dead body. Sitting here talking to a live victim was refreshing, and more. He wasn't sure if it was the refreshment or the beautiful woman that elicited the warmth, but an analysis of that would have to wait.

Darcy picked up his notebook and pen. "Let's start from the beginning. How did you end up here tonight?"

Her lower lip trembled.

"Best if we get the information now, while it's still

fresh in your mind," he said. "It'll help with the charges we're going to file against him."

Without looking at him, she nodded. "I met him in the bar a few weeks ago."

"You've known him for a while?" He began to write notes.

"Not very well. The first night I came here he introduced himself. We talked for about an hour. And then he asked if I'd come back. I said I would and I did about a week later. We talked again, this time for a longer period of time. I thought he was nice." Her head bowed as she sobbed some more.

"Men like that are experts at making women believe they're nice," Darcy said, and waited for her to regain her composure.

"I met him once more before tonight. We talked all night, and then he invited me up to his apartment when the bar was starting to close. He said for a drink and more conversation. He didn't seem to expect anything."

She tried to control her crying.

"You went to his apartment," Darcy said, helping her. "Here."

"Yes. And he gave me a glass of wine."

"Had you been drinking the whole night?" He made a note that alcohol had been involved. No surprise there. They'd met in a bar.

"I had two in the bar."

"What about him?"

"He drank more than that."

Darcy bet he had. "How much more?" He'd be tested during the arrest process.

"Um…I don't know. Maybe four?"

"Okay. What happened after he gave you the wine?"

If he'd met her anywhere else, he wouldn't think she seemed the type to hang out in bars. She had a refined way about her.

"We talked for a few minutes and then he kissed me. I didn't like it. I don't know why, so I said I was going to leave. That's when he lost it. He turned into a completely different person. He tried to talk me out of leaving, and when I kept insisting, he grew angry. At that point I knew I'd made a mistake. I tried to leave and he stopped me. I fought. He's a big man. Strong. He tore off my blouse and removed my skirt. My shoes fell off as I fought him. I couldn't believe what was happening. And then you came in." She raised her head and looked at him, grateful and full of peace all of a sudden.

She had really blue eyes. Her blond hair fell softly over her shoulders, shiny and fine and thick, only slightly messy from her fight.

"If you hadn't come along, he would have raped me."

He didn't know what to say. He was stymied over his attraction to her. This had never happened to him during an investigation.

"Why were you here?" she asked. "How did you know to come to his apartment? Is he wanted for something else?"

"No." He found his voice and, cleared his throat. "We were questioning the bartender about a different case when we heard you scream."

She stared at him. "Lucky me."

"Yes. I'd say the timing couldn't have been better."

She smiled and then winced when it pulled her lip too much. She met his gaze again. "I can't thank you enough."

"No need to thank me. Part of the job," he said.

"What kind of cop are you?" She checked out his shirt, tie and slacks. "No uniform."

"I'm a special victims detective."

"Special victims?"

"Yes." The coincidence was uncanny. Except he didn't believe in coincidence. "Domestic violence. Murder. Rape...."

Slowly, she nodded. "Wow."

As the chemistry heated between them, Darcy grew uncomfortable. He was just getting over his divorce. How could he be attracted to another woman so soon? Was it her hero worship that was doing this to him?

No. It was her. She was pretty and nice.

Realizing he'd tuned out all the activity around them and that he'd stopped taking notes, Darcy quickly refocused.

"Do you come to this bar regularly?" he asked.

"No," she scoffed. "I came here that one time with some friends after my divorce was final. It was supposed to be a celebration."

"Ah. I had one of those myself."

"You're divorced?" She looked down at his hand.

"Not even a tan line." He held up his hand for her inspection.

"I'd say congratulations but it doesn't feel like that to me."

"Me neither." Why did this keep getting so personal? He was supposed to question her as a professional officer of the law. Instead, he felt as though they were about to go on a date.

"I loved my husband and I thought he loved me," she said. "I found out he didn't when he told me he met someone. I think that's why I lost my ability to make good judgment."

"Temporarily." Her marriage had ended the same as his.

"What happened with yours?" she asked.

"Hey, Casanova," his partner called. "Time to go."

Glad to be spared having to talk any more about that, he glanced back at his partner.

Darcy faced Avery again. "You'll need to go to the hospital so that your injuries are recorded."

She nodded in understanding.

"Some officers will be there with you," Darcy said. "The paramedics can take you if you like." He'd offer, but his partner seemed to want to leave and this was getting too intimate for him.

"I have my car here. I can take care of that myself."

He nodded, and then did something he normally didn't do. He took out his business card and gave it to her—for a personal reason.

Blinking his eyes open, Darcy checked his digital clock: 3:00 a.m. His cell phone chimed the ringtone he had set for unknown callers.

Reaching over, he looked at the number. He didn't recognize it. But it was 3:00 a.m. What if it was urgent?

He answered to the frantic sound of a woman's voice. He couldn't tell what she was saying.

Swinging his feet over the side of the bed, he sat up. "Who is this?"

After a few panting breaths, she said, "Avery."

Avery Fletcher, the sexual assault victim. "What's wrong?"

He stood and went to his closet to get dressed.

"I thought I heard something. And I woke up from a dream." She started crying.

She'd come in the day before to give her statement. More of that attraction had brewed until she'd begun answering questions, reliving her ordeal. Though she hadn't actually been raped, she'd gone through a frightening experience.

Living alone, she was clearly having trouble adjusting to normal life.

"Do you want me to come over?" Holding the cell between his ear and shoulder, he put on jeans.

"Yes," her fragile voice said.

"Be there in fifteen." He finished dressing and drove fast toward her downtown apartment building. All the way there, he questioned the wisdom of doing that.

Avery let him into her top-floor apartment. High ceilings had crown molding. Gold-shaded light fixtures hung in a cluster of three over the living room. There, dark hardwood floors offset a charcoal couch with white textured pillows, checkered wingback chairs across and a gray-and-white-mosaic rug with modern coffee table between. The far wall was one large window and there were two small armchairs with a petite block table between them. The kitchen was to his left and had gold granite countertops and stainless-steel appliances. No clutter.

Yesterday she'd told him she was a nurse at the University of Northern North Carolina Hospital. Not the caliber of Duke, but still ranked high. And she had a bit of a commute from here. He tried not to dwell on the coincidence that Thad was falling for a nurse, too. They were best friends, though. This could be for real.

"This is nice."

She glanced over her living room. "I didn't spend much on the furniture. I just like to decorate."

It looked pricey. "Remind me never to show you my place."

She laughed. "A true bachelor, huh?"

"Big TV. Something to sit on. Bed. Nothing on the walls."

His wife hadn't been much of a decorator, certainly nothing like Avery, but she'd filled the house a lot better than he could. Avery's talent for decorating gave her more of a feminine essence, much more than his wife. Funny how it took meeting Avery to realize that.

The moment stretched on and grew awkward.

Avery was the first to break the silence. "Look. I'm really sorry I called you and made you drive all the way over here. I'm okay now. I just got scared."

"It's okay. Mind if I have a look around?" She'd said she'd heard something, or thought she had.

"No." She stepped aside. "There isn't much. This and a bathroom and bedroom down here and a loft up there." She pointed to a railing that overlooked the living room.

He went there first. She had a desk up there and another artful set of armchairs with a table between. Double French doors led to a balcony. He checked the handle and found it locked. Downstairs, he went into her bedroom. The brown comforter with beige floral stitching was rumpled with white sheets and pillows, a teal throw near to falling off the end of the bed. There was a brown and white feinting couch angled near the window and a brown dresser with beige, round knobs adjacent to that against the wall. He stepped over frieze carpeting toward a walk-in closet. After checking that, he peered out the window. Lights illuminated a swimming pool.

Back in the living room, he saw her still standing near the entry, arms folded and one hand rubbing her arm as though she were cold.

"I feel silly," she said.

He went to stand before her. "Don't. You were attacked the other night. You have every right to be cautious."

She met his eyes as she registered that he'd seen a lot of terrible things in his line of work. He'd seen what rape did to a woman. Some worse than others. And then there were the countless murders.

"Well, thank you for coming over."

"Do you have a family member or friend who can stay with you for a while?" he asked.

"I just moved here. My husband took a job in Raleigh last year." She averted her gaze, but he could see her disappointment at the thought.

"Where are you from?" She didn't have a Southern accent.

"Utah. Salt Lake City. I grew up in Park City. My father ran a bar there. Popular ski town."

"I've heard of it." He liked that she came from a mountain town, small and simple.

"That's how I met my husband. He came to Park City to ski."

And then moved her to Salt Lake and then Raleigh.

"I met my wife at a grocery store." He grunted a laugh. "She was buying okra. That should have been my first clue that she wasn't right for me."

"Ugh. Okra." Avery made a face and waved a hand in front of her nose and mouth.

And then another awkward moment passed.

"Would you like something to drink?" she asked.

"Sure. Might as well make it coffee." He'd have to go in to work after this.

He followed her to the kitchen and waited while she prepared a pot of coffee.

"So, what happened with you and your wife?"

As a familiar pain gripped him, he couldn't answer right away. She turned with cream and sugar, putting them on the kitchen island as she noticed what must be on his face. Regret. Sadness. Bitterness.

"She found someone else," she said.

Darcy nodded. "Pretty common, I guess."

Avery poured two cups of coffee and came to sit next to him, dumping cream and sugar into her mug. "It shouldn't be."

He dumped cream and sugar into his coffee, too. "I don't want to get married again."

It took her a bit to organize what must seem to her a blunt thing to say. She was probably wondering why he'd said it.

"Is this your first divorce?" she asked.

"Yes."

"Mine, too. But I'm not going to let it ruin the rest of my life." She sipped her coffee and looked straight ahead. "Marriage is the least of my concerns right now. It hasn't been long enough. I still need time." Then she turned back to him. "Why don't you want to get married again? I mean, how do you know you don't want to?"

This time he faced straight ahead. "When I married my wife, I felt sure she was the one I'd spend the rest of my life with. I loved her and I believed she loved me."

"I felt the same about my husband. That's what makes it so hard. It's the betrayal that hurts. You were sure, but they weren't and never told you. They weren't truthful with you. That's what keeps going through my mind. Why did he marry me if he wasn't sure?"

"Some people convince themselves that they're sure," he said.

"Right. Maybe your wife didn't foresee herself being drawn to someone else. Maybe she had good intentions starting out and couldn't admit to herself that she'd made a mistake until it was too late. I bet she never really meant to hurt you. My husband didn't mean to hurt me. Yeah, they should have confronted the issue sooner and been open with us, but they weren't. They made a mistake. It's a mistake, that's all. Getting married to us was a mistake for them." She had a soft way of soothing his angst.

"I'm against marriage now, too," she continued. "But someday I hope my heart heals enough to let someone else close. I'll be a lot more careful, but someday I'd like to have what I thought I had with my husband."

"You're a brave woman."

"Give it time. I bet you'll change your mind. Especially if you meet someone who feels the same as you."

Her words rang true between them. So far they seemed to feel exactly the same. Except about marriage. He was dead set on never exposing himself to that again.

Still, as he met Avery's eyes, something disagreed inside of him. Resisted what his mind demanded. And that was dangerous ground for him.

He stood up. "I better get going."

When her face sobered and she glanced around the apartment, he saw that she was still afraid.

"Maybe you should consider moving back to Utah," he said. "You'd be close to family there." And far away from him.

"I like it here. I like my job. I like my new apartment. I can fly to see my family." She faced him, rubbing her arm the way she had when he'd first arrived. "I won't let what happened chase me away."

He understood that. Unable to move toward the door, he waited.

"This is going to sound forward," she said, and he half expected her to say what came next, "but will you stay until morning?"

It was already morning. "Sleep on your couch?"

"No. With me. In bed."

Chapter 6

Late afternoon the next day, Thad met Darcy at a coffee shop downtown. Seeing his friend yawn for the third time, Thad asked, "Late night?"

Darcy told him about the situation he and his partner had interrupted and the call he'd received last night.

"And you went?" Thad watched his friend self-consciously avert his eyes and then his toughness returned.

"Did you stay the night?" Thad asked.

"She was scared."

"You stayed." Thad could see Darcy was interested in the woman. So soon after his divorce, he wondered if it was for real.

"I slept in my clothes."

"What about her?" Thad teased.

"She slept in hers, too."

"You like her."

"That isn't why we're meeting today."

Thad was the same way with him when he'd talked about Lucy. Both of them had met women that had them on the defensive.

"Sorry," Darcy quickly amended. "Meeting her caught me off guard. It's not that I'm falling for her or anything. We just have a lot in common. Talking to her is so easy."

If that wasn't a contradicting statement, Thad didn't know what was.

"She's a nurse," Darcy said, more of an announcement.

Thad stared at him, not liking the insinuation. What was he quietly suggesting? That they both were drawn to similar women?

"What have you got on the shooter?" he asked more abruptly than he intended.

Darcy didn't press the issue. He slid over an envelope. "A reporter I keep as a friend for times like these hooked me up with an agent working the investigation. Said he was someone who might talk. The agent isn't talking to the press, but he might to another law enforcement officer. I think the reporter is hoping I pass along anything I might find."

Thad opened the envelope and took out a ballistics report as he listened to Darcy.

"I met with the man a couple of times, and he agreed to give me copies of this report. It confirms the gunman was in the building across the street."

Nothing he and Darcy hadn't already deduced from the evidence. Thad read on as Darcy narrated.

"The angle of the strike to the wall pins it to a thirteenth-floor office space. There are several empty spaces in the building. It's old and in need of remodeling. The landlord is having trouble attracting renters. The shooter broke into the office. The agents searched it and found no evidence other than some footprints in the dust on the floor."

"Are there any surveillance cameras that may have captured the shooter entering the building?" Thad looked at the photos of the room; it was completely empty. He also studied the photos of the shoe print. The report said it was about a size ten. Common.

"That I don't know."

"And what about the type of shoe? What is it?"

"Don't know that, either."

"Your friend gave you this to shut you up." Thad put the report back into the envelope and dropped it onto the table. It was just enough information to possibly satisfy them but not enough to lead them in any particular direction. Thad suspected that if he or Darcy asked for more, they'd get a big fat "no" for an answer.

"Why?" Darcy asked. "Why bother giving me anything?"

"That's what I'd like to know."

Darcy stared across the table at him as he thought. "The chief hauled me into his office before I left to come here. He warned me to stop asking for data on the investigation."

"He knew?"

"Yes."

Wade Thomas was always one step ahead of them. Every time he or Darcy obtained any information, Wade found out. How was he doing that?

"Something doesn't feel right about this," Thad said. "It's almost as if the feds already know who the shooter is."

"Then why not arrest him?"

"Evidence?" Maybe they were waiting for the right time.

Thad could see how that was possible. But still, this whole thing had a stench to it, and he wished he could sniff it out.

"We need to keep what we learn quiet. Don't discuss this with anyone other than me." Darcy leaned forward a little and spoke in a low tone. "I wouldn't even tell your mother that you're working on this."

He didn't think she'd expose anything they uncovered. She may even be told he was looking into it. And if she wasn't, Thad was more concerned for her recovery. Worrying her with his and Darcy's speculation was unnecessary at this juncture.

"I'll be careful." He turned his attention to another matter that had bothered him ever since the literacy program. "Have you looked into what I asked you about?"

Darcy leaned back, easily shifting into the new topic. "This morning."

He'd found something.

"Rosanna Bridger…" Darcy began.

After meeting with Darcy, Thad went to find Lucy at the Winston estate. He was at odds with how he felt and his instinct to protect the little girl Sophie. Maybe it was her trouble with learning to read, something brought on by the tragic loss of her mother. Her situation touched him. It would touch anyone. He was also doing this for Lucy. In fact, he was pretty sure that was the main driver.

He'd had to work a whole day and now it was around dinnertime. He'd called his mother to check on her and she'd told him he could talk to Lucy over dinner. While he was leery of her motive, he'd been eager to tell Lucy about his conversation with Darcy. And it wasn't a conversation that should be conducted over the phone.

As he stepped into the dining room, he spotted Lucy already there, sitting in skinny jeans and a silky green-and-blue blouse. This was her third day at the estate, and she was sleeping in the room right next to his. His mother again. He was going to have to have a talk with her.

"Mother told me you'd be here." He looked around the formal dining room. Four floor-to-ceiling windows brightened the room during the day. The table was long, with two floral displays on the polished wood surface. Lucy sat beside him rather than at the other end where four chairs on each side would have separated her from him. "Did she arrange for us to sit in here?"

"Yes."

She looked as uncomfortable as he felt, and his mother's meddling annoyed him. "Sorry."

He didn't sit down. One of the waiters appeared.

"We'll eat in the media room," he told the man, who nodded once and turned to tell the other servants.

"They're serving fish Pontchartrain and some other fancy dishes," Lucy said.

"There's a buffet table down there. And a television. A big one." He extended his hand, looking down at the scoop of her blouse, which was casual enough but could pass for tonight's occasion. Had she dressed up for him or the formal dinner?

Keeping her hand and ignoring her questioning eyes, he took her through the house.

"Why did Kate arrange this dinner?" she asked when they reached the basement and walked down a wide hall lined with paintings.

"I told her I needed to talk to you, and she…used the opportunity."

Passing a large wine cellar visible through glass, he entered the media room. Leather chairs faced the television. There were two pool tables, a shuffleboard and dartboards. His favorite room.

The only drawback was that the staff was setting up a table down here. They must have moved it from storage. His mother kept things like that on hand for parties.

While the servants set the table, much more casually than upstairs, Thad turned on the TV and found a college basketball game.

Lucy eyed him strangely. "Background music?"

He chuckled. "Just trying to tone it down a little."

She smiled, a white-toothed, radiant smile. "What do you need to talk to me about?" She went over to the table that the servants had finished setting.

He went to sit across from her. A servant showed him a bottle of wine and Thad indicated it was fine.

"I did some checking into Sophie's foster mother, Rosanna Bridger," he said.

He had to wait out her reaction, first surprise, then curiosity before she asked, "Why did you do that?"

Taken aback over why she'd asked him that question, expecting her to be eager to learn about Rosanna, Thad realized her intention. She wasn't being confrontational. She was trying to get him to admit he might be making a mistake deciding to forego a life with kids and the marriage that came with that.

"She's an innocent child," he said neutrally.

"So you'd do it for any child?"

"Yes."

Lucy looked skeptical.

Thad couldn't tell her he'd done it for her, too. Because he'd seen how much she cared about those kids and how that reflected in the way she gave everything she had to teaching them to read.

"I thought you were antifamily," she said, again without confrontation. Was she teasing him?

She sipped some of the red wine.

"Other families, no. Just my own." He didn't want kids and he didn't want to get married. He'd seen a few couples get lucky and find that rare love that lasted a lifetime. So many thought they had it, only to end up in a failed marriage that ended in painful, court-complicated divorce. He didn't believe in forever love. He didn't believe he'd find the kind of love that would last a lifetime, either. And he wasn't a gambler.

"I might understand why you won't marry, but why no kids?" Lucy asked.

After he marveled how closely her thoughts mirrored his, he said, "Bringing kids into a relationship that in all likelihood won't last doesn't seem right to me. There's enough dysfunction in the world—why add to it?"

"Why follow everyone else into doom and gloom?"

As in marriage and love. Doom and gloom. He ignored her teasing. "Yes."

"What if you love the woman you're with?"

"Then I'll stay with her and be faithful to her. I just won't do it legally."

"Because you're that sure it won't last?"

"I don't know how long it will last. I don't want to risk it not lasting. I'd be glad if it lasted. But I won't risk having kids in case it doesn't."

"People know when they're in love," she said.

"My parents were in love. Every married couple I know who divorced were in love when they married."

"They thought they were," she contradicted him. "They didn't really know."

She felt strongly about the matter. Well, so did he, and they didn't agree. "I don't believe I will ever find someone I feel that sure about."

"People who don't look for it are the most likely to find it," she said.

"Then why are you looking?" he asked.

That sparked a little fire in her eyes. "What did you find out about Rosanna?"

At least they could stop talking about love now. "She's going through a divorce. The husband was recently arrested for drinking and driving and he cleaned out their bank accounts."

"She's having financial problems," Lucy said sympathetically. "Do you think she's going to have to give up Sophie?"

"I don't know if I'd go that far."

With her contemplative frown, Lucy didn't seem convinced.

"We'll keep an eye on her."

She blinked slowly, and he felt her warm appreciation. "How do you propose we do that?"

"We'll think of something."

His use of *we* filtered between them.

"There might be hope for you after all, Thad Winston," Lucy murmured.

Her meaning struck him squarely in the same instant he saw her realize she'd spoken the thought aloud. He had a tender spot for a child and endeavored to see to her well-being. While having a tender spot for a child may not be unexpected, what it did to his heart was.

* * *

Late that night, Lucy gave up trying to sleep. Everything Thad had said kept going through her head. He obviously cared about kids or he wouldn't have made the effort to check on Sophie's welfare. What troubled her and kept her from sleep was his certainty over not ever wanting a family. It was so opposite to what she was looking for, she didn't understand how she could be so moved by his protectiveness. It was probably the cop in him, nothing related to the potential to be good husband material.

She should take his word for it when he said he wouldn't have a family of his own. Why, then, did she feel there was a chance he was wrong?

Slipping into her robe, she left her room, passing a glance at Thad's room next to hers. The door was open but it was dark inside. She made her way downstairs. The Winston estate was a nearly ten-thousand-square-foot palace. When she'd first arrived to the white brick exterior trimmed with black shutters, she'd chastised herself for not realizing Kate would live somewhere like this. Security used the guesthouse during their work shifts. There was a grand front entry and a side entry that they all used.

Lucy passed that on her way into the kitchen. Through a wide archway, she stopped short on the cool, white marble floor.

Thad stood on the other side of a big, nearly square island, his bare chest visible above the dark granite countertop. One of the double doors of the refrigerator was open behind him. He made her breath falter before she noticed him preparing a root beer float.

She tightened her thin, silky robe, making sure the

curvier parts of her flesh were covered. Pendant lights hung from brown decorative tiles trimmed into the high ceiling above the island. Plants topped an expanse of white cabinets and a white-trimmed double door led to a patio, the glass dark now. She was glad it wasn't bright in here.

"You're a late-night grazer, too?" he asked, lightening the mood.

"Only when I can't sleep." She walked around the island.

"What do you eat when you can't sleep?"

"Root beer floats," she said.

He chuckled, a breathy sound, deep and masculine.

"I'm serious." Root beer floats were her favorite. They were cool and refreshing and sweet but not too sweet. While he sobered with a stunned look, she said, "There's something about chunky vanilla ice cream and the burst of carbonated root beer." She kissed the tip of her fingers and tossed the gesture of delight toward him.

He still stared at her. "What else do you like?"

She put her hands on the granite countertop beside him and to the right of the sink. "Leftovers. Cold pizza. As long as it isn't a frozen dinner, I'm happy."

Leaving her briefly to retrieve another frosty mug from the open freezer drawer, he scooped her some ice cream and poured the root beer. It didn't fizz too much.

"You're good at this." Leaning her hip on the counter, she lifted the mug and sipped.

He leaned his hip on the counter, too, so that they faced each other. "I had lots of practice when I was a kid. We didn't go out to ice cream shops much." He joined her for a taste.

Making root beer floats wasn't a science experiment. It was something to talk about. She felt silly, flirting like this. It spawned a thought.

"I rode my bike to an ice cream shop every week when I was ten," she said, and then decided to torture him some more. If one could call it torture. She was starting to think his antifamily claims were more of a product of phobia. "One time I was sitting at an outdoor table with a friend when a boy from school came over and knocked the ice cream off my cone. He was a year or two older than me. I asked him why he did it and he said it was because I was a girl. I waited for him to leave and followed him on my bike. He went to a convenience store and got a slushy. I got one, too, and came up behind him in line. When it was his turn to pay, I put my slushy down on the counter. That's when he saw me. I told him he owed me for knocking my ice cream cone. 'I'm not paying for that,' he said, and then the cashier asked if it was true, had he knocked my ice cream cone off? And the boy muttered something and paid for my slushy."

"Is this another one of your stories? I can't tell. It sounds real," he teased.

Lucy laughed a little. "You can't ride a bike with a drink in your hand so we stood outside. He kept eyeing me and I kept glaring at him. Then a car drove up. A woman got out and took her baby to a pile of wood outside the store. She didn't see us. We were on the side of the store where our bikes were. She left the baby there and ran back to her car and then drove off. The boy and I were sort of stunned for a few seconds. But then the boy went to pick up the baby. I went inside to tell the clerk. The boy held the baby until the cops came. A couple of days later, I ran into the boy in school. He told me his parents were going to adopt the baby and he was going to have a baby sister. He seemed happy about it. I thanked him for the slushy and he said, 'You're not so bad for a girl.' And I said, 'You're not so bad for a boy.' Just like a *Leave It to Beaver* episode."

Thad stared at her for a while when she finished. Then a sly grin inched up his mouth. "You made that up."

The sight of what that grin did to his handsome face captivated her. After she got ahold of herself, she asked, "How'd you know?"

"The ending gave you away. *Leave It to Beaver?*"

"Most people believe me."

"Why do you tell stories like that?"

She enjoyed entertaining. She'd joined the theater in school and had almost pursued an acting career. The uncertainty of at least moderate success had stopped her. That and talks with her parents, who'd educated her on the downfalls of trying to become an actress. They hadn't discouraged her. They'd supported whatever she decided. They just armed her with all the knowledge she needed to make up her mind.

"Even boys who claim they don't like girls end up liking them," she finally said. "The truth always comes out. There's always some kind of truth to my stories."

Some of the slyness melted away as he looked into her eyes, knowing exactly what she meant. He took a step forward. "Why couldn't you sleep?"

His low, raspy voice tingled nerve endings that craved him. She couldn't stop her gaze from dropping to his bare chest, lightly haired, hard with muscle. Try as she might to shut off her attraction, she couldn't.

"Why do you ask?" she hedged. Answering that question would brew more trouble.

"Because I'm afraid it's the same reason I couldn't." The next step he took toward her put him within inches of her. She felt the heat of his smooth, hard chest and yearned to touch him, to feel the contours of his biceps, his abdomen. Rippling sinew dipped below his shorts. Lifting her eyes, she saw that his had grown darker with desire and was sure it was a response to her own.

"Sophie?" she asked hopefully.

He shook his head. Taking the mug from her, he set it down on the counter. Then he slid his hand along her neck and cupped her head. "I wish that was the reason."

Oh, no.

He pressed his mouth to hers. She brushed her hand over his chest, satisfying a burning urge to do so, sucking in air through her nose. Nothing else mattered but this. She put her other hand on him and felt all of his muscled torso.

He slid his arm around her, his hand holding her rear and pulling her against him. He changed the angle of his mouth and kissed her much deeper. Hot, sizzling passion coursed through her.

Moving her along the kitchen counter, he positioned her so that his hips pinned her there. Now his hand was free to roam up her body to capture a silk-draped breast. The lapels parted with his seeking hands. The robe slipped down her shoulders. He stopped kissing her to look down.

Lucy was mesmerized watching him.

He picked the delicate strings lacing the bodice until they loosened and he had room to slip inside. He cupped her breast, his thumb rubbing the nipple.

Lucy dipped her head back with the erotic sensation of his hand on her. He took the invitation and kissed her neck. She felt him push the thin strap off her shoulder. Cool air touched her breast. The silky, knee-length nightgown was loose enough to push the other side down, too. Now her chest was nearly as bare as his.

Kissing her mouth briefly, he bent his head to her breasts. Lucy lowered her head to watch, her hands gliding down his biceps to his forearms. She could feel his muscles move as he caressed one breast while he took the other with his mouth. His tongue flicked her nipple.

She moaned. A modicum of coherency remained in her.

Thad stopped what he was doing and looked up at her. Standing straighter, he was so close and his burning hazel eyes kept the fire in her stoked.

Thank God, he was stopping. She wouldn't have been able to herself.

"Are you going to tell another one of your stories?" he asked.

"Do I need to?" Her breasts touched his chest and her hands were still on his forearms, his hands now on her waist.

As he looked down between them and then back up at her face, he seemed to realized the significance of what had just occurred.

"No." He stepped back as she laughed and adjusted her silk nightgown and pulled up the sides of her robe.

Humor worked to diffuse the situation, but Lucy began to feel dread for the coming days. He would not be her choice in a man. She enjoyed teasing him at his expense on his misguided views on family. They may heat up the sheets, but she was serious about finding someone who could share her plans for the future. She refused to roll the dice on Thad. What if he never changed? Wasn't it impossible to change a man? She wouldn't even try.

"I'll take this up to bed." She lifted the mug and turned. "Lucy."

He sounded serious. She looked back.

Thad stared at her, whatever he had intended to say remaining inside him. "Good night."

She left without replying. Tonight was a mistake. He knew it. She knew it. What they'd each do about it was another matter. And that's what frightened her the most.

On her way up to her room, Lucy caught sight of someone in the shadows of the formal living room. A man. A big, tall man, who was just standing there.

Chapter 7

Thad trailed Lucy, leaving his root beer float behind. As he passed the formal dining area, he spotted her standing rod-stiff in the threshold of the formal living room. Beyond her, he saw a man. Moving forward with quick instinct, he pulled Lucy back and stepped in front of her, catching sight of her wide eyes. Seeing the man had scared her.

The man bent and turned on a light.

It was Secret Service agent Jaden Mayfield, six-three, short cropped brown hair and slightly over two-hundred pounds. He wore jeans and a polo shirt, similar attire to what the other agents wore while on duty protecting his mother, more casual than usual since they were out of the public eye.

"Mr. Winston," Mayfield greeted. "Sorry if I startled you and Miss Sinclair. I just finished my rounds and was about to check the house."

Had he come through the front entrance? Wherever he'd come from, he'd have had to walk a good distance in the dark before reaching the formal living room.

"Do you always check the house in the dark?"

The agent kept an impassive face. "Not always. I like to listen first. I thought I heard something."

Maybe he'd heard Thad and Lucy in the kitchen. Maybe something else had him standing in the living room in the dark as though Lucy had caught him by surprise.

Lucy moved to stand beside Thad, her body not as stiff and eyes less alarmed, still holding the root beer float. She probably thought Cam had broken in. Instead, it had been Agent Mayfield, the man who'd replaced Daniel Henderson after he'd been shot.

"Excuse me. I'll finish up." The agent passed them to leave the living room and presumably check the rest of the house.

Lucy turned from watching the agent's retreat to Thad.

"What was he doing when you first approached?" Thad asked.

"Just standing there in the dark. Is that odd?"

"Just standing there? Yeah, a little."

"Maybe he heard me coming and stopped," she said.

"Maybe." Thad couldn't shake the feeling that he hadn't, that the agent hadn't heard Lucy. Her feet were bare.

"I'm just glad it wasn't Cam," Lucy said.

"Come on, I'll walk you to your room."

She eyed him warily but turned and walked up the grand staircase to the upper level. He stayed a good distance from her, walking behind her and careful not to let any part of him touch her, lest the flames flare up again.

At her room, he stopped her before allowing her to enter and searched the room. Assured no one was there, he went back to the doorway, where she stood just inside with a humorous smirk toying with her mouth and eyes, holding the mug with both hands, sparkling green eyes that he'd sunk into as he succumbed to powerful desire. Kissing Lucy had been the most incredible experience he could remember in a long time. Which was disturbing.

But not as disturbing as the behavior of the Secret Service agent.

"Are you always this cautious?" Lucy asked.

"My mother's never been shot before."

She lowered her eyes contritely. "I suppose I'd be the same way."

He was on high alert at all times. Vigilant and protective. And he'd remain that way until the gunman was caught.

"Good night," he said to her again, the same thing he'd said earlier when he'd stopped himself from saying something stupid like "see you at breakfast." As though he planned on taking her as his woman. Taking her, period. Taking her over and over again.

"Good night," she answered, and it warmed him despite his will for it not to. He wasn't a family man and she'd joined an online dating site to find one.

As he turned to head down the hall, the thought of that chafed him. There would be a lot of men who'd be interested in dating her. Cam had been a dud, but the next one may not be. He may not be a family man and she may not be interested in being with him because of that, but did that mean they couldn't explore something casual? No. Lucy was not that kind of woman. And he was not the kind of man to involve himself with someone like her. He wasn't against living together, but she would want more. He had relationships and wasn't against living with someone. The only glitch was that until he was an old man, he expected his relationships to end. That didn't have to be a bad thing. It would probably be mutual. Finding the perfect mate wasn't easy. People either got lucky or they pretended to be. The ones not pretending were few and far between. That was the problem he had with marriage. And children tied a couple together whether the love was genuine or not. Thad didn't believe he'd ever be one of those lucky people, and he absolutely refused to pretend. His father had pretended and look where that had led. To his mother's broken heart and never-ending bad press.

Thad had reached the living room again and looked around for Agent Mayfield. Confirming he was alone, he began to search the room, going over every square inch. None of the furniture was out of place. Nothing had dropped on the floor. He didn't find any hidden surveillance.

Going over to the windows, he peered outside. All the lights that were supposed to be on were. The gatehouse guard was in his place.

As he started to turn away, he saw the lock on the window was up. The window was unlocked. He pushed the lever back down and tested its sturdiness. All of the other windows were locked. All of the windows but this one.

Thad looked back to where the agent had turned on the light. It was steps from here. Had he heard Lucy approach and had just enough time to get away from the window?

He looked back at the window. Why would he unlock a window?

To allow the gunman access so he could have a second try at Kate Winston?

It was wild speculation, but Thad wasn't taking any chances. He checked the security system and went through the large house to check every window on the lower level. The security system was still operating, and all of the windows were locked except the one in the formal living room. Had the agent been interrupted before he could disarm the security system?

Thad found Agent Jaden Mayfield with his feet up in the library, reading a sports magazine, finishing up his shift. He didn't like the man. He didn't trust him.

The agent's brown eyes looked up when he heard him enter.

"Can I have a word with you?" Thad asked.

The agent swung his feet off the ottoman in front of one of the black wingback chairs and set the magazine down. "Sure."

Was it Thad's imagination or did the man seem nervous?

"I found a window unlocked in the living room," Thad said.

The agent's eyes grew marginally bigger before relaxing again. "I checked them earlier."

"But not tonight?"

"No. I did a walk-through."

He made it seem so casual. It wasn't casual to Thad. His mother's life depended on the thoroughness of the agents protecting her.

"Did you unlock the window?" Thad asked in his most direct tone.

The agent grunted. "Why would I do that?"

"Did you?"

Agent Mayfield met Thad's hard stare. "No."

Thad wasn't sure he believed him.

"With all due respect, Mr. Winston, I know you're Kate's son, but I don't need anyone questioning me on how I do my job."

"I didn't question you about your job. I asked you if you unlocked the window."

"And I told you I didn't."

Thad would check the video recordings and see if anything showed up.

"There are a lot of experienced people working to find your mother's gunman, Mr. Winston. I'll be sure and check the windows on a regular basis and make sure all of the other agents do the same."

Thad decided it was time to ease up. "Thanks. I appreciate that."

With one more look back, Thad left the room, vowing to keep a close eye on the man.

The next morning, Thad went down to the kitchen, where he heard voices. Sam stood in front of the coffee machine, his muscular friend Mike Harris leaning against the counter next to him. The two had met in the military. On the counter were two plates with the remnants of eggs and potatoes. Whatever meat that had been prepared with it was gone.

Sam stopped talking when Thad approached them. He was two years older than him and opposite in many ways. Blue eyes where Thad's were hazel, buzz cut where Thad's hairstyle was longer and less orderly. They were close in height, though.

Thad leaned a little and extended his hand to Mike. "Been a while."

Mike shook his hand. "Yeah."

"How are you doing?" Thad asked.

Mike exchanged a look with Sam. "Better every day."

Thad saw how his brother withdrew with that reply. He kept all that had happened to him bottled up and Thad worried that would have an adverse effect on him and his quality of life. His mom said Sam just needed time. He'd come around eventually. Thad hoped she was right. Victims of violent crimes did need time to come out on their own. It wasn't uncommon for victims to withdraw into a world of silence, at least when it came to their trauma.

"We have a full house." Sam veered the topic away from the seriousness of his and Mike's capture. "Mom said you're sweet on her home care nurse."

First Darcy and now his brother. When would people stop bringing up the sexy nurse? "Mom's condition is making her hallucinate." Or gave her time to be more observant about her sons. And right now, her focus was square on Thad.

"She is pretty hot. I saw her with Mom yesterday." Sam wiggled his eyebrows. "Don't let that one pass you by."

Thad didn't engage. Kissing Lucy last night rushed back to haunt him. He couldn't believe how strong his desire had been, how completely she'd drawn him in.

"Have you noticed anything odd about one of the agents—Jaden Mayfield?" Thad deliberately changed the subject.

Sam sobered. "No, why?"

Thad explained what he and Lucy had stumbled upon and that the window had been open.

"You think he unlocked it?" Sam asked, incredulous.

"I don't know. Why would he? I checked the security videos and nothing was out of place. The gate was secure, nobody was missing in their patrols and the electronic system was online." It would have been impossible to get past security to reach the window last night.

"They let you see the videos?" Mike asked.

Thad did his best to appear contrite. "No."

"You sneaked in and had a look yourself?" Sam laughed wryly. "I should have been a cop instead of enlisting in the army. You're having all the fun."

"Sam…"

"Anybody could have left the window unlocked," Sam said, back to being serious. "Maybe one of the servants opened it for fresh air and forgot to lock it."

That was possible. "Yeah. It's probably nothing."

"I think you should spend more time going after Mom's hot nurse."

The glimpse of Sam's sense of humor was an encouraging sign that he was recovering, but Thad was in no mood to talk about Lucy. Not after last night.

"Having a male bonding session?" a familiar female voice interrupted.

Thad turned and saw Lucy enter the kitchen, aware of how Mike took notice of her, and almost hearing him agree with Sam. Lucy was hot.

"Lucy, this is Mike Harris and my brother Sam." Thad made the quick introduction, reluctant to hang around for the coming exchange.

She stuck out her hand, and Mike took it. Sam received the same greeting.

"You're in the military?" she asked. "I overheard…"

"Yeah, but may not be staying in," Mike answered.

"Why not?"

It was an innocent question, but one that wasn't received well by either man.

"Sam and Mike were both held captive in a foreign prison for three months," Thad explained. "They've been home for almost six months now."

"Oh." She looked remorsefully from one man to the other, resting on Mike. "I'm so sorry. I didn't know."

"It's okay," Mike said.

"Are you getting the help you need now that you're back?" she asked.

A caregiver at heart, Lucy didn't have any qualms about confronting touchy subjects, and this was a touchy one for both men. At least, it was for Sam.

Mike glanced at Sam, who gave no reaction. "We've considered it," Mike answered, seeming to warm to Lucy. She did have a way about her. She genuinely cared and it showed in her eyes and the way she spoke, not overdone. Just matter-of-fact and full of kindness.

"Aside from the treatment we endured while in captivity, we're suffering from some memory loss. I'm not sure how much of that I want to remember, though." Mike again looked over at Sam, who still wouldn't contribute to the conversation.

"Memory loss?" Lucy moved into the kitchen, finding a cup and then going to the coffeemaker. Mike was closest and lifted the pot and poured her some.

"Thanks."

"You're welcome," Mike said like a man affected by an attractive woman.

Thad watched while Lucy's sympathetic gaze softened Mike like an injured bird in her palm.

"I'm not sure I would, either, but you need help getting past something like that," she said.

"Maybe." Mike's eyes traveled briefly over her upper body before meeting her caring eyes again. He was taking too much of an interest in Lucy. Okay, so she was hot. But she was his.

As soon as that thought came, Thad shut it down. Why was he thinking of her as his? Not in the sense that she was his girlfriend, he rationalized. He had noticed her first. And, yes, he had flirted with her, still was at times. Maybe that's where the idea came from.

"I know some people who work with memory loss. There are some exercises you can do to help restore it. Would you like me to give you his name? If not, I can give you some links to resources online."

Thad saw how Sam perked up with the mention of that.

"I'd like the online links," he said.

"I'll send them to Thad and he can pass them along."

"You must have really caught Kate's attention to have her bring you here as her home care nurse," Mike said.

"Oh, I don't know about that. I was her nurse at the hospital, that's all."

"What made you decide to get into nursing?"

Thad wondered if he'd have to step in. He felt like taking Lucy by the arm and escorting her out of here.

"My father is a doctor," she answered. "I guess I saw how happy he was every time he saved a life."

"Most people can't handle the gore."

"That took some getting used to. But when you work with it every day, it becomes routine and clinical. It only bothers me when they die." Blowing on the hot coffee she held, riveting each man in the room as her lips pursed, she sipped her coffee.

"Did you just come by for breakfast?" Thad asked Mike, more of a confrontation.

Three heads turned to look at him.

"Uh-oh." Sam's mood brightened. "You're homing in on his girl."

Mike smiled. "I guess this is when I tell you you're a lucky man. She's a great catch."

His good-humored response tamed Thad's tension. Lucy's stirred it up again.

She put down her mug of coffee. "Hey. I'm nobody's catch. Thad and I aren't seeing each other."

"Yet," Sam said. "One thing I know about my brother is that he needs something other than sports to keep him warm at night."

"Well, then, maybe there's hope for me," Mike carried on the banter while Thad inwardly cringed. If only he'd kept his mouth shut.

"Lucy." Mike took her hand and gave the top of it a peck of a kiss. "It was a pleasure." When he straightened, he shook Thad's hand. "Thad."

"Mike."

Mike then gave Sam a brief hug and pat on the back. "Thanks for breakfast. Let's get together again soon."

"Plan on it. I'll give you a call."

"I should get going, too." Sam went to Thad and leaned in for another man-hug. "Take my advice, Thad."

Don't let Lucy get away or something like that. Thad ignored him. When Sam left the kitchen, Lucy asked, "What was that all about?"

"He's conspiring against me," Thad answered. And seeing Lucy all dressed and ready for the day, he wondered if he'd be conspiring against himself before long.

"Oh." She nodded uncomfortably. "Um…about last night…"

He put up his hands. "Yeah. Sorry about that. It was just…"

"Late," she said for him.

"Yeah…late."

"The root beer floats…" She was still nodding.

"Who can resist the charm of that?" Smoking-hot charm. He could think of so many other things that would lead to that than an innocent root beer float. "Well, I better get going. I made plans to go to a hockey game with Darcy." He backed toward the archway leading out of the kitchen and to the side entrance.

"It's still morning."

Caught, he stopped and didn't say anything. Never had a woman had him so weak-kneed.

"Who's Darcy?"

"A friend. Cop. We went to the police academy together. He's getting past his divorce."

She stepped forward. "Oh. You'll be perfect for him."

"Very funny."

She smiled and stopped close to him. "You like sports."

He thought her comment was more of an observation. "It's going to be a great game."

"No, I mean, you *really* like sports."

"Yeah…" he hedged. What was she getting at? "Football. Basketball. Hockey." Pretty much all of it.

"You're almost obsessed with it. You work and watch sports. No time for women."

"I wouldn't go that far."

"I think sports fill the gap. What if you spent that time with me instead?"

He didn't even have a reply for that. What had gotten into her? That was a bold thing to say. Did she mean it?

Was she flirting? Leading him? Did she want something to come of them? Thad had mixed feelings about that. He could see himself being with her, maybe even for a long time, indefinitely, even, but she was after a ring and strollers. He got a cold flash just thinking of it.

She moved closer still. "Scared?"

He frowned at her easy perception of where his thoughts had gone. She was on a mission, and he was the target. "No." He wasn't afraid of marriage and children, he just didn't believe they were for him.

"I think you are." She put her hands on his chest, sliding them up. Her eyes were alight with mischief. This was the playful side of Lucy, the side that told stories.

Lured into whatever had compelled her to be this way, he didn't fight the instant warming that she'd deliberately ignited.

"You're afraid to trust any woman with a future. Sports are safe. You can pour all your attention into that and never risk a thing."

"Where is all this coming from?" That kiss?

"Just an observation. You have trust issues."

He didn't like how that came with a sting of truth.

She reached up and traced her finger along his lower lip. "Yeah." That finger trailed down his neck to the V of his long-sleeved shirt. Her palm flattened there, caressing him a little before going still. Then she rose up to put her mouth right beneath his. "If only someone could show you how good it could be."

"You mean…you?" He was hard.

"Yeah," she said in that sexy voice. "You should try giving someone a chance."

"I'd give you a chance." But only if she could go into it casually.

"At what?"

"This," he said. "Last night." And more.

She drew back a fraction, far less flirtatious. "But not a chance at marriage and kids."

He regretted the change in her. "It doesn't mean we can't have something special together."

She recoiled, stepped back as though a hot iron had just burned her. "You holding back isn't special to me."

Would he hold back with her? Hold back marriage and kids, but she meant more than that. She meant the whole emotional package that came with those two terrifying obligations. When he realized apprehension had attached itself to his thoughts, he wondered if, somewhere inside of him, he'd decided that, with her, the whole emotional package was attainable. Or was it the other way around and he felt threatened by her? Threatened that she'd lure him into marriage...

He didn't reassure her that he wouldn't hold back. He couldn't. The idea that she threatened him had him all mixed up.

With a disgusted sigh, Lucy went around him and left the kitchen. On her way she tossed over her shoulder, "Have fun at your *game.*"

Lucy had to go into a bathroom to get ahold of herself. Why couldn't she take a step back from Thad? And why had she tempted him that way, put herself against him, caressed him like a lover? Had she wanted to make him respond? Feeling his hardness had given her immeasurable satisfaction. It had encouraged her. Could a man respond that way, so quickly and so poignantly, without love fueling it?

Yes.

She'd be a fool to believe otherwise. It hadn't been any special feelings toward her that had made him react, it had been a purely male response to a woman teasing him with the possibility of sex.

Bracing her hands on the bathroom counter, she looked at herself in the mirror. It wasn't like her to do things like that, much less let her emotions get to her this way so powerfully. She normally took life's curveballs in stride, with a story or a joke to go with it. She always moved on without a scratch. Why was Thad so different?

One kiss and she was a mess. Well, it was more than one kiss. It was more than a kiss....

That sank her mood lower. She contemplated packing her suitcase and leaving. But she'd made a commitment, one Kate was paying her a lot of money for. She couldn't back out now. She was stuck here in this estate until Kate was fully recovered.

Taking a deep breath and forcing the lump in her throat to loosen, she left the bathroom and went to make sure the servants had brought Kate her breakfast.

"There you are," Kate greeted as she entered the master suite. There was a tray over the bed with a plate of oatmeal, fruit, yogurt and a glass of orange juice.

She sounded stronger every day. "Sorry I'm late."

Kate waved a hand as she finished a bite of oatmeal. "If it wasn't for the physical therapy, I'd be just fine."

"The physical therapy will make you heal faster."

"It doesn't feel that way." Kate winced as she moved her upper body in an attempt to stretch.

"You're supposed to be sore." Lucy began picking up around the room, needing something to do while she waited for Kate to finish eating. She couldn't stop analyzing what Thad had said, and what he hadn't said. No way would he ever consent to marriage and children. He refused to entertain even the possibility. While she felt on the verge of falling truly in love with him, he remained in control. He might say he loved her, but what kind of love would it be if he denied her what she craved? He wouldn't love her fully if he refused to give them a chance. A real chance.

She couldn't predict what he'd do if they kept having encounters like the one they'd had last night. Even more unsettling, she couldn't predict her own response if they did, and didn't think she'd be able to resist him. The burn of tears surged forth. She should have stayed in the bathroom until she was sure she had control of her emotions.

"Lucy?"

Realizing Kate had been talking, Lucy jerked herself to attention, wiping under her eyes to make sure no tears had escaped. "Sorry."

"What's wrong?"

What was the matter with her? Why was she all weepy over Thad? "Nothing." It was just a kiss.

A kiss that had knocked her world off its axis. A kiss that had shown her how strong her attraction was for Thad. Too strong.

"All right. What's he done?" Kate demanded.

Lucy focused on Kate. "Who?"

Kate did a half roll of her eyes. "Thad, of course. What's he done now?"

"Nothing. He's done nothing. Really. I'm fine."

Kate studied her for a moment. "Don't let all his talk about marriage never working get to you."

"I'm not." Lucy felt silly now. "We don't talk about marriage." Well, that was a lie.

"Thad's attitude stinks. I warned you about that."

"Really, Kate, I don't know your son that well."

"Stop cleaning. The staff will do that."

Lucy stilled and faced her.

"I've been meaning to talk to you and Thad about something. I was going to wait until I recovered a bit more, but now is as good of a time as any." She waved her over.

Lucy went to sit on the chair beside the bed.

"We have a house in Carova Beach," Kate began. "When I'm better I plan to go there for a visit. But usually I send someone there to get the house ready. With the assassination attempt, I have to be careful with who I choose."

Uh-oh. Lucy had a bad feeling about this. She shifted in her seat.

"I was going to ask Thad to go, and I'd like you to go with him."

"But I'm here to take care of you."

"And you are. You can go when I'm back on my feet."

"I really don't see why I should go along."

"Thad told me about that man who waited for you after you were finished working," she said. "I don't think, and I'm sure Thad would agree, that you should be alone right now."

"What about you?"

"Thad also told me about his concern over one of my security agents. The window was left unlocked. It could have been an innocent mistake, but it could have been more. I need someone I can trust to secure the beach house for my visit."

Lucy understood that. But going to a remote beach house with Thad wasn't in her best interest right now.

"I'm concerned for your safety, and mine," Kate said. "And Thad could use some time with you, to see what a real woman could do for him. It might even change his mind about love." Kate smiled with well-intended deviousness.

Her motive was purely as a matchmaker and nothing less. Lucy could not ignore that.

"Why do you think I'm any good for Thad?" she asked. "I mean, I know I deserve a good man. I'm not insecure and I have a lot to offer. But Thad isn't interested in the same things I am." Not when it came to love.

"Having a family?" Kate asked derisively.

"Yes." Didn't she see? It would be futile for Lucy to carry on any kind of relationship with him. Especially when her feelings were already so deep.

"That's precisely why you're perfect for him." Kate scrutinized her again, and Lucy felt exposed. Thad's mother understood what had her so down. "Come here." Kate reached her hand toward her.

Lucy stood and went to her, and Kate took her hand.

"Thad doesn't know it yet, but you're right about marriage and he's wrong. You can teach him that, and if the two of you fall in love, everyone benefits."

And if only one of them fell in love, what then? "Are you sure you're not trying to arrange a marriage for us?"

Kate let go of her hand. "Lucy, my dear, I wouldn't push the two of you if I wasn't sure of the way he feels about you. Thad has never been in love before. When he falls in love, he's going to realize that marriage and love go hand in hand, and children are the celebration of them both."

Lucy stared at her while the possibility of Thad being a viable suitor for her mushroomed. Could he be just like one of the men she'd choose on her online dating site, one who shared her desires for the future?

What would happen if Kate was wrong? What if Thad stuck to his beliefs? Where would that leave her? If she dove into this headfirst and really went after him, she might very well end up with a broken heart.

"I'm sorry," she said with the shake of her head. "I'm not the one for him. If he ever falls in love—" which she did not believe he would "—it will have to be with someone else."

Kate's face fell with disappointment. "I understand. It was worth a try."

"Are you finished?" Lucy indicated her breakfast, eager to get things back to business.

"Yes."

"Then let's get you up and walking." As Lucy lifted the tray off the bed and set it aside, Kate's proposition plagued her.

Or was it temptation?

Chapter 8

For about an hour now, Thad had watched the office building across the street from the hotel where his mother had held her fund-raiser. Traffic crawled and people clogged the sidewalks. No federal agents lurked. No one noticed him, either. Thad put down the newspaper he'd used to disguise his true purpose and stood from the café patio table. Dropping a tip on the table, he lifted a briefcase and headed for the street.

Waiting for traffic to pass, he crossed and entered the building. Inside, there was no one in the lobby. There was no security desk. No security at all. No wonder the shooter had chosen this as his position to try and kill Kate Winston. Taking the elevator to the thirteenth floor, he walked down the hall. A door ahead had an X of yellow police tape blocking entrance. There was no one guarding the door. He passed a darkened office space, visible through windows on each side of double doors. Across from it was another vacant space.

A man exited the office at the end of the hall. Across from that was the yellow taped door. That was the only occupied office on this floor. There was a janitor's cart parked along the wall but no sign of the janitor.

Thad slowed his pace until the man reached the elevators. At an enclave of the public restrooms, Thad ducked behind the wall and waited. The man disappeared and the hall fell quiet again.

Putting his briefcase down, Thad crouched and retrieved a lock pick. The door was aged and not sophisticated. Another plus for the gunman. It took him a few minutes to maneuver the lock pick, but at last it slid the bolt open. Thad turned the knob and entered, stepping over the tape and bending to fit through the opening. He looked in the hall to make sure he wasn't seen.

Closing the door again, he faced the open space of the vacant office. There were four enclosed offices on each side and six cement support columns between. Facing the street was a wall of windows. Thad went over to them.

He could clearly see the twelfth-floor ballroom of the historic building across the street. There was an event taking place right now. People sat at tables that faced the front of the room, some kind of business presentation taking place. The hotel hadn't wasted any time cleaning the space up and reopening for scheduled events. He couldn't see the projection screen, but he did see a raised platform where a podium might be placed, where his mother had stood.

It gave him a helpless feeling, a sick feeling, to stand here as the shooter had, taking aim at his mother. He clenched his fists.

Examining the window frame, he leaned close, looking for trace evidence. The shooter would have had to open the window to take his shots. The agents would have searched for fingerprints. Seeing nothing telling, he turned his attention to the floor, crouching to scan every square millimeter.

Nothing. The agents wouldn't have left anything behind.

Standing, he faced the office once more. Well, he'd had to confirm it and he had; there was nothing here.

Going to the door, he opened it a little. The janitor cart was still there. Other than that, the hall was empty. He stepped through the yellow tape and shut the door. When he turned, he saw the janitor emerge from the men's bathroom, a fortyish African American man with salt-and-pepper hair.

"I thought you all finished up in there," he said.

"We did. Just had to check something."

"You catch that man yet?"

Thad shook his head.

"Didn't think so. I've been waiting for somebody to ask me to go make an ID. Haven't yet."

Thad's mind went on full alert. "You saw the shooter?"

"Yeah, well, least I think I did. Saw him leave the office much the way you just did, minus the tape, of course. Thought it was odd, considering that the space is vacant and all."

"You described the man to an agent?"

"Oh, yeah, and an artist drew up a picture of him."

The feds had an artist's sketch of the shooter. Why were they keeping it a secret? Why wasn't the picture on the news? Prickles of foreboding trickled up his spine.

"When did you talk to the agents?"

"After I heard what happened, I told my boss, who contacted someone. Then they came to me the day after the shooting."

Thad hadn't heard about that. No one had told him. He doubted his mother even knew. She would have mentioned something like that. His feeling that there was something wrong with the investigation intensified.

"What did the man look like?" he asked.

The man's brow furrowed. "You haven't seen the picture?"

"No. I was just moved to the case today. That's why I came by."

He hesitated, obviously questioning the validity of Thad's statement. "He was a little shorter than you. Brown eyes. Wore a hat the day I saw him. Short hair. Fit guy."

Thad would give anything to see the artist's sketch. "Did you talk to him?"

"I said hello but he just walked down the hall."

"Have you seen him again?" Thad asked.

"Just that one time. You have any leads?"

"No. Thank you." Thad turned to leave, full of bombarding questions and the sixth sense that the description was familiar.

Thad went straight to Darcy at the station.

"You're kidding," Darcy said after he finished telling him what the janitor had revealed. They'd gone into a conference room for this conversation.

"Do you think Chief Thomas knows?" Darcy asked.

Thad stared at him, thinking the possibility was real. He didn't have to answer. "What if the shooter has already been identified?" Darcy asked the question that plagued Thad.

"I don't know." They could at least have an idea of possible suspects. "The description matches Cam Harmon."

Darcy cursed, as frustrated as Thad over the information that had been withheld and wondering how much more there was. "What about Jaden?"

"Maybe they're working together. Leaving the window open, helping him to get into the estate, since dating Lucy didn't work."

"Right. Except there's a problem with that theory. Why date Kate's nurse to get close to Kate?"

It did seem to be a stretch. But it was too coincidental. "Maybe she'd bring him to her room one day or night. It would have been a way around security."

Lucy had met Cam right after Kate was shot. Cam could have gone to the hospital before the day Thad had seen him there, cased it out and decided to use Lucy. He may have seen how well the two were getting along. And then Lucy had been hired as Kate's home care nurse and she'd stopped seeing Cam. Was Cam now working his way in through Jaden?

"Do you think we should tell Chief Thomas?" Darcy asked.

"Yes. If he does nothing, then we know he's in on it."

"In on what? An assassination attempt? How many people want her dead?"

If several people were involved in a conspiracy to kill a potential presidential candidate, this was bigger than he imagined.

"There's only one way to find out." Thad left the conference room.

"Get ready for a flogging," Darcy said from behind him.

Thad glanced back, catching his meaning. Going to the chief would reveal he and Darcy hadn't done as ordered and steered clear of the investigation. But Thad didn't care. He'd do anything to protect his mother.

Reaching Wade's office, he knocked on the glass. The chief looked up and waved them to enter.

Thad did, and Darcy closed the door behind them.

"I thought you were taking a leave, Winston," Chief Thomas said without looking up from the papers on his desk.

"Something's come up."

Removing his reading glasses, Wade eyed him with disapproval.

"The FBI has an artist's sketch of the shooter," Darcy announced.

Wade's hard eyes moved to him. "And how, might I ask, do you know this?"

"I went to the vacant office where the gunman made his shots," Thad said. "I ran into a janitor there, who told me he saw a man leaving the office the night of the shooting. He gave a description."

"I thought I told you not to investigate that case." Wade stood, anger beginning to brew and storm over his brow.

"He shot my mother," Thad said simply. Did he really expect him not to investigate? When Wade didn't dispute that point, Darcy went on.

"There's more. We think the shooter could be Cam Harmon."

"Cam Harmon." Wade looked as if he were searching his memory.

"The man Lucy Sinclair met online after my mother was shot," Thad reminded him, wondering if Wade had truly forgotten or if he was deliberately minimizing this.

"Online?" Wade questioned. "How would Harmon have known she was on a dating site?"

Thad had already considered that. "He could have heard her talking when she was away from Kate's room." The security would be too tight there, and Lucy wouldn't have been alert to someone spying on her.

The chief nodded haphazardly, not really buying the likelihood. But he leaned on his desk with his hands. "All right. I'll pass this along to the FBI. On one condition."

He had Thad's undivided attention. Would he really pass the information along?

"You stop investigating the shooting," Chief Thomas said. "I can't keep having to tell you that. You must leave it up to the feds. Understood?"

"Understood," Thad said. "Thank you, sir."

"Get out of my office."

Darcy led Thad out into the main office area, where talking and the tapping of keyboards echoed off the high ceiling and nearly bare walls.

When they were out of sight of Chief Thomas, Darcy stopped. "How do we know if he tells the feds?"

"We wait to hear about an arrest."

Darcy nodded, not satisfied. "Where's Lucy?"

"At the estate." Where she was safe. Unless Jaden had something to do with all of this and he and Darcy had just sent agents after the wrong man…

On Friday in early March, Lucy almost forgot her hair appointment and had rushed out of the estate. Now leaving the salon with bouncing, shining auburn hair, she walked toward her car. Haircuts always made her day.

Speaking of day, it was beautiful outside. Not a cloud in the sky and it had warmed into the sixties. She breathed in the fresh air. Reaching her Subaru, she was about to open her door when a man called, "Lucy?"

Immediately recognizing the voice, Lucy turned.

Cam stood in a navy blue suit, brown eyes and cropped blond hair a good disguise for the kind of man he truly was.

"Do I need a restraining order?" she asked him.

He put his hands up. "No. I just want to talk."

Her pulse knocked her rib cage as she opened her car door. He always said that. "Leave me alone."

She looked around the parking lot. There were a few other people walking to and from the strip mall where her salon was located. He'd be foolish to try something now.

"I'm sorry for the way things turned out between us."

His apology held an eerie tone. They barely knew each other and he made it sound as though they'd been together for months, maybe even years.

"All that talk about stay-at-home moms." He grunted a laugh. "It was stupid."

Of him? She couldn't argue there.

"I'm going to leave you alone for a while, okay? Give you some distance. Then maybe a few months from now, we can try again."

He made her sick to her stomach. "No means no, Cam," she said. "I don't want to see you again. Ever." She leaned toward him and pointed her finger. "That means *never*. How much clearer do I need to make it?" What was it going to take before he finally left her alone?

His gaze remained steady on her. And then he stepped forward.

Lucy opened the Subaru door and sat on the driver's seat. But as she pulled the door to close it, Cam took hold of the door frame. Forcing it open wider, he stepped into the open space and crouched with eyes that gleamed menace.

"How much *clearer* do I have to make it, Lucy?" he asked.

She dug into her purse for her cell phone.

"You and I will be together again," he said. "If I have to lock you in a room, I will."

Real panic began to rear up inside her. She believed he would do that—if given the chance. "You're crazy." She retrieved her phone and navigated to the keypad.

Cam gripped her wrist and pried the phone from her hand, throwing it to the floor on the passenger side.

When she turned to him, he grinned. "I always get what I want. And I want you."

"Go to hell, you psychotic bastard!" she hissed. Provoking him like this probably wasn't wise, but she'd be damned if she was going to let him treat her like this! She leaned over, stretching her body to reach for her phone.

Cam grabbed her hair and pulled her back. With his other hand, he pushed her back against the seat. His face contorted with rage, brown eyes feral and mouth pressed tight.

She cried out in pain, the force of his grip on her hair stinging her scalp.

"I'm tired of you talking back to me. You're going to learn how to do what I say, and when. Do you hear me?"

Dear God, the man was certifiably insane! "Get your hands *off* me!"

His jaw clenched and his eyes flared with uncontrollable rage.

"Is everything okay?" an old woman's voice interrupted.

Cam turned his head and Lucy saw the elderly woman in a long floral dress with an old-fashioned white purse hooked over her elbow. The smartphone in her hand hinted to a little twenty-first century spunk.

"Is this man bothering you, honey?" she asked Lucy.

Obviously he was with his meaty hand clenching her hair. The old woman must have known it.

Cam let go of her hair and stood.

"Do I need to call the police?" the old woman asked in her frail voice, her thumb poised over the phone that she must have prepared with the numbers 9-1-1.

With limited options, Cam looked down at Lucy. "We'll be seeing each other real soon."

She refrained from replying with a threat of her own and he strode away.

Nearly slumping with relief, Lucy got out of her car, a tremble running through her body. The old woman approached.

Lucy put her hand on top of the open door. "Thank you so much."

"Should I call the police, honey? That man should be reported."

"No. He won't bother me again." Uncertainty shrouded that claim. *We'll be seeing each other real soon....*

"All right, if you're sure. If it were me, I'd report it."

"I already did." To Thad.

The old woman turned to her big, long Lincoln town car. "Young men these days." She shook her curly, short, gray-haired head. "Aren't what they used to be." She looked at Lucy as she opened her car door. "I pity you."

Lucy smiled. "There are a few good ones left."

When Thad's face came to mind, her smile slowly faded.

After Thad left the station, he drove to find Cam. He wasn't at work, so he drove to his residence and waited.

Now he saw him arrive and park in the driveway. Not long after that, another car appeared, this one parking in the street.

Thad recognized Jaden when the driver got out and wasn't surprised. He and Cam were working together.

He waited for almost a half hour before Jaden left the house. He seemed agitated. So agitated that he didn't notice Thad in his car. He also didn't notice him following.

A few minutes later, Thad parked in the street two doors down from Jaden's place of residence, an average neighborhood of thirty-year-old homes. Jaden didn't make it inside. What must be his wife opened the door and started yelling at him. Thad rolled his windows down. He heard her shouting from here, but couldn't discern what she said.

He shouted something back and she began beating on his chest. This time Thad could hear what she yelled. "Stay the hell away from me!"

He took hold of her wrists to stop her from hitting him but didn't hurt her. When she pulled back, he let her go and stood on the front porch step, the front door open.

Then his wife reappeared with a suitcase that she hefted out the door. Jaden stepped out of the way of the tumbling luggage. It rolled off the steps and onto the lawn.

The Secret Service agent was having problems at home. How complicated were they? Was this a typical failing marriage or was more going on?

Jaden's wife slammed the front door shut. Jaden stood there for a while as though undecided over what to do. Then he lifted the suitcase and took it to his car.

That evening, Thad waited in the guesthouse, made available to the security team for whatever needs they had during their work. There were two other agents in the kitchen, no doubt wondering why he was waiting for Jaden.

Finally Jaden arrived, fifteen minutes late. He saw Thad and stopped.

"I need to talk to you," Thad said, standing from the living room chair.

"If this is about that window..."

"It isn't. Let's go into the parlor." Thad went to the small room off the entry and living room and waited just inside for Jaden to pass him.

Closing the double doors, seeing the two agents watching from the kitchen table, he faced Jaden, who stood in front of a two-chair sitting area.

"Having trouble at home?" Thad asked.

The caught look and lengthy hesitation revealed enough. "I don't have to talk to you about that."

No, but he'd have to talk to someone about it soon. Divorce was reportable when you had a security clearance. "I saw you with Cam Harmon today."

Anxiety flickered in Jaden's eyes before he masked it.

"I was going to go have a word with him when I saw you drive up," Thad said. "Imagine my surprise."

"So I know Cam. Big deal." He walked to the window that overlooked the front yard of the guesthouse.

"How did you meet him?"

Jaden didn't answer, only continued to peer through the window, the sun setting and casting shadows.

"Have the two of you been friends long?" Thad persisted.

Again, Jaden refused to respond, but turned to face him.

"Maybe you just met, like right after my mother was shot?"

Jaden folded his hulking arms and smirked, still without engaging in the one-sided conversation.

"Are you helping Cam kill my mother?"

"No." His firm answer held some truth to it.

"What are you doing with him, then?"

Lowering his arms, Jaden stepped forward, stopping close to Thad so that they were eye to eye. "If I were you, I'd back off."

"Or what?"

"Sticking your nose where it doesn't belong is going to get you in big trouble."

"With who? You?" And who else?

Jaden didn't answer. Instead, he walked to the door and left Thad standing there.

Lucy helped Kate stretch in preparation for her afternoon physical therapy exercises. Now Saturday, a week into March, Kate was slowly getting stronger. She'd also noticed something preoccupied Lucy again, and this time it wasn't Thad.

"You might as well tell me what happened," Kate said, trying yet another tactic. Asking her what was wrong hadn't worked. Neither had asking what had her so quiet.

Lucy walked with her toward the walk-in pool. She held Kate's arm as they stepped into the water and went in to their waists.

"It isn't Thad, is it?" Kate guessed. "You seem worried about something."

"Let's swim to the other side." Lucy stayed close to Kate, who grimaced as she started to swim. Lucy swam with a side stroke to the other end of the pool. There, she held on to the edge along with Kate.

"I might be able to help," Kate said.

Maybe, with all her security. But if Thad found out, he'd take action, and she was beginning to think Cam was a lot more dangerous than she'd estimated until now.

"Is it that man who stalked you?" Kate accurately surmised. "Who is he?"

Lucy relented. Kate knew enough to tip off Thad, and Thad would only come asking her questions.

"I joined an online dating service. That's how I met him. I went out with him a few times."

"Are you still on this site?" Kate asked.

"Yes." Her account was still active.

"You're dating other people?"

Other than Thad, she realized Kate meant. "No. Not anymore. I—I mean…I—I'm dating, but not right now." She looked away as she wondered if the reason she'd stopped checking her online account had anything to do with Thad.

"Did this man confront you again?" Kate rested her arms on the pool edge with her body horizontal to the water's surface, her feet moving just enough to keep her afloat.

Lucy told her what happened and as she did, Kate lowered her feet. That was the only indication that the savvy politician was appalled.

"Does Thad know about this…that he attacked you again?"

"No, and I'm not sure he should. I think if I just lay low for a while Cam will lose interest and move on to someone else."

"Someone else he can hurt?"

Lucy hadn't thought of it that way. Cam hadn't hurt her that much. He'd gotten physical with her but would he try to rape her or worse?

"Did this occur when you went to your hair appointment?" Kate asked.

Lucy had told her where she was going. "Yes."

After a moment of calculated thought, Kate said, "Well," and then reached a wet arm and put her hand on Lucy's shoulder. "We'll take care of that."

How? "I don't know what Cam is capable of. Thad working alone may not be enough."

"Thad won't have to work alone."

Kate had resources Thad didn't. She could protect her family.

Family?

It sort of felt that way....

"There you are."

Lucy's heart palpitated from heated awareness as she heard Thad's voice. She moved to hold on to the edge so that she faced him as he approached. The next thing she registered was Kate's pleased observation.

Thad made everything worse by crouching by the pool's edge and looking at Lucy with heated regard, as though he were glad to see her or had missed her while he'd been away.

"That man Lucy dated from her online site accosted her after her hair appointment yesterday," Kate announced.

"Your mother needs to ease up on her pain medication," Lucy tried to quip. When Thad's masculine appreciation of Lucy in a swimsuit abruptly fled, and his brow turned stormy, she added, "It was nothing. He came to apologize and say he would leave me alone, that's all."

"He scared her," Kate said. "I don't think he's going to leave her alone. But Lucy is concerned you'll get hurt protecting her."

"Why did you go to your appointment alone?" he demanded, not acknowledging his mother's comment.

"It's okay, Thad," Kate said. "I'll make sure she's got security the next time she has obligations like that."

Thad wasn't satisfied. The way he continued to look at her told her so.

"Were you followed?" he asked.

"I watched for that, but I didn't see anyone."

"Cam isn't exactly an expert," Thad said. "So if he didn't follow you, how did he know you'd be at your hair appointment?"

Awed that Thad had considered that, Lucy only stared up at his handsome face.

"You think Cam knew she had an appointment?" Kate asked.

Thad turned to his mother but didn't answer.

"What have you not told me?" Kate asked.

"Jaden and Cam have been talking. They know each other," he said.

"But Jaden is new to the security detail," Kate said.

"I don't think he's the shooter."

"But you think Cam might be?" Lucy was stunned.

Thad stood. "That's what I intend to find out."

Chapter 9

With many questions racing in her brain, Lucy walked up to the front step of Rosanna Bridger's two-story townhome. Paint had begun to chip and weeds grew through cracks in the driveway before the single-car garage. There were toys junking up the yard. Lucy had never been to Rosanna's home before, and seeing its condition worried her. So had hearing the woman's voice when she'd called yesterday evening.

That Rosanna had called her at all surprised her. But she'd explained how fond Sophie was of her and that she had no one else to turn to. She'd confessed the state of her marriage. Her husband would be moving out today and she didn't want Sophie around when that happened.

As she stepped up to the door, she heard arguing.

"Hurry up and get that kid out of here," a man said in an angry, snide tone. "I don't have all day and Harry is on his way with the moving truck."

"Lucy will be here any minute," Rosanna answered in a strained voice.

Lucy rang the doorbell. What kind of environment was Sophie living in?

Rosanna opened the door. "Lucy. Hi." She opened the door wider. "I can't thank you enough for doing this."

Lucy looked past her to the man standing in a small living room filled with boxes. Paper plates with food still on them littered the coffee table. Last night's dinner?

"I'll get Sophie." Rosanna vanished up the stairs.

The man watched Lucy, his gaze going all over her body before resting on her face. After dealing with Cam, she was hypersensitive to strange men who gave her a bad feeling.

"How do you know Rosanna?" the man asked.

"I'm sorry, you are…?"

"Layne Bridger. Soon to be single."

Lucy didn't even spare him an acknowledgment for that statement.

"How do you know her?" Layne asked. "She doesn't have many friends here."

Rosanna had explained she'd moved from Minnesota where she was from because her new husband had gotten a job here in North Carolina. They'd only been together for two years.

"I met her through the literacy program."

"Ah." He raised his head in a half nod. Lucy couldn't tell if it was in mocking or if he was impressed. "You're one of those do-gooders."

"Isn't that what you are?" she asked sarcastically, not appreciating his insult. He had been mocking her.

Just then, Sophie came bounding down the stairs.

"Lucy! Lucy!" She ran up to her and threw her small body against her.

Lucy laughed and crouched to her level to give her a hug. "Hey there, little pumpkin. Are you ready to go have a sleepover at my house?"

Sophie's smile expanded to gigantic proportions. "Yeah!"

"Here's her bag." Rosanna handed a flowery duffel to Lucy, eyeing her uncertainly. Was she threatened by how much Sophie liked Lucy? Were things so bad with her home life that it had created a wedge between them?

"Come on, honey." Lucy took the girl's hand and said to Rosanna, "You have my number...."

"Yes. Thank you again." Rosanna walked them to the door.

Lucy took Sophie outside and to her Subaru, putting the duffel in the backseat. Sophie knew the drill about sitting in the back. She planted herself behind the front passenger seat, happy as could be.

Lucy got in and began driving. "How are things at home, Sophie?" It was time to start picking for information.

Sophie's happy glow dimmed some. "Okay."

"Just okay?"

She glanced up at Lucy, then turned toward the window. Her feet didn't quite reach the floor and she bobbed them up and down.

"Rosanna and Layne aren't getting along, huh?" Lucy coaxed.

"No. They fight."

"Layne is moving out this weekend, so things should get better."

Sophie shrugged.

"Why don't you like it at Rosanna's house?"

Again, Sophie shrugged, feet still bobbing.

"It's okay, you can tell me. I won't say anything to Rosanna."

Sophie's feet stopped moving. "She yells at me."

"Rosanna does?"

"She never wants me to be around," she blurted in a louder voice, eyes looking at Lucy with a desperate plea. "She never plays with me or lets me play at friends' houses and she never lets me watch TV!" The torment poured out from her tiny body. "It's boring there! Rosanna doesn't want me. Nobody does!"

That well and truly sliced a gash in Lucy's heart. "Oh, sweetie. It might seem that way, but Rosanna does want you. She's just going through a rough time right now. You wait and see, once Layne moves out, you two will have fun together again."

"It's not fun there." Lucy barely heard her quiet voice.

She took her shopping and then out for dinner. It was getting late when they arrived at the estate.

When Lucy retrieved her bag and walked with Sophie toward the side entrance, Sophie gaped at the huge home.

"You *live* here?"

"Just for a while. I'm taking care of someone who was injured and just released from the hospital. That's what I do. I'm a nurse."

"I want to be a nurse when I grow up." She skipped along toward the side entrance.

"Do you?" Or was she just saying that because she had a case of hero worship going on with Lucy?

"Yes. My mommy was a nurse. Rosanna told me you were a nurse."

"Did she?"

"Yes. My mommy had brown hair, too."

Oh, this poor child. Losing her mother at such a young age.

When they entered the house, Sophie continued to gape as Lucy declined the help of a servant and took her up to the room Kate had prepared for her.

Inside the white-and-pink room, it was fit for a princess.

"Wow!" Sophie yelled, bouncing into the bedroom that had been designed especially for kids, with its pink comforter and pictures and a rug. Lucy wondered if the items had been placed here just for Sophie. There were toys in an open trunk and a dollhouse left open.

Lucy put the duffel down on the bed while Sophie dropped before the Victorian-style, yellow-and-white Princess Anne dollhouse. The interior was fully furnished.

"I asked for some monster girl dolls for my birthday," Sophie said.

Monster girl dolls was the latest trend in dolls. Times sure had changed since Lucy was a kid. "When's your birthday?"

"March 15."

This week? "I'm sure Rosanna will get you them."

"No." Her head whipped back and up to see Lucy. "She said I couldn't have them."

"Why not?"

"She said she can't afford them."

Because Layne had cleaned out her bank accounts. Lucy was uncertain how much she should intervene. Part of her contemplated taking her for herself and part of her warned to be careful. Winning Sophie over too much might harm her. Lucy would have to return her to Rosanna.

"Will you get me those monster girl dolls?" Sophie asked.

Lucy couldn't respond right away.

"You said Imagene gave us those books. Can she give me those dolls?"

The drawbacks of making up stories…

"I don't know, Sophie."

"Will you ask her?"

She hesitated. "I'll try, okay?"

"Okay." She was back to being the happy girl again, pretending she had the dolls she wanted, her hands curled as though she held two and moved them through the elaborate miniature house.

"What happened to my mommy?" Sophie asked.

The question took Lucy aback and she had to spend a few seconds to think it through. "Well, she was in a bad car accident."

Sophie turned with a blank look. Had no one explained this to her? Likely someone had tried but she didn't understand.

"A man in a big truck ran into her car while she was driving. He didn't mean to. That's why it's called an accident."

Sophie stopped playing and stared down at her hands. "Where did my mommy go? Why doesn't she come and get me?"

Why doesn't she come and get me. Lucy swallowed a wave of sorrow for the girl, her eyes burning with near-tears. She knelt beside Sophie. "Well…she can't, honey. She died in the accident."

"Why do mommies have to die?"

Lucy touched her shoulder. "Everybody dies. Usually that isn't until we're all very old. It's when accidents happen that they're taken from us sooner than they should be."

Sophie looked down at the lower level of the dollhouse, her young mind trying to process a grave topic.

"You know, every time you think of your mom, she's here with you. You keep her right here." Lucy pointed to her own heart. "As long as she's there, she'll always be with you. She won't be able to talk to you, and you won't be able to see her, but she'll be here. She's here right now."

A glimmer of hope lit in Sophie's eyes. "She is?" She searched the room.

"Yes, but remember, you can't see or hear her. You can just feel her." Lucy pointed to her heart again. "Right here."

When Lucy withdrew her hand, Sophie pressed hers there.

Lucy had to leave before she started crying in front of Sophie. "Get your pajamas on. I'll be back to tuck you in, okay?"

"Okay." Sophie pretended to play with a doll a while longer. At first her motions were mechanical, but as the imaginary doll went up the stairs and into a beautifully furnished master bedroom, she seemed to fall into another world, the tragic loss of her mother receding to a dark corner of her small head.

Listening to Darcy talk on the phone with his new girlfriend, Thad suffered the glaring evidence that his best friend was falling in love. So fast? It was like a bad movie he couldn't stop watching. The smile on Darcy's face stayed after he disconnected the call and stared off into space. Thad imagined a cartoon character with big, round eyes and red hearts floating up over his head. Desks surrounded the one where he sat, phones rang, detectives talked, and Darcy was oblivious to it all. Worse, he seemed to have forgotten Thad stood next to him.

Sitting on the office chair beside his daydreaming friend, Thad cleared his throat.

Snapped back to the real world, Darcy straightened some papers and put them back into a folder on his cluttered desk, two computer screens and a keyboard sticking up from a bed of papers, folders and books.

"We were talking about Cam confronting Lucy outside her hair appointment," Thad reminded him, not missing his self-conscious preoccupation with the papers. Moving them to other piles on his desk would hardly tidy things up.

"Right. Yeah. I'll get the paperwork going to charge him for stalking. We may not have enough evidence."

They had Lucy's phone records, and Thad had witnessed the first confrontation in front of the hospital, but Lucy hadn't gotten the old woman's name who'd witnessed the confrontation in front of the hair salon. She had no pictures, nor had she reported the second incident to police.

Maybe the threat of charges would be enough to scare him away from Lucy. Thad had a feeling it wouldn't.

Noticing Darcy drift off into another daydream, he gave up trying to get any work done. "Things are going pretty good between you and that girl."

Darcy's attention came back to him. "I talk to her every day. We've gone out a couple of times. Dude. I can't get her out of my mind."

Wow, every day. "Do you want to?"

"No. Yes. It's so soon after my divorce." His uncertainty was palpable, but Thad didn't think his uncertainty extended to his feelings for the woman.

"She makes me feel so good," Darcy continued, getting that dreamy look again. "Am I just desperate or is this for real?"

Thad had no idea, and he was the wrong person to ask. "Just go with it." That's what he always did. Stay in the now and enjoy it while it lasted.

"This is different," Darcy said.

He could tell his friend was torn over this. "How? Do you think you're falling in love with her?"

When Darcy could only answer with silent resignation, Thad controlled his alarm. "Already?"

"I know it's crazy, but Avery is… I don't know… She's so…perfect for me. She's having a rough time getting over what happened to her, and we're taking it slow, but we talk about everything."

"Are you hearing what you're saying? Taking it slow? You just met her."

"It doesn't seem like it. It seems like I've known her my whole life." His whole face corroborated his claim.

Thad had never experienced anything like that. Or had he? Being with Lucy felt like that, only it was different. With her, there was this burning cauldron of… not lust…attraction. Pure attraction. The kind that led to something deeper. Unlike Darcy's relationship with Avery, his with Lucy was slow to develop. He couldn't say she was perfect for him because she had opposing beliefs. But there was something about her that drew him to her. Her literacy charity. Her caring nature. The way she teased him without being insulting. If he were to make the stretch and say they had things in common, it was their service to the community. Didn't that qualify as the same belief structure? Was it only his issue with marriage and babies that didn't mesh?

When a resounding affirmative response resonated inside of him, he tensed. That removed, his relationship with Lucy had a striking resemblance to Darcy and Avery's.

Darcy chuckled as he observed Thad. "Maybe we should plan a double wedding."

Thad pushed the office chair back and stood. "I'm not getting married."

"Fine. Don't get married, but you're falling in love, my friend. There's no stopping it. The same is happening to me, so I know."

That only instilled fear and panic in Thad. And then he wondered why. Why did falling in love with Lucy give him the instinct to run the other way?

Because she wanted a family. A traditional family. Thad wasn't against sharing part of his life with someone. "Till death do us part" wasn't realistic. And he was a realist when it came to marriage. Marriage didn't last. Period.

"Easy, there, fella," Darcy teased. "You should see your face."

"I'm okay."

"You're more than okay. You're falling in love." He chuckled some more. "I can't believe it's happening to us at the same time."

"It's not happening to me." As the words tumbled out, he wondered why he felt he had to say them. He wasn't against falling in love. It was the same principle. Enjoy it while it lasted; that was his motto. But would Lucy force him into marriage if he did fall in love with her?

Darcy patted his shoulder. "You go ahead and keep telling yourself that."

"Thanks for being a friend, Darcy. I have to go." He walked away to more of Darcy's chuckles.

This morning his mother had mentioned she needed the house in Carova Beach prepared for a visit and needed someone she could trust. She suggested he take Lucy there. All this talk about falling in love had him tempted to agree. Take Lucy somewhere isolated and let all his guard down with her. Spend an entire day naked in bed…

In the hall leading to the exit, his cell rang. Not recognizing the number, he answered. "Winston."

"You don't know when to back off," a man's voice said. He didn't recognize it.

"Who is this?"

"Someone who's going to teach you when it's time to back off."

Thad stopped walking as he realized Jaden had said those exact words to him. *Back off.*

"Jaden?" he asked, but the connection had already been broken.

As he put his phone away, he spotted Wade Thomas through the glass wall of his office. He was staring at Thad. He'd seen him talking to Darcy and he didn't like it. More than a chief of police trying to keep his men in line, Wade looked at him as though he knew who had just called him.

Thad contemplated going into his office and asking him point-blank. But what good would that do? If the chief was innocent, Thad would only push an already thin boundary. If he wasn't and he knew more about this investigation than he was letting on, he would simply deny it.

* * *

Thad entered the estate, plagued by the threat he'd received. What would the caller do to teach him when it was time to back off? Making his way deeper into the home, Thad climbed the stairs to go to the bedroom where he was sleeping to change into something more casual. Unlike Darcy, he preferred soft shirts and jeans over the dress pants and shirts with strangling ties. He removed his jacket on the way. At the top of the stairs, he almost bumped into Lucy.

She wiped her eyes, tears springing from them. When she saw him, her quiet sobbing broke into something more wrenching and she flung herself against him, arms going around him.

Thad dropped his jacket and wrapped her in his arms. "It's okay. I've got you." What had happened? Had Cam gotten to her again?

Her outburst calmed as fast as it had come on. She sniffled and leaned back. "I'm sorry." She moved to step away but he kept her firmly where she was.

"What's wrong?" he asked.

Lucy wiped her eyes again.

Reaching into his front pocket, he retrieved a handkerchief and hung it up in front of her.

She took it from him. "Really? You carry a handkerchief?"

"Crime scene investigator. It gets used at least three times a week." He grinned when she moved the cloth away from her face with a grimace. "I have a rotation and this one is clean."

She blew her nose. "Who uses them? You?"

"No. People I talk to who know the victim."

"Oh." She kept the handkerchief and lowered her

hands, curled and now resting on his chest. "Sophie is here."

"Here?" The bedrooms were filling up fast. Pretty soon there wouldn't be any left. Kate in the master, Sam in one, he and Lucy in two more, and now Sophie. There was only one more room left.

"Rosanna called." Lucy explained how Sophie had come to stay here for the night. "She seemed so scared when I picked her up, and Layne…"

Rosanna's husband. Soon to be ex-husband. "What about him?"

"I didn't like him. Sophie doesn't, either."

"Why don't you like him?"

"It's just a feeling. And he seemed to hit on me."

Thad ignored the instant jealousy that information inflicted on him. "Rosanna is the one who filed for the divorce. Maybe he's not happy about having to move out."

"Maybe." She didn't seem convinced.

"That's why you're crying?"

"No." Her eyes bloomed fresh tears but they didn't spill over. "Sophie asked about her mother. She doesn't understand where she went."

"And you had to try and explain." That would be hard on anyone. Sophie was an innocent child.

Thad kissed Lucy's forehead. "She'll be all right." Especially while she slept in a room that was right next to his and across from Lucy's. A real family affair…

Just then his mother appeared at the end of the hall, using the wall for support. Seeing them, she stopped.

Thad set Lucy apart from him. "Mother. What are you doing up?"

"I heard crying."

"Lucy was upset over Sophie's situation. She's okay now," Thad said.

"Yes. I'm okay now."

"I can see that." Kate wore a triumphant smile.

Now she'd never leave him alone until he agreed to take Lucy with him to get the Carova beach house ready for her visit.

Late that night, Thad woke to the cries of a young child. Waking the rest of the way, he realized it was Sophie.

Leaping off the bed, he ran into the hall. No one else had gone to see to Sophie. Going by instinct, he went into the girl's room. Sophie sat up in bed, her face a contortion of misery, mouth open with a long wail ringing through the room. She'd wake everyone in the house with that set of lungs.

He went to her and sat on the bed. "What's the matter?"

She reached for him with her tiny hands. A child seeking comfort from him was a new experience. He gathered her in the blankets and lifted her onto his lap, where she snuggled close, her wails easing a bit but still crying.

"What happened, Sophie?" he asked, bringing his face down so he could see her teary one. The sight touched something deep inside of him. He wiped her face with his fingers.

"Layne came to get me."

Thad glanced around the room. Had he broken into the house? Impossible. Security was tight. Then he thought of Jaden.

"He was hairy and had green eyes." Sophie sniffled, no longer crying and now intent on impressing upon Thad what she'd seen. "They glowed."

"You had a nightmare?"

"He came after me," she said, traumatized by the realness of her dream.

"Layne can't get you here. You won't see him anymore. When you get home, he'll be gone."

"You promise?"

"I promise."

She relaxed on his lap, leaning back to look up at him. "I don't like Layne."

"Yeah, neither does Lucy."

"He fishes."

That's what the girl didn't like about him?

"I don't like the fishing house," Sophie said.

The fishing house must be a rental or second home Layne frequented. "What don't you like about it?"

"It smells like fish."

Thad smiled. "Do you like Rosanna?" The investigator in him made him ask. That and an inexplicable protectiveness.

Sophie didn't answer.

"Do you?" he pressed.

"I like Lucy."

"Who doesn't like Lucy?" Thad couldn't stop his chuckle. "But what about Rosanna?"

"She's okay."

"Better than Layne."

The little girl nodded emphatically, eyes big with certainty. "Lots better."

"Well, that's good. You won't have to live with Layne anymore, just Rosanna."

The animation faded from Sophie's face and she looked down.

"What's the matter?" Thad asked.

She raised her eyes, so solemn and full of gravity no child should have to bear. "I want my mommy."

A spear drove through his heart at her declaration, followed by a fierce impulse to do something about her sorrow. He'd never felt anything like it before.

Thad rubbed her back gently. "I know you do. I wish I could bring her back to you."

Sophie snuggled closer to him again. "I like you."

She liked him. He watched her eyes close, a gesture of utter trust in the adult who held her. Thad didn't want to let her go. He waited while she drifted off to sleep, staring at her sweet face, overwhelmed by her loss, wishing he could find a way to fill the void. No child should lose their parents, the only family they had. Sophie had been thrown into a cold world and desperately sought warmth.

Thad was concerned over her aversion to Layne and her increasing withdrawal from Rosanna. Rosanna's situation may have been suitable when she'd first taken Sophie into her home, but that was no longer the case. This poor child was adrift and in need of a soft place to land. And damn if Thad didn't entertain giving that to her.

Lifting her, he set her down on the mattress and adjusted the blankets so they weren't twisted. She made a little groaning sound and then fell into deep sleep again. Thad stood and looked down at her, torn apart inside.

His rational side argued that he'd never been against kids. He was only against bringing them into a family that was doomed to break apart. But what was his answer to Sophie's situation? Her mother had died. Her father hadn't stuck around when she was born and would never claim responsibility for her. She had been brought into a dysfunctional family and now had no family at all.

Thad could turn away from marriage and babies and

prevent an emotional breakup of his own, but what was he supposed to do when a child who wasn't his was left motherless and the foster home where she lived was no longer a safe haven?

"Now you know why I cried," he heard a woman's voice say from behind him. Lucy.

She stood in the doorway. How much had she witnessed? Enough. His wall shot back up into place. "She had a nightmare." With that he walked to the door. Lucy stepped out of the way, and he passed her.

In his room, he closed the door, but not before seeing Lucy once more. She knew what comforting Sophie had done to him. The lock to his heart had been opened, and his beliefs questioned.

Chapter 10

The next day, Thad drove Lucy and Sophie to Rosanna's house. It had been pure drama getting Sophie into the car. She didn't want to leave. Thad was supposed to meet Darcy, but he'd called to push the time back so that he could go with Lucy to drop the child off. Just one look at Lucy confirmed that she felt the same as he did. Were they doing the right thing by taking her back to her foster mom? Lucy said Rosanna had sounded stable on the phone. Happy, revived, relieved. Layne was gone. She'd reclaimed her life and was eager to get Sophie back.

He looked in the rearview mirror as he had several times already. Sophie's eyes were red but she'd stopped crying. Such a young mind didn't understand what was happening to her. She was being yanked from one home to another, never having time to adjust, settle in and feel safe. He couldn't shut off the nagging instinct to do something. The more time he spent with Sophie, the stronger that instinct became.

He pulled to a stop in front of Rosanna's house and got out. Lucy did, too, and opened the back door.

"Come on, Sophie," Lucy said.

"No!" Sophie whined. "I don't want to go!"

Thad opened the other back door and retrieved Sophie's overnight bag.

"We have to do this," Lucy said.

"I don't want to live here!"

"Out of the car, Sophie," Lucy said in a sterner tone, but it sounded forced. She didn't like doing this.

Sophie began crying again, but she climbed out of the car.

Lucy knelt down with her hands on the child's shoulders. "I'll come and see you."

Thad walked around and stood over them, torn apart inside. A couple of tears ran down Lucy's face.

Sophie cried, deep and genuine. This was more than a childish tantrum. Sophie was hurting.

When she reached her little arms up toward him, wailing unintelligible pleas, he dropped the bag and lifted her up into his arms. She cried against his shoulder while he rubbed her back.

"It'll be all right, Sophie," he tried to comfort her.

"Take me back home," she sobbed, leaning back to look at him. Her wet face and sad, red eyes broke him.

He looked down at Lucy, who stood up and wiped her tears, crying outright now.

"Why can't you take me home?"

Thad looked at her. "I would if I could."

"Is everything okay?" a woman asked.

Thad saw Rosanna standing on the sidewalk, worriedly observing the scene.

"Rosanna's here, Sophie," Lucy said. She'd regained control, although it was obvious she'd been crying.

Sophie's cries eased and she looked back.

"Hi, Sophie," Rosanna said. "I baked some cookies for you. And I thought we could watch a movie together."

Sophie turned back to Thad. Her sweet eyes heavy with innocent despondency.

"Lucy and I will come and see you," he said, wondering what had made him.

"Promise?"

"Promise." He kissed her temple, and then she hugged him, her tiny arms squeezing him around his neck.

Touched more than he could handle, he put the girl down, and she all but dragged her feet toward Rosanna.

Rosanna took her hand. "Things are going to be so much better around here. You'll see."

Until she had to be yanked out of this home and into another once she was adopted. Thad didn't know what to do with the helplessness he felt.

Lucy knelt to hug her and then stood beside Thad.

Rosanna tugged Sophie toward the house. The little girl's lower lip quivered as she looked back at them.

When she disappeared inside, Lucy turned to him and cried. He held her and for the first time noticed a car parked across the street. A man was inside and he was taking pictures.

Late that night, Lucy couldn't sleep. Piling all the pillows behind her, she gave up and sat up on the bed, turning on the TV with a remote. Not only did Sophie's heart-wrenching tears haunt her, so did the man who'd taken pictures of them. As soon as Thad had noticed him, the man had spun the car around and sped off. Who would do that and why?

Flipping channels for several more minutes, Lucy gave up on finding anything that would take her mind off Sophie and the strange man. Letting her head fall back, she stared up at the ceiling.

Thad barging through her bedroom door effectively changed her focus. Fully dressed in jeans and a leather jacket over a white T-shirt, he had an urgency about him. What had him so wound up? Cam? His mother's shooter?

"I just got a call from the station. A 9-1-1 call was placed by Rosanna…"

Sophie.

9-1-1.

That was something she hadn't expected. Lucy sprang out of bed as Thad went into her closet.

"What happened?" She quickly dressed in what he started throwing at her. A pair of jeans came first.

"Rosanna's been murdered."

Murdered? He threw a thin, soft sweater at her next. No bra. The shock of his announcement sank in.

"Where's Sophie?" she asked.

Finally his eyes met hers, helpless and grim with bad news.

The stab of apprehension took her next breath. "Where is she?"

"I don't know."

"She's missing?" *Oh, God…*

"It appears that way."

Kidnapped? "Why would anyone take her?" And who? It didn't add up.

And then she recalled the stranger parked in the car

and taking pictures of them…of Thad holding Sophie. Of Lucy crying. Sophie crying…

Clearly Sophie and Lucy meant a lot to him. Lucy was harder to get to at the estate, with all the Secret Service agents roaming around. Sophie, on the other hand…

Minutes later, Thad raced to a stop in front of Rosanna's house, where police had already strung up crime scene tape. He knew the officers there and some of the other crime scene investigators. He hadn't been called officially because he was still on leave.

"We should have kept her with us," Lucy said, breathless. The scene frightened her. It should. He dismissed the thought that they were behaving like worried parents. Under less serious conditions, he'd expect Lucy to tease him or tell one of her stories. If only that were the case.

Rosanna was dead and Sophie had been kidnapped— he had to assume this was related to the threat he'd gotten.

Thad faced her, putting his hands on her shoulders. "I think you should wait out here."

In a daze, Lucy nodded.

Reluctantly, Thad left her and approached a detective he'd worked with on other scenes who stood at the front door. After greeting him, he went inside. He saw Rosanna facedown on the floor, a pool of relatively fresh blood beneath her. He'd seen it many times before, but this time it felt more personal.

"She made the call after the child was taken," the detective said. "She was stabbed three times in the chest."

And as she lay dying, she'd called for help, knowing that Sophie had been kidnapped. "Murder weapon?"

"Haven't found it."

"Any witnesses?"

The detective shook his head. "None so far."

"Who took her?"

"The ex, or soon-to-be. She told the operator."

Thad nearly closed his eyes. At least he had a lead. A solid one.

When he imagined what the little girl might be enduring, a cold sweat broke out in him. Quickly following that, brewing rage. He would do anything to bring Sophie back to safety. Anything.

Surveying the scene and taking in every detail, Thad spotted some photos on a white bookshelf. Going there, he looked at each one and stopped when he saw one of a birthday celebration. He couldn't tell whose it was, but Layne was in it. He stood on a balcony. The day was sunny and in the background was a river. It looked like some kind of vacation home. There was a planter shaped like a fish, and a fish wind chime hanging from a jutting soffit.

"Do we know anything about this?" he asked.

The detective came over to the shelf. "What about it?"

"Did Layne have a vacation home by a river?" *A fishing house,* as Sophie had called it.

Suddenly, a feeling in his gut had his feet moving.

He went back outside to Lucy. She hugged herself, guilt-ridden over not keeping Sophie with them. He felt a little of it himself. He was relieved when Lucy had taken her back to Rosanna. The child would no longer be around to challenge his views and his reason for having them. Now he struggled with doubt over whether those views were justified, or even real.

A scream emanating behind them caused them both to turn around. A woman tried to break through two officers blocking her attempt to gain entry to the home.

"Rosanna!" she cried.

Police tried to calm her. Letting her inside would not only disturb the scene, it would gravely upset the woman.

"I'm her mother! Rosanna!"

One of the officers spoke to her and Thad could tell when he revealed that Rosanna was dead. The woman crumbled to the ground and screamed louder and much more gutturally.

Thad went over to the group. "May I?"

"Sure," one of the officers said.

Thad crouched before the woman and told who he was. "Ma'am?"

The sobbing woman looked at him. With tears shining on her face, she said, "You have to find Layne. He did this."

Lucy turned her head sharply toward him, and he nodded once to let her know that's what he'd learned when he'd gone into the crime scene.

"Rosanna was afraid of him," the woman said. "He threatened her more than once." She leaned with her hands on the lawn and cried again. "Get him out of the house, I told her. Get him out. We thought she'd be safe once she did." She resumed her sobbing.

Thad was certain he wouldn't take Sophie to his new residence. "Did Layne have anywhere else he could go other than here or at his new home? A vacation home? There's a picture inside of a place where he fishes."

The woman regained some of her composure. "Yes. He fished a lot. Near Jordan Lake. His parents have a place there." She gave him detailed directions on how to get there but didn't know an exact address. It was enough.

"Do you have any idea why he'd kidnap Sophie?" Lucy asked.

And Thad understood the reason she'd asked. He wondered the same. And the image of that man taking pictures kept running in his head.

"No." The woman shook her head. "He didn't care much for kids. Not like Rosanna. Rosanna loved children. She wanted some of her own someday." More tears spilled free. "He must have done it to spite her."

But Rosanna was dead. If Layne had killed her, why take Sophie? Rosanna was no longer alive to care. No, the man who'd taken pictures had discovered what Sophie meant to him. More than even Thad had had time to comprehend.

"Thank you." Thad stood and said to the policemen, "Take care of her, would you?"

The one closest to him nodded. "We will."

Thad took Lucy's hand and hurried to his car. There, he called Darcy, who could help him find the place Layne's parents owned. Sophie could be anywhere. This was a shot in the dark, but it was the only one they had.

Lucy saw the average-sized house as Thad drove by. There were a few lights on, but no activity was evident from here. After they were out of sight from the house, Thad parked.

"Wait here," he said.

But Lucy got out with him. "I'm coming with you." If Layne hurt Sophie, she'd kill him.

Not arguing, Thad pulled out his pistol from the holster he hadn't bothered to cover when he'd left the estate. He'd put it on over his T-shirt. Going to the front door, he tried the handle. It was locked. Listening, he heard no sounds. No cries from a child. No talking.

Around the back, he kept to the side of the house, the

roar of the river a hundred yards from there. He saw the balcony he'd seen in the picture. There were stairs leading up to it. He tried the sliding glass door on the lower level. It also was locked.

Lucy trailed behind him, searching the darkness in case anyone appeared. They crept up the stairs. The blinds covering the windows on the lower level were all closed.

Trying the balcony door, the handle turned. Thad looked back at Lucy and mouthed, "Stay here." When she nodded, he pushed open the door. He heard a television from somewhere down the hall that played a cartoon.

An instant later, a man's form jumped out from the enclave of the kitchen, holding a pan. It was Layne. Thad blocked the swing and then drove his fist into Layne's sternum. When Layne grunted and bent over slightly, Thad grabbed his wrist and used his weight to force him backward, slamming him against the stainless-steel refrigerator.

Thad pounded Layne's wrist to the metal refrigerator door until the frying pan dropped and clattered to the tile floor. Then he rammed his knee into Layne's chest and chopped his throat with the side of his hand. That sent Layne to his knees.

Pointing his gun at Layne, he demanded, "Did you hurt her?"

Lucy appeared inside the kitchen. Seeing that he had Layne under control, she ran down the hall toward the sound of the cartoon. She vanished into a room, and Thad heard Sophie begin to cry and say her name.

"I've got you," Lucy said, emerging into the hall carrying the crying child, who clung to her. "I won't let you go, I promise."

Something in Thad shifted, the love Lucy had for the child touching the cold spot in his heart. Sophie trusted her and returned the love. The sight of them and the realization of that love choked him.

Sophie wailed unintelligible things, a patchy account of what had happened to her. Layne had come into her room and put something over her mouth that made her go to sleep. She woke up here, and he'd threatened to kill her if she made a single sound.

He'd drugged her. A child. That was so dangerous. What if he'd given her too much? Fury roiled, and Thad had to force himself to stay under control. The only positive in this was that Sophie hadn't been aware of what happened to Rosanna. She may have heard the struggle and perhaps Rosanna screaming, but she hadn't seen her body. Still a traumatizing experience, but it could have been worse. She'd woken in a strange place, kidnapped by Layne, a man she didn't like. She'd been scared.

Rage propelled Thad to kick Layne, planting his boot on his chest and banging him backward against the refrigerator.

"Why did you do this?" Thad needed him to talk about the man who'd taken pictures.

Layne looked up at him, lip bleeding.

"Why?" Thad yelled.

Lucy put her hand on Sophie's head, making sure she didn't see what Thad did to Layne, and then talked into the girl's ear to calm her.

Thad leaned down and yanked Layne's head back with one hand and pressed the barrel of the gun to his temple. Layne was no hardened criminal. If he'd killed Rosanna, it was a crime of passion.

"Tell me now," Thad said.

Layne looked up at Thad's face, at his eyes, and relented. "I was paid."

Just as he'd thought. "Who paid you?"

"You're Thad Winston, aren't you?" Layne asked rather than answering.

Had he recognized him from a picture or because of who his mother was? Maybe both.

"He warned me that you might come after me," Layne continued.

"Who paid you?" Thad repeated.

Leaning against the refrigerator, Layne stretched his legs out in front of him and wiped his lip. Thad kept the gun aimed at his head but allowed him to get more comfortable.

"He wouldn't tell me his name," Layne said. "He just offered me a lot of money." Layne explained about the call he'd received and although he'd been skeptical, he'd met the man an hour later, when he'd given him cash.

"Half today, half after the child was delivered," Layne said.

"What did the man look like?" Thad asked.

Layne thought for a moment. "He wore a hat and sunglasses. He wasn't as tall as you and had on a dark suit."

That wasn't much to go on and Thad hadn't gotten a good look at the man who'd watched them before he drove away, which had been right after he'd been spotted. He hadn't seen the license plate, either. "After you had Sophie, what were you supposed to do?"

"He was going to contact me to arrange giving her to him. He hasn't yet."

Thad had gotten here in time. "How was he going to contact you?"

"My phone. Cell phone."

Thad searched him. Not finding the phone, he scanned the kitchen.

Finally having calmed Sophie enough to put her down, Lucy picked up a cell phone from the kitchen island and showed it to Thad.

Layne had agreed to kidnap a young girl for money without knowing who hired him or why. He hadn't set out to murder Rosanna. He'd been desperate for money. And once embroiled in the plan to kidnap Sophie, there was no turning back.

Hearing sirens outside, Thad was assured of Layne's arrest, but without a solid lead to identify the man who'd paid him to kidnap Sophie. He could only vow to protect Sophie from further harm. And that came with another kind of danger—one to his heart.

Chapter 11

Darcy lay propped up on his elbow, looking down at Avery's pretty face as she slept. Her thick, soft blond hair fanned over the pillow and one fine breast. Over the past week, he'd spent every night with her here at her apartment. They hadn't had sex until last night. He was still in awe. The sex had clinched what he'd begun to suspect. Avery hadn't been ready before last night, but he had been ready since the day he met her.

He'd gone slow with her, spent more than an hour loving her before spreading her legs and doing what he'd dreamed of doing for days. It had been better than he'd imagined. She'd been timid that first time, the aftereffects of nearly being raped. The second time, she'd climbed on top of him. Together they were a couple of 1.3G fireworks.

The night before last, she'd worked a night shift at the

hospital while he worked his latest murder case. She'd gotten back to the apartment at 6:00 a.m., about fifteen minutes before he'd arrived. It was so refreshing to be with someone who understood his irregular schedule. She could change hers to match his. She had a sweet arrangement at work.

Just then her eyes fluttered open.

"I love you," he said, and kissed her.

Still groggy and waking up, she blinked a few times and kept looking at him.

"I've been lying here watching you sleep, thinking about that," he said. "I'm sure of it. I love you. I can't believe how fast it happened, but I do. I'm madly in love with you." There. It was out in the open.

"Darcy..." she finally said, sounding hesitant.

He controlled the wave of dread. "You don't feel the same?"

"I..." She sat up, holding the sheets to her chest.

He sat with her. Maybe he shouldn't have been so honest yet.

She looked at him, her beautiful blue eyes uncertain but full of desire. "No. I do feel the same...but it scares me."

It scared him, too. He kissed her. "Good. Let's go find breakfast. I know a diner that's open 24/7." It was 2:00 a.m.

She got up with him. He started the shower. They'd developed the habit of taking showers together. Quiet and averting her eyes from him, she stepped under the spray with him. She had a big enough shower for the two of them. It was separate from the tub.

He turned on the stereo, and a jazzy tune played. She laughed at his playfulness and looped her arms over his shoulders while water rained down on them. He kissed her, enjoying the wet contact.

"Darcy..." she breathed.

"Yes." He moved her so that her back was against the wall.

"Stop doing this to me."

"I'm going to do this to you." He lifted her, and she wrapped her legs around him with a soft, sultry laugh.

He found her and pressed her to the wet tile wall with each thrust, holding her waist. After she came, he quickly followed, the love he felt making the build and release so much more powerful.

"Darcy," she whispered.

"I know." He kissed her softly, tenderly.

Neither of them had to voice what they felt. This had come on so fast. What had him worried was that he might be more prepared to deal with it than Avery. He didn't like thinking about losing another woman he loved. This was so much different from his marriage, but he was afraid he felt more for Avery than he had for his wife the entire time he was with her.

Darcy sat across from Avery at Gracie's Diner. At first glance it looked like a good place to get botulism, but once inside, the aroma beckoned and the food never disappointed. He knew the owner, Gracie. She ran a tight ship. This place was clean. There wasn't a corner that didn't shine.

Avery looked over the restaurant. Chrome, black cushioned stools and booths formed an L around an open kitchen. Framed pictures of various cartoon characters cluttered the walls. Gracie didn't have the decorating sense that Avery did.

"How did you find this diner?" she asked.

"It was near a crime scene. Been coming here ever since."

"I love it."

At her mention of the word *love,* Darcy grew uncomfortable. He'd felt so sure she was on the same page as him. He still thought she could be, but he shouldn't have said anything. It wasn't like him to blurt out what he thought and felt.

"Darcy." She reached over and put her hand on his. "Do you think we're reading too much into this?"

Why did she think they were exaggerating? Because their divorces were so fresh?

"I was ready to be alone for a long time before I met you," he said.

"So was I." She looked down, drawing her hand back. This was really bothering her. Sex had changed the dynamics.

Gracie carried two plates over, her short, curly, white hair unruly, big-hooped earrings swinging, and chewing gum just like a scene in a movie.

"Here ya are," she said, putting the plates down with a clank as she eyed Avery. He'd already introduced her, and Gracie had asked if she was his new partner. When he'd said no, she'd absorbed every detail about Avery. She'd seemed surprised Darcy had brought her so early in the morning.

Darcy looked down at his and Avery's plates. Steaming eggs smothered in spicy green chili. Avery loved Mexican food as much as he did. They had identical plates, right down to the whole wheat toast—hold the butter.

"Thanks, Gracie." He hoped she'd leave them alone now. No such luck.

"Kate Winston was released from the hospital, I heard," she said.

"Yes, she was." Gracie was always chatty when he came in, catching up on the latest news.

"Heard on the news that your friend has been by her side the whole time."

She didn't have to say Thad's name for him to know that's who she'd meant. But why was she pointing that out? "It's his mother."

Gracie smacked her gum. "Is he part of the investigation? I heard the feds were leading it."

She'd heard a lot. "He's doing what he can." Darcy couldn't talk much about that. Chief Thomas had too many eyes and ears as it was.

"Well, if anyone can catch that shooter, it's you and Thad." Gracie turned to Avery.

"Did you know he came here to my restaurant every day after some gang members killed a teenage boy in my parking lot?" she asked Avery.

Avery shook her head, but exchanged a knowing look with Darcy. That was the crime he'd responded to, and what had kept him coming back.

"Made me and my workers feel a lot safer," Gracie said. "Saved my business, too. Customers came back and liked knowing an officer of the law was spending a good portion of his day here."

"It wasn't that long." Why was she making a special effort to boast for him?

"All morning. Every morning." Gracie turned to Avery. "He was here before the first worker arrived. Most times that was me."

"You just think it's sexy to have a cop in your restaurant."

She hooted a laugh and patted his back. "It's good to see you recover so quickly, Darcy."

So that's what she'd been leading up to. He'd brought a beautiful woman into her diner in the dark hours of morning. He should have expected that.

"You have yourself a fine man," she said to Avery. "I'd hang on to him if I were you." She winked at Darcy.

While Avery looked bashful at that comment, he endured her not-so-subtle praise. They always talked when he came in. They were friends. Darcy leaned back against the bench seat in resignation.

"You two enjoy." Gracie left the table.

"You're well liked in this community," Avery said.

And he felt like asking if that would make her admit she loved him. He let her eat awhile, seeing that she was slow in doing so.

After a while, she gave up. Putting her fork down, she leaned back like him. "What are we going to do about this?"

"About what?" He knew, but he hedged anyway.

"Us. Last night. This morning." She flung her hand as she spoke.

"Nothing. Live."

"We both just got divorced, Darcy. My husband cheated on me."

"My wife cheated on me."

"Exactly. We're damaged."

"Why do we have to look at it that way?" Darcy sat forward. "Why can't we look at the good in this?" The connection. The sex.

She angled her head, uncertain but accepting his reasoning.

"Do you enjoy being with me?" he asked.

She blinked, their passion from last night reflecting briefly in her eyes. "Darcy…"

"Do you? And not just the way we were last night. Do you genuinely like being with me?"

She took a few seconds to consider his serious question. "Yes. You know I do."

Relief flooded through him. Then he wasn't wrong about her, about them. "I enjoy being with you, too. So what do you want to do? Stop seeing each other?"

"No."

"Are you sure?" He held her eyes in a demanding gaze. She had to tell him the truth. "I need you to be honest with me right now."

Another blink revealed her feelings. She feared what had sparked between them, but she truly did not want to stop seeing him. "Yes. I'm sure. But…" She averted her gaze.

Somehow he had to reassure her.

Darcy put his hand on top of hers where it rested by her glass of water. She looked at him again, turning her hand to entwine her fingers with his.

"Even if this is just a Band-Aid that helps us both get past our divorces, I don't see anything wrong with that. We hang out together, make each other feel good and live life. If it ends up that we decide to split, then we split. If it ends up we decide not to…we don't."

"No pressure," she said.

"No pressure." Would she place pressure on herself by resisting love? He had to make her face her fear.

"I see us going on the way we are and falling more

and more in love," he said. "I see us getting married and having kids. And that's something I never thought I'd say to any woman ever again."

Her hand tightened in his and she looked uncertainly at him, afraid of the intensity of what they had together.

"I won't tell you I love you until you're ready," he said. Just like she wasn't ready to have sex until last night.

She relaxed again. "Okay."

"Don't be afraid."

She sighed and slipped her hand from his. "I'll try."

Seeing her resistance linger, he wasn't convinced. What could he do to make her trust him? Trust in them as a couple?

Just then, his cell rang.

"There goes that moment," Avery muttered. She knew as much as he did what his ringing cell phone meant at this hour of night.

"Jenkins."

"It's me, Darcy."

"Thad?" He shared a perplexed look with Avery.

"I think Wade Thomas had something to do with my mother's shooting."

"What?" Darcy struggled to remove cash from his wallet. He always had a lot of cash on hand in case he had to pay and run.

Avery took the wallet from him and removed the correct amount. He almost didn't hear what Thad told him about the kidnapping of a young girl. She was behaving as though she were already his wife. And she didn't even know it. He vowed to make her that, and he'd use love to his advantage.

Fifteen minutes later, Thad met him at Avery's apartment. She had to get ready for work and his day was about to begin at the same time. While she went into the bedroom to change, Darcy headed for the kitchen, where Thad sat on an island stool.

"You look tired. Coffee?" Darcy went into the kitchen.

"Sure." Thad explained in detail everything that had occurred.

Darcy started the coffee brewing. "Why Wade Thomas?"

He went to stand opposite of Thad at the island. "It's a gut feeling. The way he keeps us off the investigation. The way he always finds out what we're doing. It's almost as though someone were keeping him informed." Thad told him about the man taking pictures.

Okay, that made sense. It explained how the chief could be keeping tabs on Thad, and even Darcy.

Thad ran his fingers through his hair, elbows on the table. He knew the danger of implicating the chief of police. If they were wrong...

"Why would he send someone to kidnap Sophie?" Darcy asked.

"To stop me."

"He can order you to do that." He already had. Maybe that's why he'd taken it to the next level. He was getting worried Thad would find out too much—assuming Wade was behind any of this. It seemed like a stretch to Darcy. Until he recalled the pictures of Thad and Lucy returning Sophie.

"Sophie means that much to you, huh?"

"Don't give me a hard time about that right now," Thad snapped.

Darcy held one hand up. "Hey. You know you're thinking it, too."

Thad met his look and didn't argue. He couldn't. No

one would have used that child against him if it hadn't been obvious she was important to Thad.

"You want to catch your mother's shooter. I get that," Darcy said. "But I think you should hang back. Be an observer for a while. See what the police get on Layne. Maybe he'll feel like talking."

"He claims he doesn't know who paid him."

Darcy could see Thad believed him. And he agreed it seemed as though the shooter wasn't working alone. But the chief of police?

Thad lowered his arms and met Darcy's gaze. This was the most frustrating part of investigative work. The dead ends were growing more numerous and it seemed as if they'd never solve the case.

"What do you want to do?" Darcy asked.

"Talk to Wade."

That bold? He'd go straight to the chief and start asking questions? Darcy admired his smart friend. That wasn't something Darcy would try. He'd take a more conservative approach, gather evidence first and then confront.

"Be careful," Darcy said.

"Careful about what?" Avery appeared, dressed in her uniform and tennis shoes. She leaned in for a kiss, and he held her head for a longer one than she'd have given, enough to get him by until he could see her again tonight.

"I thought you didn't have to work today." He deliberately avoided answering her.

"I had a message asking if I could cover for someone. I figured you'd be working today anyway." She glanced at Thad.

"I might be."

She kissed him again. "Thanks for breakfast."

He grinned because he knew she wasn't talking about the diner or the food. "I'll call you."

She gave him one more peck on the mouth. "Okay."

When she left, he noticed Thad looking at him as though he couldn't believe what he'd seen. Love was surrounding him and it was beginning to have an effect on his friend. Good. It was about time. If there was one thing Thad needed, it was love, the kind that would never fade away. And it seemed to Darcy that love had found him, not just with Lucy, but a little girl named Sophie.

Thad knocked on Wade Thomas's open office door. Wade looked up and his head jerked back a fraction. He hadn't expected Thad to come see him. He waved for Thad to enter.

Thad did.

"I didn't expect to see you so soon."

"Something's come up."

The chief stared at him for a while, making his own deductions. "I thought we had an understanding."

Thad wasn't supposed to be investigating his mother's shooting. "That was before I rescued a seven-year-old girl from Layne Bridger." He watched Wade's face closely.

Chief Thomas didn't alter his expression. "Who?"

"The girl's foster dad. He kidnapped her and said someone paid him to in order to teach me some kind of a lesson." He went into detail of all that had occurred.

Wade revealed nothing of his emotions. "I take it this girl is someone special to you."

He was getting sick of everyone pointing that out. "She's someone special to Lucy."

"The nurse." Wade put down the pen he held. "Why are you in my office telling me this?"

"You didn't know about this?"

"The kidnapping?" If he was acting he was good at it. "No. Must have been outside our jurisdiction." Wade studied Thad, dissecting him, trying to figure out why he was here.

"She was kidnapped because of my interest in my mother's shooting," Thad said.

"You're still nosing your way into that?"

Thad gave no reply.

Wade's brow furrowed and he stood. Moving around the desk, he came to stand before him. "How many times do I have to tell you to stay out of it?"

"Did you have anything to do with the kidnapping?" It was risky for Thad to ask that question. Darcy had known it, but he hadn't tried to stop Thad. Like Thad, he knew it might be the only way to get answers.

As he expected, Wade grew even angrier. "Are you accusing me of something, Winston?"

"I'm asking you if you had anything to do with Sophie Cambridge's kidnapping."

"Why would I have anything to do with that?"

"You keep warning me to stay out of the investigation. How far will you go to see that I do?"

"You're crossing the line. I didn't know about the kidnapping of a little girl until you walked in here and told me."

Wade seemed to be telling the truth. Either that, or he was a good liar.

"Somebody really doesn't want you sticking your nose where it doesn't belong," Wade said. "Have you received any other warnings?"

"A phone call."

Wade studied him some more. Then he went over to his desk and wrote some names down. "You went against orders by continuing to look into the shooting," Wade said, leaving the pen there. "But I'm going to overlook it." He picked up his phone and pressed in a number. "Chief Thomas here. I need you to check some phone records."

Wade was going to help him? Thad hadn't expected this. A guilty man wouldn't try to help.

Wade told whoever he'd called what Thad had told him, and then asked him to get the case information from the Pittsboro police.

When he finished, he hung up the phone and looked at Thad. "I'm going to pass whatever I get on to the FBI. Can I count on you to stay out of this from here?"

"If you let me know what you find out in Sophie's kidnapping case, yes."

Wade nodded. "If anything else happens, let me know. Meanwhile, go back on leave, Winston. I don't want to see your face around here until you're ready to come back to work and do what I tell you."

"Yes, sir."

"And the next time you accuse me of anything as heinous as kidnapping a seven-year-old girl, I'll fire you. Do we understand each other?"

"Perfectly." Thad left the office, still not sure he could eliminate Wade from his list of suspicious characters. What if Wade never shared the information?

Chapter 12

The night after rescuing Sophie, Lucy tucked the girl in and kissed her on her cheek. She was already drifting off to sleep. They'd read a book, and she could barely keep her eyes open. Brushing wayward strands of light brown hair from her face, she stood from the bed, so glad that Sophie was no longer under stress. She was content and safe.

Turning the lamp off, Lucy left the room in the dim glow of a Tinker Bell night-light. Pausing at the door, she looked back at the sleeping girl and wondered for the hundredth time what she was going to do with her. She'd made arrangements to temporarily foster her, but what then?

Making her way down to the informal sitting area, Lucy walked in to find Kate and Thad there. Kate was moving around on her own now. She didn't need a home care nurse anymore, but had insisted Lucy stay anyway. She suspected there was another reason for that, and that reason was sitting on the white designer sofa in jeans and a gray thermal T-shirt. His golden-green hazel eyes went into a smolder when he saw her.

"How is she?" Thad asked.

"A lot better." Lucy went to sit beside him, Kate occupying the adjacent chair.

"That poor child," Kate said. "She's been through so much for such a young age."

Lucy met Thad's look and wondered if he was as affected by the little girl as she was. He had a fierce protective streak when it came to Sophie. He cared for her. Lucy was sure of that. He hadn't admitted it yet, though. Would he ever? Or would he stubbornly stick to his belief that marriage and kids weren't his calling?

"She sure is attached to you, Lucy," Kate said.

The observation only intensified Lucy's conundrum.

"You, too, Thad," Kate added.

Beside her, Thad turned stiffly to her without responding. Thad had periodically checked in on her and Sophie. He'd even watched a movie with them—most of it. And then his phobia had taken over and he'd had to leave. Lucy was okay with that. He took the family time in doses, each one bigger than the last.

"He's becoming a real dad." Lucy couldn't stop herself from teasing.

"I've always said he'd make a good one," Kate said.

"I'm sitting right here," Thad interjected.

"Sophie adores you," Kate told him. "The three of you would make a lovely family."

Lucy watched the observation bounce off Thad's wall of indifference.

"My mother and I were discussing the possibility that the gunman who'd tried to kill her may have been involved in Sophie's kidnapping," he said.

"Go ahead, change the subject," Lucy said, a little put off by his stubbornness.

He smirked at her and nothing more.

"I've been briefed on the case," Kate said. "No one suggested Wade Thomas has anything to do with it. He isn't involved in the investigation any more than you are, Thad. And you yourself said you could find no connection between him and Cam Harmon. There's nothing to indicate the two are friends or have met before."

Lucy wondered if Kate was being briefed about everything or if those informing her simply didn't know any more than she and Thad. If Wade had hired Cam, he'd keep his association secret. But how likely would it be that Wade would go so far as to arrange for Kate's assassination, or even be a part of it?

"There's nothing to indicate he has extreme political views, either," Thad said.

"The chief is just doing his job," Kate insisted. "He was told to stay out of the investigation. He may have people who keep him apprised of developments, but he's doing what he's been told. This isn't an ordinary attempted murder case. I recently announced my intention to run for president. Wouldn't you make sure an attempted assassination investigation was controlled and that crucial information didn't leak out?"

"Maybe. But I wouldn't turn away help."

"You would if you risked media coverage."

Thad sighed, hands entwined on his lap as he leaned forward. Kate had a valid point, but was she being too blithe?

"Would the agents working the investigation tell you everything?" Thad asked.

If there was foul play going on within law enforcement, they wouldn't.

"If they aren't, somebody's head is going to roll." Kate could appear the most docile, unassuming woman, and then in an instant become the hard-hitting politician she was. "I'll get someone I trust to take a closer look."

When Thad gave a nod, Lucy knew he was satisfied. Lucy, too. Kate wasn't going to be blithe about this. She'd check every angle, and hopefully the results supported what she thought: that Chief Thomas was only doing what he was told.

Thad leaned back against the sofa, more relaxed than he had been since Lucy had joined them.

"Meanwhile, I want you to stop carrying on your own vigilante investigation," Kate said.

And that had Thad tensing all over again. He sat forward, his forearms on his thighs. "Why?"

"It's too dangerous. Sophie was kidnapped to send you a warning and it's one you should heed, at least for now, at least until my inside man can gather some meaningful intel. We need to know what we're dealing with. Who is involved? Did someone pay the shooter or is the shooter working alone? These questions need answers."

It seemed to Lucy that there was more than the shooter involved. Cam's background matched the shooter's. Jaden was a suspicious character, and now Thad thought Chief Thomas knew more than he let on. Were they all linked somehow? Lucy didn't see how. Why would Chief Thomas help assassinate Kate, a presidential candidate?

"Let me do some checking," Kate pleaded with Thad.

"Go to Carova Beach for a few days. I'll let you know what I find when you get back."

"No. I'm not leaving you here."

"I'm surrounded by security. I want you to go away for a while, and I need someone I trust to get the house ready for my visit. I'll be fine here."

"I can't leave you alone until the gunman is caught. What if something happens and I'm not here?"

"Thad, you're not the only one who can protect me. Sam is here, and I have plenty of Secret Service agents."

One of whom Thad didn't trust. Lucy could tell he would not leave his mother unprotected and he felt he would do the best job of it. Part of her was relieved, since Kate had suggested she go with him. Another part wondered if a few days in Carova weren't exactly what he needed to let his guard down with her.

"Ask your friend Darcy to stay here while you're gone," Kate suggested. "You trust him, don't you?"

Lucy saw how that made an impact on Thad's resolve.

"Take Lucy and Sophie with you." Kate pushed and wouldn't let up until Thad agreed. That both excited Lucy and made her nervous. "You'll keep them safe that way. Cam won't be able to harass her and no one will be able to hurt Sophie. She'll be able to play on the beach and see new things. It will get her mind off what she's been through."

After contemplating his mother for endless seconds, Thad turned to Lucy in silent petition.

"She has a good point," Lucy had to concede. They would all be safe in the Carova beach house, and if Darcy stayed here at the estate, Thad wouldn't have to worry about his mother.

"It's just for a few days." A tiny smile pushed at Kate's mouth.

"All right," Thad relented. "We'll leave on Friday."

Lucy would have plenty of time to get Sophie's things and pack.

"It's Sophie's birthday this weekend," Lucy verbalized her realization. "I'll go shopping for the monster dolls."

"I'll arrange for a dollhouse to be delivered to the beach house," Kate said.

Lucy looked at Thad the same time Kate did.

He met each one and then said, "I'll get her a bicycle. There are adult bikes already there."

This had the feel of a real family vacation. Lucy couldn't tame her smile.

"I can't wait to hear all about it when you get back," Kate said.

Now brooding, Thad stood. "I'll call Darcy in the morning."

He strode from the room.

Kate waited until he was out of earshot. "You just might be the best thing to walk into his life."

"I wouldn't bet on it."

Thad headed for a storage room where Security kept their records, beset by the prospect of spending a long weekend at the Carova beach house. His mother was right. He should let her try to get information, and Lucy and Sophie would be safe if he took them away for a while. Not knowing who paid Layne to kidnap Sophie bothered him.

The house was dark and quiet at this hour. The agents were at their posts for the night and none would come near the file room. He'd copied one of the keys so he could monitor the video recordings without anyone knowing. Unlocking the door, he entered the ten-by-eleven room lined with shelves and a few file cabinets. The shelves were half-full of file boxes and in the center was a rectangular table with a computer. Sitting on the stool there, he logged in as he had every night since catching Jaden in the dark living room. Navigating to the daily video files, he scanned through them.

Thirty minutes later, he finished. Nothing of significance had occurred. Closing the file, he opened the live feed and checked all the cameras. He almost closed the one monitoring the side entrance next to the kitchen when he saw Jaden appear and unlock the door. Looking around him, he left as quickly as he'd come.

After making a file of the portion of video showing Jaden unlocking the door, Thad saved it to a jump drive he always brought with him on his surveillance rounds. Shutting the program down, he left the file storage room. He went to the bathroom down the hall and waited. Sure enough, Jaden stepped into view and entered the storage room. He didn't see Thad hidden in the darkness.

A few minutes later, Jaden left the room. Thad returned to the storage room and confirmed Jaden had deleted the recording of him unlocking the door and tampering with the security system.

First going to the side door to relock it, Thad then headed for the guesthouse. There, he went inside without knocking. No one was up at this hour. He found the agent in charge and woke him. The man had slept here most nights since the shooting.

Todd Matheson was never surprised when he was awakened at all hours of the night. But he was surprised to be awakened by Thad.

"There's something you need to see." Thad handed the man his laptop case when he sat up on the bed.

"Give me a second." Todd dressed in jeans and a long-sleeved Henley and then booted his laptop.

"What's wrong?" he asked.

"You'll see."

Todd let Thad put the jump drive in the computer and navigate to the video file. The agent in charge watched Jaden unlock the side door with an increasingly tightening mouth. When the file finished playing, he cursed.

"He also disabled the security system for that section of the house." Thad saved a copy of the file to Todd's desktop and then removed the jump drive. "He's trying to allow someone access." The gunman, most likely. Had the same person paid Layne to kidnap Sophie? Was he also paying Jaden?

After a moment, Todd said, "We'll keep this between you and me for now."

Jaden was finished as a Secret Service agent. Todd wouldn't reveal how he'd discovered Jaden's betrayal. Thad wasn't supposed to be involved in the investigation, but Todd had been briefed on Sophie's kidnapping, the way Cam was stalking Lucy and the fact that Thad had seen Jaden go to Cam's home. That would help Thad catch his mother's shooter and anyone working with him.

Leaving the guesthouse, Thad walked down to the gatehouse and found it unmanned. A chill ran down his spine. It had been manned when he'd checked in the file storage room. He pressed a button on the gatehouse console that set off the internal alarm system. The agents in the guesthouse would be alerted, as well as his mother in her bedroom. Anyone else in the house wouldn't know an alarm had been set off.

Thad ran toward the house. Through the side entrance, he held his gun up and moved stealthily into the living room. Nothing moved. He raced up the stairs, hearing agents behind him. Sophie was still asleep in her room. Lucy's was empty.

Kate appeared in the hallway as agents swarmed her. His mother was all right. Lucy was missing.

Sam emerged from his room, still fully dressed and looking as though he'd gone out for the night and had just gotten home. "What's going on?"

"Lucy's missing." Thad turned to search the rest of the house.

"I'll help you." Sam told him which sections of the house and grounds he'd search and that he'd meet him on the side driveway.

When no sign of Lucy presented itself in his search, Thad ran to the file storage room. There, he took another look at the files surveying the driveway and gatehouse. The footage repeated after one minute. The cameras watching the gatehouse had been disabled, so no live feed had been recorded. While Thad was talking to Todd, Jaden had driven away, secure with the knowledge that he wouldn't be seen. He must have done something with the guard on duty.

But why unlock the side door? He could have abducted Lucy and gone through the gate. He didn't need the door unlocked. Thad didn't have time to figure that out. He had to find Lucy and he had to find her fast.

Jaden had to have taken her. Thad had seen Jaden at Cam's house. Had Jaden taken her there? Again, the unlocked side entrance didn't jive. Was any of this related to

Sophie's kidnapping? Maybe it was all linked somehow and Thad just hadn't put the pieces together.

Hurrying to the side driveway, he found Sam waiting there. He shook his head at the same time Thad did. They had both found nothing in their searches.

"I have an idea," Thad said, heading for his Charger.

When Sam got in the passenger side, Thad explained about seeing Jaden at Cam's house and the side entrance door.

"He could have been trying to throw you off," Sam said.

That could be possible, if Jaden knew Thad was onto him and knew he'd been watching. Thad had a feeling it was more than that, but he considered the possibility.

"He may have known I'd go talk to the agent in charge," he said. But Jaden wouldn't have predicted Thad would wait near the file storage room. He wouldn't know Thad had made a copy of the recording.

"There's one way to find out," Sam said.

Catch Jaden.

As he drove, Thad recalled that Sam hadn't gone to bed yet. "Where'd you go tonight?"

"Mike and I went to Ted's Steakhouse for dinner and then ended up getting coffee. We talked awhile."

All night. They must have talked about their captivity. Thad didn't press him for more details. If Sam was opening up about what happened to him and Mike, it could only do him good.

His cell phone began to ring.

"Thad. It's Mike Harris."

Mike Harris? He exchanged a look with Sam and put his phone on speaker. "Mike, I have Sam with me. Where are you?"

"Right now I'm parked in front of a house." He told them the address. "After I dropped Sam off, I saw a security agent put Lucy into his car and drive through the gate."

"Did the security agent see you?" Thad asked.

"No. I was parked a good distance away on the driveway. At first I wasn't sure what he was carrying. By the time I realized it was a woman, and it was Lucy, Sam had already gone into the house. I thought about going in to get him, but the agent drove through the gate. I decided to follow. I don't think he saw me."

Mike wasn't close to the investigation. He didn't know that Thad and Lucy had seen Jaden in the living room or that the window had been left unlocked and the security system tampered with.

"The agent dropped her off here," Mike continued, "and some other man carried her inside."

Cam. Just as Thad had suspected. Jaden had kidnapped Lucy...for Cam.

"We're two minutes from you. Call the police." Thad pushed his Charger to its limit.

Lucy woke to an aching head. When she went to investigate, she discovered her hands were tied. Next, she discovered her feet were tied and she was lying on a bed. Craning her neck, she struggled to see through the darkness. Was the room windowless?

A light came on and she saw Cam straighten from a lamp on a nightstand. She shut her eyes and pretended to still be unconscious. The last thing she remembered was going up the stairs to bed. Kate had already gone to hers.

Opening her eyes a slit, she saw that Cam had gone

toward the door. He must have just put her on the bed and thought he had to wait for her to wake up.

When he left, Lucy twisted her wrists. The rope tying her was too tight. Her hands were numb. Sitting up on the bed, she reached with her bound hands and frantically tugged at the knot tying her feet. She had it loosened when Cam appeared in the doorway.

"Ah. You're awake." He approached.

Unable to finish untying the knotted rope around her feet before he reached the bed, Lucy lay back and kicked him against his chest. Catching him off guard, he stumbled backward and fell.

Lucy struggled against the rope around her feet. It loosened some more. She kicked free and scrambled off the bed as Cam got to his feet with a curse.

It was hard to run with her hands bound in front of her. She made it through the bedroom door and down a narrow hallway. It was so dark in here. There was a light on in the living room. The house was a ranch with a large, open great room that had a high, gabled ceiling. As she raced for the front door, she noticed all the windows were boarded up.

Reaching the door, she was horrified to discover it lacked a door handle and the dead bolt could only be opened with a key.

Turning, she leaned against the door and used her teeth to loosen the rope around her wrists. Cam appeared in the great room, walking slowly. His confidence told her all too well how much danger she was in. He was certain she couldn't get out. Not without a key and not without a fight.

She finished loosening the rope and tossed it aside. "I told you this would happen," Cam said.

That he'd lock her in a room? This was more than a room. He'd turned his entire house into a prison…for her.

Could she fight him off before he had his way with her? She'd try to reason with him first.

"What kind of end do you think this is going to come to?" she asked with serenity she did not feel on the inside.

His head cocked to one side as he neared. He came to a stop in front of her.

"That depends on you." He reached out and brushed her hair away from her face. It was all she could do not to swat his hands away. "On how well you behave."

She felt as if she were about to vomit.

"What do you want me to do?"

"Well…" He folded one arm in front of him and propped his elbow on his forearm, putting his chin in his fingers as though thinking deeply, albeit full of mockery. Before she could block him, he swung his hand out and smacked her alongside her face. The blow sent her stumbling off balance and she fell. On her hip, she stared up at him.

"To start with, you can stop untying yourself and trying to run away. I'll untie you when I want to untie you."

Anger swirled and sparked inside her. No man had ever hit her. She would not do as he ordered. He was sick in the head and she'd fight him to her last breath. Even as she rebelled, his craziness gave her a dose of reality. Could she fight him? He was a big man and stronger than her.

Getting to her feet, she glanced around the room. There was a standing lamp, some books on a bookshelf, and an electronic picture frame. Her options were minimal. As Cam walked toward her, she went to the standing lamp. Picking it up, she swung. Cam blocked it by grabbing the pole, but the base clipped him on his face. She pulled the lamp but he held firm. Letting that go, she went to the bookshelf and started hurling books at him. He knocked a couple away but she got him with two others. His face grew stormier as he marched toward her.

If she didn't get away now, he was going to seriously hurt her. Unable to control her panic, she ran around the couch. In the kitchen, she opened drawers until she found the knives. She almost had her hand around the handle of one when Cam grabbed her hair and yanked her backward. She sailed across the kitchen and banged into the table, the corner of it digging painfully into her side. She fell into one of the chairs, toppling it over as she crashed to the floor.

Crawling away, she scrambled to her feet, pushing the table askew to block Cam's advancing steps. She had to hurt him before he hurt her. Or killed her…

When Thad and Sam arrived at Cam's house, they spotted Mike standing outside his car. He'd parked in front of the neighboring house. Thad parked behind him. Mike hadn't gone to the house. Probably smart, since help was on the way. But Thad wasn't waiting for the police. He alighted from the car and ran with his gun drawn toward the house. Seeing there was no handle on the front door, and the windows were boarded up, a sick feeling roiled his stomach.

Sam tapped his arm. Thad looked to where he indicated. The garage. Maybe there was a side door. Sam wasn't armed and neither was Mike.

"You two stay behind me," Thad said, and led them around the side of the house. There was a side door in the back, and Sam and Mike kicked it until it broke off the frame.

Thad rushed in. Like the front door, the inner garage door didn't have a knob, but someone inserted a key and began to unlock it from the inside. Cam had heard them kicking down the door.

Sam and Mike scattered to either side of the door and Thad stood between them. The door opened and Thad aimed his gun as Cam peeked his head to look into the garage. Seeing Thad, he ducked out of sight and tried to slam the door closed. Thad shoved his foot in the doorway, blocking the attempt. His black combat boots protected his feet. As a cop, he always wore good shoes. At times like these, it paid off.

Pushing the door open, he hurried inside, swinging his gun in each direction. Cam wasn't in the kitchen.

He heard sirens as he emerged into the living room and saw Cam holding Lucy with a knife at her throat. Other than that and the frightened look in her eyes, she appeared to be all right. She was fully clothed. There was a cut on her face and a faint bruise was forming but Cam hadn't had enough time to do what he'd planned.

"Drop that gun or she dies."

"In two seconds you're going to be surrounded by law enforcement," Thad said.

"Drop it!" Cam's eyes were wide with crazed uncertainty.

Crouching, Thad slowly put his gun on the floor. He heard Mike and Sam go into the garage to intercept police. Shortly after, the kitchen filled with uniforms yelling, "Raleigh Police!"

Thad stepped back and out of the way. While Cam was distracted with that, Thad picked up his gun and aimed.

He was a good shot. He practiced a lot. It was a sport to him, one that came in handy with his work, too.

Cam stood behind Lucy, his right arm pinning her to him, and his left hand holding the knife. Thad fired for his elbow and hit his target dead-on. Cam gave a shout and could no longer hang on to the knife. It fell to the floor.

Lucy took the opportunity and twisted free of Cam and ran to Thad. He wrapped his arm around her. Police rushed forward and Cam was thrust to the floor and handcuffed. He'd receive medical attention and be taken to jail. Cam glared at Thad as he was being cuffed. All the policemen here knew Thad, and Mike and Sam had probably informed them he was in here. Any other man, they'd have gotten him under control at gunpoint. But in this case, Cam was the only one on the floor. Thad saw the menace directed at him and only felt victory. He'd saved Lucy. He'd gotten here in time. Even without Mike and Sam, the first place he'd have come was Cam's house. He may have had to fight harder and longer, but the end result would have been the same.

Lucy rested her head on Thad's shoulder and watched Cam's arrest, safe and secure against him. He tightened his hold, giving her the comfort she needed and letting Cam know she was more to him than his mother's nurse.

While police patted him down, Cam glared harder at Thad. Lucy's obvious welcome of Thad's embrace left no doubt who she preferred and Cam's sick mind couldn't accept that. Lucy belonged to Thad.

Leaning back, Lucy put her hands on his chest and looked up at him, staying close in the wake of her ordeal. It stirred primitive male instincts that made him keep her against him.

"Are you all right?" he asked to be sure.

She nodded in the safety of his arms. "How did you find me?"

He told her about Mike and guided her toward the garage. Outside, Sam and Mike waited. Lucy went to Mike first, wrapping her arms around him for a hug. "Thank you."

Wearing an awkward grin, he mumbled, "You're welcome," and stepped back.

"Sam," she said.

"I just came along for the ride."

Lucy laughed a little and hugged him anyway. Then she moved back to Thad's side, her arm going along his back. He held her beside him, struggling with how warm she made him feel.

Chapter 13

Tracking down Jaden had been easy. Mike had, indeed, been stealthy in following him to Cam's house. The special ops soldier had managed to remain unseen. Thad had found an unsuspecting Jaden at his home. His car was in the driveway and lights were on inside the house. Jaden hadn't known he'd been followed, wasn't aware Cam had been arrested or that he'd been caught tampering with the security at Kate's estate. So desperate for money, Jaden hadn't taken into consideration that Thad had seen him at Cam's house. He may know Cam, but he wasn't the one who'd planned to hold Lucy captive. He'd thought he could get away with his part in the crime.

With a team of agents that Todd had assembled standing by in cars parked out of sight, Thad knocked on Jaden's door. Todd had agreed to help instead of excluding him in Jaden's arrest. He'd told him that Jaden had deceived the gatehouse guard and relieved him for the night. Todd's team spirit convinced Thad he was one of the good guys, and a good man to have on his mother's security detail.

Jaden answered the door with a look of perplexity.

"You and I need to talk," Thad said.

After searching the front of the house, Jaden didn't resist when Thad pushed the door open wider and stepped inside the newer home he'd rented after his wife had kicked him out. Sparsely furnished and nothing on the walls, only a chair and a TV decorated the small living room. An overhead light hung in the middle of the room, blinding in its brightness. There was no dining table and the overhead light was on in there, too.

"What brings you here at this hour?" Jaden asked.

Thad couldn't decide which question to ask first. He wanted to keep Cam's arrest secret for now.

"How much do you know about my mother's shooting?" With Jaden's cautious look, Thad said, "You're a member of her security detail. They keep you abreast of any progress made in the investigation, don't they?"

Jaden eyed him a bit longer. He must know there was a reason Thad was here. He was concerned about why but not concerned enough. "They told us the shooter is still at large. I'm not involved in the investigation. Why are you asking me about that?"

"Do you know who the shooter is?" Thad asked, more of a taunt than a question.

Jaden's brow twitched with intensifying confusion... and worry. "Why would I?"

The guilty ones always got nervous. "Leaving a window unlocked and then the side door... It's almost as though you were trying to let someone in." The slight blanch of Jaden's face revealed enough. He hadn't anticipated being seen at the side door.

"Why did you do it?" Thad asked.

"That's what you came here to ask?"

"Why did you unlock the door?" Thad demanded.

Jaden held his silence. But after a few seconds, he said, "You can't prove I did anything."

Thad reached into his front pocket to show Jaden the USB device. "Actually, I *can*."

Looking from the jump drive to Thad's face, Jaden's nervousness became palpable. Now his concern mounted.

"How did you get the guard to leave the gate?" Thad asked.

"I don't know what you're talking about. I left the estate and came straight here."

Liar. "Why did you unlock the door?"

"I didn't mean to. I was checking it. If I unlocked it, I didn't mean to."

"Who do you think you're talking to?" Thad was an experienced crime scene investigator. The reminder of that registered with Jaden.

"I didn't do it on purpose," Jaden insisted.

"What about the gatehouse guard?"

"What about him?"

"He said you let him go for the night."

"He's lying."

Thad angled his head to show his disbelief.

Jaden said nothing, but he had to know he was caught by now.

Thad walked into the living room, going to the back of the sofa and facing Jaden again. "I know you're having trouble at home. Your wife is leaving you and you're close to bankruptcy."

Jaden faced him but didn't move farther into the room. "Digging into my personal life?"

"Did you do it for money?" Thad asked.

Jaden had no reply for that.

"How much did Cam pay you to kidnap Lucy?" Thad dropped the magical question. He watched Jaden process how Thad might have come to learn of this.

"I saw you at Cam's house, remember?" Thad helped him.

Jaden started to back toward the door.

"I wouldn't go out there if I were you."

Pausing, he looked toward the window, and then went there. When he saw nothing outside, he looked back at Thad.

"Mike Harris saw you leaving the estate with Lucy tonight."

Jaden turned from the window, his skin pale. After a long, desperate moment, he said, "I'll tell you where she is." He realized the trouble he was in and thought he could bargain his way out of it. Or attempt to.

Thad wasn't ready to reveal that Lucy was safe. "Why did you leave the side door unlocked?"

"I told you, I didn't mean to do that."

"Was leaving the window unlocked an accident, too? And what about the security system? Did you accidentally shut that off?" The man had to know he'd get nowhere denying his guilt.

Jaden's jaw clenched and released in his tension. "I'll tell you where Lucy is. Just let me go."

So he could run from the law? Thad wasn't that kind of cop. And this was too personal to be lenient. "I need a few more questions answered."

"Okay." Jaden looked hopeful that if he answered his questions Thad might let him go.

"Cam paid you to bring him Lucy," Thad said. "Did he also pay you to kidnap Sophie?"

"No. Cam approached me after Lucy moved in at the estate. I didn't know about Sophie's kidnapping."

Thad could see and hear the truth in that reply. Jaden hadn't been involved in Sophie's kidnapping, only Lucy's. That meant someone other than Jaden was behind this. Jaden was another dead end. Cam must have discovered Jaden's situation—that he needed money—and made him a proposition. Could Cam be the shooter? Thad didn't see how. He'd been busy holding Lucy prisoner. He hadn't gone to break in to the estate.

"Who did you leave the door open for?" Thad asked.

"I keep telling you—"

"You keep telling me a lie!" Thad roared.

Jaden met Thad's eyes and didn't budge.

"Who else is paying you?" Thad asked in a calmer tone.

"No one. I don't know what you're talking about. I don't know who kidnapped the little girl and I didn't leave any door unlocked."

The first might be true but Jaden did leave the door unlocked. Thad realized he could ask a hundred times and Jaden wouldn't give in. He seemed too afraid to. He wasn't afraid to talk about Lucy, but the door was another matter.

Maybe the police would have better luck. Thad headed for the door.

"Don't you want to know where Lucy is?" Jaden asked.

With a glance behind him, Thad opened the door and held up his hand to signal the agents.

"What are you doing?" Jaden asked.

Thad moved out of the way as agents burst into the house. Jaden tried to escape out the back, but there were agents there waiting. Now he'd understand that Thad had already known where Lucy was and Cam hadn't gotten away with what he'd planned.

That Friday, Lucy yawned as they neared Carova. They'd gotten a late start. It was dinnertime and she was starving. Thad must have read her mind…or gotten tired of Sophie repeatedly asking if they were there yet from the backseat of the car. He turned into the parking lot of an Irish pub. It was on the way and a convenient stop.

Beneath soft lighting, the hostess led them over rugged wood floors and through a maze of heavy wood tables. The wood chairs had green cushions on them. Clovers decorated the walls between historical pictures of the town.

Sophie took hold of Lucy's hand as they walked to their table. A young couple saw them, the woman smiling fondly as she took in the trio. They looked like a real family. With her light brown hair and golden-brown eyes, Sophie could pass as Thad's daughter. Lucy's hair was darker and she had green eyes, but people would think she'd taken after her daddy.

Thad put his hand on Lucy's lower back to guide her ahead of him, the gesture intimate. Daddy loved Sophie's mommy.

If only it were true…

They sat at a booth with Lucy and Sophie on one side and Thad on the other. An elderly woman sitting with her husband smiled over at them, adoring them as the other woman had.

"We must look like we're a family," she couldn't resist saying, knowing Thad would struggle with it.

He glanced around and saw the elderly woman give him a nod of greeting. He awkwardly nodded back, then sent Lucy an unappreciative frown.

She laughed a little.

"What's funny?" Sophie asked, pausing in her drawing. The pub had a kids coloring page.

"Nothing." She lifted the menu and began to read. "What do you like to eat, Sophie?"

"Um…" Her young eyes lifted as she thought. "I want…mac 'n' cheese with French fries."

"Okay, you got it. The culinary delight of mac 'n' cheese and fries coming right up." She looked at Thad, who noticed her playfulness and a flicker of a grin almost emerged.

"What can I get for you?" a waitress asked. She was young and short with beautiful, bright blue eyes and hair in a bob much like Sophie's, the same color, too.

Something about her struck Lucy as familiar. She couldn't place her, though. She'd never been to this pub before and didn't know anyone in the area.

"You're Thad Winston, aren't you?" the elderly woman's husband asked, interrupting their order.

Thad looked over. "Yes."

"We heard about your mother. How is she doing?"

"Much better, thanks for asking."

"That's good. Did they catch her shooter?"

"No, not yet. But I'm sure we will."

The man missed Thad's inclusion of himself in the investigation. "Damn crazies out there. Kate Winston would make a fine president. She's got our vote."

"Thanks, I'll be sure to tell her."

That seemed to please the old man immeasurably. He didn't interfere any further.

"You're Kate Winston's son?" the waitress asked.

"Yes."

"Wow. We have a celebrity in the house." She beamed a smile.

"I wouldn't go that far. I'm just her son," Thad said.

Lucy had never thought of him as a celebrity. He was humble and down-to-earth. A sports fan and a cop.

"What can I get you folks?" the waitress asked.

"Mac 'n' cheese!" Sophie burst out.

"With fries," Lucy added.

The waitress wrote the order down and Lucy ordered a hamburger. Thad asked for the same. It was French fry night.

The waitress walked away, going over to the kitchen where an older man stood. A little taller than average in height, he had graying dark brown hair and a ruddy complexion, he resembled the girl in certain ways. Lucy wondered if they were related.

"Does she look familiar to you?" Lucy asked Thad.

He looked where her gaze was fixed and then turned back to her. "No. Why?"

"She seems familiar to me." She watched as the man grew surly with the waitress. He looked over at her and Thad.

"That man recognizes us." She watched him exchange words with the waitress, who seemed taken aback and then argued with whatever he'd said.

Thad looked at the waitress and the man again. "Really?"

Lucy didn't have to answer. The man came over to their table.

"Thad Winston, are you?" he said. Animosity hung in his tone. He struggled to control it.

What was this all about?

"Yes," Thad said. "I'm sorry, you have me at a disadvantage. I don't believe we've met before."

"You may not know me, but I know you. I told my granddaughter not to serve you. I'll send someone else over. Unless you'd like to go somewhere else?"

"I don't understand. Why won't you let your granddaughter wait on us?" Thad asked.

"Name's Patrick O'Hara. That's my granddaughter Shelby. She's too precious for the likes of you."

"Why are you so angry?" Lucy asked. "Shelby looked familiar to me when she came to our table. I may have seen her or met her before."

"You tell Kate Winston I won't be voting for her." With that, Patrick O'Hara, who probably owned the pub, stormed away.

"What was that all about?" Lucy asked.

"Must not like my mother," Thad said.

"Maybe we should go somewhere else," Lucy said.

"Is that man going to spit in our food?" Sophie asked with the frankness only a child could get away with.

"We'll go somewhere else." Thad stood up. "In fact, we're close enough to the beach house. Why don't we pick something up at the store and make it there?"

"Okay."

"No," Sophie complained. "I'm hungry."

"We'll feed you," Lucy said. "Come on."

"No. I don't want to go."

"If we go to the store we can get ice cream," Thad said.

That smoothed the child's defiant face. "Can I still have mac 'n' cheese?"

"Of course you can," Thad answered.

Sophie scooted out of the booth with Lucy.

Lucy saw how Patrick and Shelby watched them, Patrick appearing satisfied they were leaving and Shelby looking from him to the three of them, clearly not understanding why Patrick had displayed so much anger toward them.

Lucy got out of the rental Jeep Grand Cherokee Thad had driven here and had to just stand and admire the beach house. It was a stunning piece of architecture. She hadn't expected anything less, but the beauty of this place was remarkable. Made of stone trimmed in white, it was three levels with a fanning stone staircase leading to the entrance on the second level. And it was quiet. Only wind and waves had greeted them.

Thad handed her a grocery bag with a grin. She took it and turned her attention to another bag in the back of the Jeep. Sophie carried her stuffed puppy and walked with her behind Thad to the front door. Lucy looked back and to the side of the house. Five horses grazed on patches of tall grass about a hundred yards from here. There were other houses, but they were far away. The Winston family must own a good chunk of land to keep the development at bay and the views pristine.

Lucy stepped into the entry, white and dark wood stairs to the left leading both up and down and straight ahead she saw a wide, open room with shining dark wood floors and soft yellow walls. Neutral red-, yellow- and green-striped chairs and a huge brown leather sectional were positioned before a panel of white-trimmed windows.

Leaving the entry, Lucy passed a pair of open white

French doors to a dining room on her right. Across from there was another set of French doors, those opening to a smaller sitting area, a place to get away from the noise. On the other side of the wall from the dining room was the kitchen, overlooking the living room. Dark granite countertops and white cabinets looked rich and clean, and the double-door, stainless-steel refrigerator could feed an army. An island lined with stools separated the kitchen from the living room, and a round, casual dining table sat at the end of the kitchen before the wall of windows it shared with the living room.

Sophie skipped into the living room and dropped her stuffed animal and tote bag. Dolls spilled out, and she busily fell into imaginative play. No doubt, this was the biggest dollhouse she'd ever seen. It certainly was for Lucy—this had to be a dream.

Lucy put down the bags on the kitchen island counter with Thad and began to unload groceries. There were no stores here, only beach houses, sand and ocean. They'd stopped in Corolla on the way.

Thad turned on the oven and put French fries on a cooking sheet while Lucy put a container of mac 'n' cheese in the microwave.

"I'll grill our burgers," Thad said.

This had such a domesticated feel. She followed him to the balcony door, drawn by the view. The sun was setting, giving the ocean's surface an orange sheen. Thad started the giant steel grill on the balcony. Stairs led down to the pool. There was also a hot tub.

Going to the railing, she rested her hands there and leaned over to see the back of the house. There were windows on every side, but panels of them filled the back on all levels. A wooden railed path led to the beach, breaking waves rolling up onto sand in the distance. The beach was wide and went on for as far as the eye could see.

Catching Thad watching her, having paused in his task of putting burgers on the grill, Lucy turned and went back into the house to cut tomatoes, cheese, onions and lettuce. The look in Thad's eyes stayed with her. He seemed relaxed, even with Sophie here.

The television played in the living room and Lucy realized Sophie had turned it on. She'd had to become more independent since her mother died.

She finished preparing Sophie's dinner and put the plate on the kitchen island.

"Sophie."

"Yes!" Sophie bounded into the kitchen and clumsily climbed up onto the stool. She had a spoon in hand and stirred the steaming macaroni and cheese. It was too hot to eat.

Lucy resumed getting the burgers ready. They'd bought coleslaw and potato salad to keep it simple.

"Lucy?" Sophie queried in her high-pitched voice.

"Yes?"

"Do I have to go back to Rosanna's house?"

That was a loaded question. Lucy stopped what she was doing and faced Sophie. "No, honey, you don't."

Her head tilted to one side as that news confused her. "Am I going to live with you now?"

"For a while, yes." The question singed Lucy, piercing through her core.

Sophie's head tilted again, more confusion gripping her. "For how long?"

"I don't know. We have to work it through the State."

"What's the State?"

"The people who sent you to Rosanna's house."

Instead of confusion, dislike pinched her mouth and saddened her sweet brown eyes. "I don't like those people."

"They're trying to help you."

"I don't like them."

Moving around the island, Lucy put her hand on the girl's head, smoothing her unruly hair. "Don't worry. I'll make sure everything turns out okay." She wasn't sure how she'd do that, but she'd do all she could.

"Why can't I live with you all the time?" Sophie asked.

Choked up over her helplessness and indecision over what to do about Sophie, Lucy couldn't answer.

"Don't you want me?"

Oh, that stung. "It's not that, Sophie." What could she say to avoid hurting her? Her young mind wouldn't understand.

"Why doesn't anyone want me?"

"It isn't that anyone doesn't want you."

"My mommy left. Rosanna doesn't want me. And now you."

Lucy swiveled Sophie's stool so that she faced her and took her hands. "Okay, listen to me, Sophie. Your mother didn't leave you. She died. And Rosanna…" She looked down, uncertain of how much to tell her. Not one who believed in lying to children, she went with the truth. "Rosanna died, too. She was in an accident the night we picked you up from the fishing house."

The news troubled Sophie, but she couldn't process so much terrible information all at once. She hadn't known Rosanna the way she'd known her mother. "Like my mommy?"

"Yes, like your mommy."

"Well…" Consternation and more confusion marred her face. "Then I better not live with you."

"Why not?"

"Because you'll die, too."

Lucy gathered the girl into a hug. "No, I won't. I'm not going to die. You're safe now, I promise. We're all safe."

Sophie clung to Lucy, in need of love and attention. Lucy would give her all she had this weekend and for however long she had with her.

Thad came inside just then and paused on his way to the counter, carrying a plate of cooked burgers. He was all man standing there and probably feeling awkward over interrupting what was obviously a tender moment between woman and child, two things he struggled with most. "Everything okay in here?"

"Yeah." Lucy ruffled Sophie's hair. "Just a little girl talk."

Lucy swiveled the stool back toward the counter. "Finish your meal. We're here to have fun. Forget all the rest."

Sophie lifted her spoon and dug into the macaroni and cheese. Lucy couldn't tell if all the death that surrounded her still bothered her. Her mother's death would stay with her for the rest of her life. Rosanna's she may not understand. She may think about it for a while but Lucy was confident that it would pass, and as soon as she got somewhere stable, as soon as someone adopted her, she'd flourish.

She and Thad made their plates and sat at the island as Sophie finished and jumped off the stool to go back to playing with her dolls.

Thad was quiet after seeing her with Sophie and he kept glancing over at her.

"What do you think will happen to her?" he asked in a low enough voice that Sophie wouldn't hear over the television.

"She'll be put in another foster home."

"How long will that take?"

"I don't know that, either."

He studied the girl. "I wish there was something we could do."

"I suppose we're doing all we can," she said.

When he met her eyes, she could tell he struggled the way she did.

Thad turned back to his plate but didn't resume eating. He'd already finished most of his food. Talk of what to do with Sophie had ruined his appetite. Why? Lucy wondered. Because he'd considered the possibilities? And if he had, it had probably scared him.

Lucy decided to spare him. And herself. She got the feeling he was beginning to test waters—with her. Something in him sought to find out if Lucy had what it took to make it all the way. Something strong enough to bypass his beliefs about marriage. Even if he never married in his life, long-term commitment was difficult for him. Was he contemplating whether Lucy would make a good candidate, or was worth a try?

Chapter 14

When Thad heard Sophie's cries, he threw the covers off of him and picked up the jeans he'd worn yesterday. He put them on as he stumbled toward the door. There were two master bedrooms on the third level, one on each end of the house, and two smaller rooms between. Sophie was in the one closest to Lucy. When he reached the room, he saw that Lucy was already there, comforting the girl.

The nightmares were becoming a regular occurrence. He went to sit on the other side of the queen-size bed.

"A green-eyed man came to get her," Lucy said as she held a crying Sophie. Sophie was still under the covers, her arms looped over Lucy's neck and Lucy leaning toward her to hold her close, rubbing her back and looking solemnly at Thad.

"She had the same dream the last time." He felt helpless while everything in him urged for some action that would make it all better for the girl. "We'll get her counseling. Help her get past this."

Lucy realized along with him that he spoke as if Sophie would be in both of their lives…indefinitely.

His determination to rescue the girl as though she were his own daughter instilled a bolt of panic in him. What was he thinking? None of this was a sure thing. Lucy. Sophie. Especially Sophie. The two of them together spelled family. And family he did not do without sharing a single last name. Sharing a last name meant forever. And he'd never have forever with any woman. That would take a miracle, and Thad didn't believe in miracles. He believed in reality, and reality was a lot harsher than that.

He stood up. "You've got this covered."

Sophie pushed back from Lucy, her crying subsiding for a moment. "Where are you going?"

Thad froze, looking down at Sophie's teary face, her eyes beseeching him, needing not only Lucy but him, as well.

"Nowhere," he heard himself say.

He saw Lucy's adoring smile over the child's connection to him.

"You have to chase the green-eyed man away," Sophie said. "Lucy said he'd be no match for you and that you'd chase him away."

Thad lifted his brow. "Lucy is telling stories again."

"It's true," Sophie insisted. "You can scare him away."

"Okay. I'll go scare him away." Indulging them both, he began his search in the room, spending extra time in the closet and under the bed.

"He's not in here." He went to the window and made a show of searching through the darkness. "Don't see him…wait a minute. What's that?" He looked back to a wide-eyed Sophie and a delighted Lucy. "I think I see him."

Sophie clung tighter to Lucy. "Go get him! Go chase him away!"

"You two stay here so I know you're safe." Thad opened the balcony door and ran down the stairs, glad no one was around to see him. There, he waited out of sight, timing his absence in his head. This had to be believable. A few minutes later, he ran back up the stairs and into Sophie's bedroom, slightly winded from sprinting up all those steps.

Sophie huddled with Lucy, still on the bed, frightened and expectant.

"I caught him," Thad proclaimed, feeling as if he was in one of Lucy's made-up stories. "I told him if he ever came back he'd have to go through me to get to you." He moved closer. "You were right. He was afraid of me. He's gone and he's never coming back."

Sophie looked at Lucy for confirmation.

"You heard him. The green-eyed man is gone. For good." She tapped the girl's nose with her forefinger.

Sophie relaxed and giggled.

"Let's read something and then you need to get some sleep." Lucy found a book and reclined on the bed beside Sophie.

Thad locked the balcony doors and then leaned against the frame. He watched Lucy read to the girl and listened to her animated voice. All the while he struggled with letting go of what swelled in his heart. Forever. With the two of them...

Sophie's eyes drooped and then closed. In less than a half hour, she was sound asleep. Seeing the child enveloped in so much peace, knowing he had a lot to do with that, Thad felt something shift in him. His resistance weakened. Lucy gently pulled the covers up to her chin and then turned off the bedside lamp, leaving only the night-light.

Thad went with her to the door, leaving it open as they left.

In the hall, Lucy turned to him. "You're good at that."

"At what?" He shouldn't even ask. She'd start in on him again.

"She'll never have another nightmare again, thanks to you." She leaned against the hallway wall, too dreamy for his comfort zone, but sexy as hell. This time without a robe, she wore that silky nightgown. The strings tying the bodice were loosened and teased him with half of her breasts exposed. He could see the shadow of her nipples and thighs through the thin material. The nightgown came to just above her knees.

He felt himself react, the tightening down low, the quickening of his pulse. Awareness of her sensuality engulfed him. With resistance vanishing, temptation took its place. What would it be like to forget reality for one night?

Lucy noticed the change in him. Her appreciative smile faded and a darker pleasure took over. Her eyes grew hungry.

Drawn to her, he crossed the hall. Her hands slid up his chest as he swooped down to kiss her. Bracing his hands on the wall, he kissed her softly at first, exploring her and loving how her breathing deepened. Her mouth fit his deliciously.

Was this what kissing the mother of his child would be like? He enjoyed the fantasy. It was okay as long as it remained a fantasy.

Lucy ran her tongue along his mouth. He opened for her and they caressed each other that way for a while. Fiery heat coursed through him, reaching every wicked nerve ending in him. She arched her body toward him. Her hips pressed against his growing hardness.

Kissing her harder, he ran his hands down her body, one over her breast the other down to her rear.

"That nightgown is driving me crazy," he rasped.

"You're driving me crazy." She sought his mouth again.

He kissed her while he kneaded her breast, feeling the nipple go stiff.

"Sophie," Lucy whispered.

Though the child slept, waking her to this wouldn't be the best example to make.

He moved back, and she took his hand, leading him into her room. It was nearly identical to his, only having a different color scheme. Lucy had chosen the blue hues and he took the one with green.

"Are you sure about this?" He shut the door. Even if she wasn't, he might have to convince her. This was one fantasy he didn't want to miss.

"Yes." She backed into the spacious room, walls painted a soft yellow and offset by white trim. Every room had a balcony door. Lucy had left the blinds open, and moonlight streamed in. She hadn't turned on a light when she'd gone running for Sophie.

Her gaze roamed all over his body, down to where his erection strained his jeans, all over his upper torso and back to his face.

"Are you?" she asked.

Her body in that nightgown beckoned. "Yes."

She lifted the silky thing off her and dropped it to the

floor. Completely naked, her dark, thick hair tumbling over her shoulders, she was a vision. Her breasts jutted, firm and free. A sinewy line divided her ribs and abdomen. She shaved her private area so that only a strip remained. Light from the window outlined her trim thighs, starting at the apex of her sex.

Thad removed his jeans and boxers. His erection was almost painful. He couldn't remember ever being this hard before. Maybe when he was a teenager.

As he stepped toward her, she waited. She wanted more foreplay. Standing close, he angled his head to kiss her while he touched her breasts. When that wasn't enough, he trailed kisses down her neck, over her collarbone and down to first one and then the other nipple.

She held his head, her fingers buried in his hair, sounds of pleasure whispering from her. She was holding back so that Sophie didn't hear them. That she had to hold back heated him immeasurably. What would she sound like if she let go?

He kissed her lips again, his hands on her rear, pulling her to him. She groaned into his mouth.

Then she broke free, stepping back. Turning, she moved like a cat on all fours onto the bed, presenting her rear and enticing him further. She sat on the sheets, waiting for him.

He crawled over her, kissing her as she still sat. Heat radiated between them. With one hand on his chest, she touched him with her other, curling her fingers around him and softly rubbing.

"Oh," she breathed.

He was so hard.

Thad kissed her with more purpose, guiding her down onto the mattress. He shoved pillows out of the way, fanning her hair across the white sheets. The sight of her was so erotic he nearly penetrated her right then. But this fantasy had to last.

He treated her to more kissing, then moved out of her reach, down to her feet. He kissed the tops of them and made his way up her calf, spreading her legs as he moved past her knees.

She gripped his hair as he satisfied curiosity and ran his tongue along the landing strip she kept so neatly trimmed. Reaching sweeter center, he brought her to a shivering brink and yielded to her tugs on his hair. Kissing her belly, tickling her belly button, he treated her breasts to more before lying on top of her and taking her mouth.

Her hands went from his hair down his back and to his rear, where they stayed as he began to probe for her warm wetness. He pushed into her, slow and steady, rising up from a long kiss to look into green eyes that shone in the moonlight. As he moved back and forth at the same pace, a deep rightness settled in his soul, gripping him and intensifying the explosive ecstasy they made together.

Lucy stretched her arms above her head, her fingers touching the grand wooden headboard. She was a million-dollar painting and the headboard was her frame.

"More," she breathed. "I want more."

She wanted more. Thad pushed into her with more force, thrusting over and over. A strangled sound burst from her. He clamped his mouth over hers and moved faster.

A long groan vibrated into his mouth. He kept his eyes open to watch her. She lifted her knees and now it was him who groaned. Unbelievably, they peaked at the same time, each quieting the celebration that broke free in audible release.

Thad lay on her for a few seconds before rolling to her side. He kept the fantasy alive, unwilling to let it be more than that. But try as he might to keep it at bay, it was more than a fantasy.

"That was fantastic." She rolled toward him, saw him staring off across the room, and asked, "Are you okay?"

He covered it well. Kissing her, he answered, "Yes."

Lulled from great sex, she snuggled with him and moments later fell asleep. It was a while later for him before he could put his thoughts to rest. What would morning bring? How would Lucy feel? Would she be willing to engage in his kind of relationship? Or was the most applicable question, how would he feel?

Lucy kissed Thad awake. She'd slept for a couple of hours and waking next to him had stirred her into arousal again. He'd let go with her; she'd felt it when he'd made love to her. Afterward he'd seemed to slip into negative thought, but hadn't withdrawn as she'd feared he would. She wasn't sure if anything would come of this, and she wasn't ready to think about it. All she knew was he was worth a chance.

As his eyes fluttered open, she pushed him onto his back and straddled him. The covers were askew at the foot of the bed. She waited for him to wake up more. Bending down, she kissed his sexy mouth before moving on to his chest. She kissed him everywhere the way he'd done to her. When she reached his waist, she took his erection into her mouth.

"Lucy," he murmured.

She made him rock hard in a matter of seconds. Kissing him all the way back up to his lips, she met his hazel eyes and saw them drooping, not with tiredness but with flaming passion. She loved that she could do that to him.

Guiding him between her legs, she sank down onto him. He sucked in a sharp breath. Planting her hands on his muscular chest, she moved her hips to grind on him, going slow at first. He held her breasts, caressing her nipples while he watched her—worshipped was more like it.

His response emboldened her. She moved faster. His hands moved to her hips and then her thighs. His thumb found her sweet spot and expertly rubbed, slow and in tune with her movements. Until she began to spiral into a pleasurable eddy. He sensed it and rubbed harder. Her orgasm came quickly.

Rolling with her, he took over the top position and drilled into her. Like her, it didn't take long.

Once again he lay on her until their breathing calmed. And as before she feared he'd withdraw. She saw grimness in his eyes before he closed them and kissed her.

She let him have his space and didn't say anything. When he lay on his back, she curled next to him. Their lovemaking had a profound effect on him, and Lucy wondered if she should go with it. Not try to get him to talk about his phobia of marriage and kids. He was obviously great with kids, and his trouble with marriage was a misconception, one she was starting to believe he'd overcome…with the right woman.

Was she the right woman? That she couldn't answer. But deep inside, deep in her core, she couldn't ignore the instinct that told her to forget caution, forget her determination to find a man who wanted what she wanted—a family—one she was sure about, and focus her efforts on winning Thad.

If she was wrong and failed to change his mind, then she'd have some good memories, after her broken heart healed, but good memories nonetheless. She'd also face the challenge of topping Thad. The sex would be difficult to beat.

But that's what made him worth the risk. He might have convinced himself that he could have a relationship with a woman and not marry her in preparation for the inevitable split-up, but he could never have a relationship like that with her. He'd withdraw. She hoped she was wrong but she didn't think she was. If he couldn't overcome his flaws, this would be a brief relationship. If he made progress and embraced what he felt for her, they had hope.

The sun was coming up, or sort of. It was overcast today.

"Weather report said there's a storm moving in." When other topics were too heavy, there was always the weather.

"Late winter storm." Easing away from her, he sat up on the bed. "Could be a strong one."

"Maybe we should just stay in today."

"We'll be all right. The storm won't get here until tonight. We should be home by then." He got off the bed. "Let's get ready."

It was early. They had plenty of time. He needed to escape.

Unable to meet his eyes, she kept her back to him and went to her suitcase for something to wear. Slipping into her robe, she tied it shut as he came up behind her.

"About last night."

Dreading what his comment brought to light, she turned reluctantly toward him.

"And this morning." He grinned to be playful but she saw his discomfort. He didn't like the subject any more than her. Although he had different reasons than her for not liking it, she had to give him credit for having the guts to talk to her.

"It was good," he said, and then more honestly, "Really good."

Hearing a *but* coming, Lucy stepped closer and put her finger over his lips. "Let's not talk about that today. It's Sophie's birthday." She said it as an excuse. She wasn't prepared for another diatribe about love.

"Lucy…"

"Not today."

"We have to talk about it."

So he could make sure she bought into his antimarriage philosophy? "Not today," she said with more force.

He studied her and then relented. "All right, not today."

"I'm going to get ready now." She needed to be alone.

"Right. Sure." Awkwardly, he headed for the door. There, he looked back at her and she felt his uncertainty.

He wanted to convince her to have a relationship with him on his terms. What frightened her was she actually wondered if she should.

After a pizza lunch in Corolla where Lucy endured Thad's contemplative looks and absorbed herself in Sophie's excitement, they drove to a sandy parking area not far from Carova. After Thad parked, Lucy bundled Sophie up for their wild horse tour. They were going to return to the beach house for present and cake time. The suspense was killing Sophie. She wanted to skip the horse tour.

Lucy zipped up Sophie's jacket and looked up at the darkening sky. "Are you sure we have time for this?"

Standing with his hands half-stuffed in his front jean pocket, one leg relaxed and looking like a sexy model in a magazine ad, Thad glanced up. "We might get a little cold, that's all." Did he think being here out in the cold was better than nestled in the beach house, alone with Lucy?

"Want to learn about wild horses?" Lucy extended her hand to Sophie.

"Yeah!" She skipped alongside Lucy toward the open-roofed SUV waiting for them. Thad had arranged for a private tour.

Thad followed. He'd been withdrawn all day so far, and she knew he was thinking of last night—a dream. She hadn't cornered him with questions and now she wondered if she should have. He'd tried to talk to her about it and she'd given him an out, something she suspected he appreciated, although it was hard to tell. He was a man who hid his emotions well once he put his mind to it. And he was definitely doing that today. Sophie was their distraction. After spending most of the day putting up with him, Lucy decided not to anymore.

"Sit with us," she said. "It will be warmer."

With no sign that it bothered him, he sat next to her, Sophie beside Lucy. He had his cop face on. She hadn't noticed he had one until today. Whenever things got to him and he withdrew, this was how he handled it. Kept it all to himself behind a thick shield of armor, a tough exterior for a strong man.

The driver began a narrative about the history of the Spanish mustangs that inhabited this area of the Outer Banks for about five hundred years. They were brought here by explorers. A cold gust of wind diverted her attention. The sky was darker, and out to sea, waves white-capped. The four-wheel-drive vehicle bounced and jerked over the deep sand.

Lucy put her arm around Sophie and looked ahead to catch sight of a good-sized herd of horses.

"I see them!" Sophie leaned toward the window, out of reach of Lucy's arm. The driver slowed, explaining that they couldn't get too close, as the animals were protected here.

Lucy shivered as another gust of wind whipped through the open SUV. They were exposed on all sides, except where the windshield rose up.

Thad surprised her by putting his arm around her. Checking to see how pained he was and seeing a slight smile curve up, she snuggled closer, welcoming the warmth. She couldn't tell if she'd triggered the smile or if the outing had. It didn't matter—being close to him thrilled her and she didn't stop the good feeling. He was also more relaxed than she'd seen him all day.

Sophie was absorbed in the horses and what the guide was telling them about this particular herd, which mares were expecting and tidbits of behavioral details, like how some horses liked humans more than others. She wondered if he was making it all up.

After an hour and viewing two more herds, the driver headed back to where he'd picked them up. On the way, it began to rain. Tiny pelts of rain at first, but the closer they got to the parking area, the heavier it fell. Lucy noticed Thad surveying the sky. Maybe the tour guide should have offered to reschedule. He probably didn't get many requests for private tours this time of year and maybe he needed the money.

The rain was getting uncomfortable. Even Sophie forgot all about horses and huddled close to Lucy. She held her and Thad held them both.

"It's cold!" Sophie complained.

Why did children think adults could fix everything?

"We'll be all right," Thad said. "I'll get us back to the beach house."

Lucy didn't doubt he would. Sophie didn't mind the weather at all. She was having fun searching for horses, who were now becoming scarce as they sought shelter.

The driver turned around and headed back to where they'd parked the Jeep. The tour was over, if a bit rushed. Lucy didn't mind. She'd rather get out of this weather. Plus, being close to Thad gave her a warm glow. His cop face had vanished and fondness for her had taken its place. Not afraid of the storm and not afraid of what last night and this morning meant. He was completely relaxed now.

Every time she tipped her head up to see him, he looked down, and each time he did so was warmer than the last. Who needed a jacket when his eyes and all they let her see heated her plenty? And oh, she did love his eyes, more than ever after last night.

He seemed to feel the same about hers, because when she tipped her head again, he didn't look away. Encouraged that last night hadn't been a total loss, she lifted her face more and pecked a quick kiss to his lips. The moment felt right for it. No alarm or withdrawal changed the way he regarded her. He seemed to lose himself in what they made together. Love. The fuel for it. Not wanting to own that two-ton block any more than she was sure he did, she just went with it, embraced the moment and whatever followed.

Still staring at each other, she closed her eyes when he kissed her softly and a lot longer. She could kiss him all night.

They separated when Sophie's child voice sang, "Hh-heeeyy," followed by a giggle.

Sophie may have been embarrassed by the sight of them kissing, but she eyed them with curiosity. She'd seen the love brewing there. Kids weren't stupid. They knew the real thing when they saw it.

The driver noticed, too, grinning to himself as he turned the windshield wipers to a faster speed. The rain had picked up.

By the time they made it to the sandy parking area, their Jeep rental was the only vehicle left, and the rain poured in earnest.

Lucy took Thad's hand and then Lucy's and they ran to the Jeep. The wind had really picked up, driving sheets of rain into the sandy landscape. It was hard to breathe it was so strong.

Thad took Sophie from Lucy. "Get in."

She did while he made sure Sophie was seat-belted in. Then he walked with his head turned away from the pelting rain. Sitting behind the wheel, he dripped water but wasn't daunted by it. He started the engine and drove as fast as he could through the deep, wet sand.

"It's going to get bad tonight," she said.

"Yeah." He kept his focus on the barely visible outline of the rough road. "I'll get us home."

The way he said that pulled Lucy's heart. He may not be convinced he would be lucky enough to find real love, but he cared for her and Sophie. He cared more than he realized.

It wasn't even dinnertime and a person wouldn't be

able to tell. It was so dark. Thad navigated the dirt and sand road with firm hands. They weren't far from the house. Lightning flashed and thunder rolled.

Lucy checked on Sophie. She'd dug into her tote and had her dolls out, bobbing them up and down as though they were riding horses. Her innocent trust touched her. She may know the weather was bad, but she trusted Lucy and Thad.

The jolt of the Jeep brought her facing forward again. Thad steered through deep, wet sand. For a moment Lucy thought they'd get stuck, but he maneuvered the vehicle without faltering. She could see the house ahead. Sheets of rain pelted to the ground. The Jeep's headlights had come on. The sun was probably setting but it was already dark.

Thad seemed confident he'd get them back to the beach house, but Lucy was beginning to wonder.

Chapter 15

Sitting at a table in the expansive library at the Winston estate, Darcy put his head in his hand as he read the report from someone Thad knew, someone anonymous. Thad had given him a cell phone number, an untraceable one. His contact may have really come through for them. They had to be careful that no one discovered where they were digging. Darcy had let the man loose on several people, Wade Thomas included.

The chief of police had a lot going on in his life. Thomas was a security red flag. He fit a stereotypical tragedy. In debt up to his eyeballs, ready to finish a bitter divorce, he had a lot in common with Jaden and Layne. But the three didn't run in the same circles.

"Hey, lover." Avery lightened his mood. She leaned down and pressed a kiss to his cheek. "This place is amazing. I went to the gym and stopped for coffee on my way here. All in the same building."

The estate had everything. He chuckled and stood from the desk, looping his arms around her. "Mmm, you're sweaty enough for a shower."

"Join me." She winked.

"What are you doing drinking coffee at this hour?" It was just after dinner.

"Decaf. The cook here makes them better than a coffee shop. How about that shower? Then we can go to bed early."

"I need to check something out." He kissed her quickly and moved away before he changed his mind.

"You found something?"

He'd told her about the case he and Thad were carrying out in secret. "Maybe." He gave her a peck on her mouth. "Don't wait up for me."

"You're going out?"

"I need to see what the chief is up to."

She looked disappointed but didn't complain. "Wake me up when you get back."

Because of what happened to Lucy, she'd taken a few days off work. With Jaden gone, the security detail was solid. Everyone was on heightened alert. Even Kate had agreed to stay put for a while. She was happy Thad had agreed to go to Carova with Lucy. Darcy had seen her smiling and humming a lot.

Darcy was surprised when Thad had asked him to stay here. It would take a lot for his friend to abandon the case, even for a little while. And that something must be Lucy.

"I will." With one more kiss, he left the room and then the estate. The agent working the gate would alert the others that he wouldn't be close to Kate.

* * *

Two hours later he was about to give up his watch at Wade's residence when a car pulled into the driveway. It wasn't terribly late but it was late enough to make the visit suspicious. A man he didn't recognize got out and walked toward the front door.

Darcy took pictures of the car and the man, getting a good face shot when he turned to look around. He had a special night-vision camera that Sam had given him. The army sure had some neat toys.

Wishing there was a way to listen in on the nine o'clock meeting, Darcy drove away. He was alone and wouldn't risk getting caught. The license plate and photos would be enough for now. Besides, he missed Avery. One more stop and he'd go home to her.

At the station he looked up the license plate number and got a name. Andrew Lindeman. He searched several databases and found nothing criminal on the man he'd seen. He'd get a background started on him.

On his way back to Kate's estate, he tried calling Thad but there was no answer. As he ended the call, he noticed a car behind him. If the silver Lexus sedan was a tail, the driver didn't care if it was obvious, which didn't bode well for Darcy. And it looked a lot like the car he'd seen at Wade's. He couldn't see the plate, but what were the odds that another silver Lexus would be following him?

He gave his car all the gas it would take. Sure enough, the one behind him did the same.

Darcy took a corner and headed for the freeway. If he could make it to the estate…

The car raced up to his bumper. Darcy swerved and veered around another car on the freeway. The Lexus drove ahead of the other car and then cut Darcy off. Darcy nearly lost control.

The driver of the Lexus was trying to steer him off the road. Darcy avoided a collision with a semi, staying on one side while the Lexus was forced to drive on the other. Darcy slowed, got into the lane behind the semi, then raced up behind the Lexus. He didn't have to memorize the plate. It was the same one he'd seen at Wade's.

The rear brake lights of the Lexus lit up. Darcy couldn't slow enough before ramming into the back bumper. He swerved and once again nearly lost control, doing a swerve through the grassy side before rolling back onto the highway. A car whizzed past, so close he felt the air whoosh by as it passed.

Too late, he saw the Lexus race at an angle across the highway and ram his rear right bumper. Darcy lost control then. His tires squealed as he fought to keep the vehicle straight. And then he ran into the concrete median. The car rolled three times. His driver door crushed inward, nearly pinning him.

When his car went still, he sat upright looking at oncoming traffic. Luckily, he was part on and part off the highway, close to the median.

Aware of car lights behind him, he couldn't move yet. He was dizzy and disoriented, a surreal feeling. The next thing he knew, a man appeared at his door, reaching in and dragging him outside through the window.

Dropping him on the ground, cold wind blowing, rain beginning to fall, Darcy looked up at a giant of a man wearing a hat but not concealing his face. Dead blue eyes looked down at him and a meaty hand held a pistol at his side.

Avery's beautiful face was all that came to him in that stark moment.

"Who are you?" the big man asked.

Darcy decided the best thing to do was answer all of his questions. "Detective Darcy Jenkins."

"Why were you following me?"

"Why were you at Wade Thomas's house?" He could not show fear to this man.

Watching him ascertain that Darcy didn't know why he'd gone to Wade's house, Darcy sensed the danger wane. "If you and your friend don't stop interfering, I'll have a bullet for everyone both of you love."

"Not just Kate Winston?" he dared to throw at the man.

The big man crouched, his pistol beside his leg and aimed for his kidney. "I've been real patient with you two so far. But my patience is wearing thin. Back off, or I'll kill everyone you and your friend love. Do you understand?"

Darcy understood this man was some kind of mercenary or gun for hire. "Yeah." He nodded. "Got it. Everyone we love." The man stood, smirking down at him. Cars flew by, a spray of rainwater developing. So much for Good Samaritans.

Chapter 16

The Jeep bounced and jerked through the deep, wet sand. Lucy kept looking over at Thad's grim but focused profile. He had to fight his way at a snail's pace. The windshield wipers were at top speed and water ran off them. Lucy gripped the door handle and checked on Sophie, who looked up every time the Jeep lifted her off the seat. Her dolls and a vivid imagination kept her oblivious to the severity of the storm.

Ahead, a stream of water coursed across the road. Thad didn't slow, he took it on without preamble. The Jeep sank into the depression and threw all of them up off their seats. Lucy came down hard on her butt. Water splashed high on every side of their car.

Sophie started crying.

The dolls she'd been holding had dropped to the floor,

her mouth was an open frown and tears sprouted from her frightened eyes.

"It's all right, sweetie," Lucy said. "The road is just a little wet from the rain." Boy, was that an understatement.

Straining to reach the nearest doll, Lucy handed it to the girl. "We're almost home."

Quieting, Sophie took the doll and then bent forward to retrieve her other doll.

Crisis averted, Lucy faced forward. The Jeep handled the conditions amazingly well. Dips and washed-out portions of road didn't stop them.

Finally, through torrents of rain, Lucy spotted the lights of the beach house.

"We're home, Sophie," Lucy said with as much animation as she could muster.

"Yay!" Sophie dropped her dolls and looked out the window, not possibly seeing much through the rain.

Thad drove onto the long driveway, maneuvering two mini floods streaming across and bouncing them across washed-out holes.

At last the Jeep came to a stop. They'd made it.

Lucy helped Sophie with her tote and Thad waited for them to climb the stairs first. They all ran for the door. The rain was incessant. A bolt of lightning flashed at the same time an explosion of thunder boomed. Sophie started crying. Thad opened the door, and Lucy gently pushed Sophie inside.

Dripping wet, Lucy unzipped Sophie's jacket, trying not to laugh at her adorable, crying face. "You're all right."

Her cries eased up, but she still wore a cute pout.

Lucy took off her hat and ruffled her hair. "Shower time."

After Lucy sent Sophie to change into pajamas, she came back down to the second level. Thad stood by the back windows, the television tuned to a news channel. The storm was going to intensify tonight, turning to snow by morning.

She went over to him, daring to slip her arm around him. He warmed her by putting his around her while they watched the rain in the lights over the pool. The ocean wasn't visible through the darkness.

"Darcy called," he said. "We lost cell service but I called him from the landline."

Darcy was staying at Kate's estate. Had something happened? She moved out from under his arm and faced him as he turned from the window. "Why?"

"A man met Wade Thomas at his house and then followed him." He explained what happened.

Who would do that? Who would risk being caught? Someone who wasn't afraid. That's why Thad stood here staring out the window. He wanted to go back to the estate, and it looked like the weather would stop him.

"What was his warning?" she asked.

"You and your friend better stop interfering," Thad summarized. "Darcy found out the chief is in trouble financially just like Layne and Jaden." Thad shook his head incredulously with a long sigh.

And then he'd gone to check out Wade. "How would the chief be involved?" Lucy asked.

"I don't know. None of this makes sense. I don't think Cam is involved, but Jaden could have taken money from Cam and the person who contacted Layne. He's vulnerable, and someone with the right resources would be able to find that out." Cam had.

So, Cam was just a coincidence? He hadn't met her

on purpose to try and get close to Kate? He didn't strike her as the sniper type anyway. He was crazy enough to stalk women but not smart enough to use his sniper abilities to attempt to kill a presidential candidate. She had to agree with Thad. "Who was the man who attacked Darcy?" she asked.

"Darcy is pretty sure his name is Andrew Lindeman. We think Wade hired him."

A gunman? Someone to do the serious threatening? "Could he be the shooter?"

"I think he's the one who paid Layne to kidnap Sophie and Jaden to allow the shooter access to the estate. I don't think he's the shooter."

"Why not?" Thad walked away from the window and stopped in front of the TV. "Whoever is behind this must be very rich and powerful," he said. More powerful than Wade. "It's more than a lone shooter."

"You mean like some sort of network?"

He looked back at her. "Or organization, yes."

She could see how that was possible. It did seem that there were several involved. Jaden. The chief of police. And now this Andrew Lindeman character.

"I need to get back to the estate."

Seeing Thad looking out the window again, she went to stand beside him. "You and Darcy have been friends a long time, haven't you?"

"Yes, since the academy." He turned to her, curiosity over why she'd asked in his eyes.

"Your mother is safe, Thad. You're not the only one who can protect her."

He blinked, his tension easing. "Thanks for reminding me."

He did know Darcy was capable of protecting Kate.

He had no reason to worry other than not being in control himself. He needed to let go of some of that control.

One of the security agents had told Lucy all about Darcy, his divorce and the way he'd rescued Avery. Thad hadn't told her, and she now wondered if the reason why was because watching his best friend fall in love made him take a closer look at his own love life.

"Kate said he met someone and that she's staying at the estate with him," she said.

"Yes." Again, he wore that curious look.

"They're really serious." Handsome man meets beautiful damsel...sounded familiar.

Thad didn't respond. He must have contemplated whether the same could happen to him as had happened with Darcy. And it made him uncomfortable...because he did have feelings for Lucy.

"I knew someone who fell in love like that," she said.

When Thad started to move away, she put her hand on his arm, stopping him. "She was in a bad car accident and had to go through extensive physical therapy."

Thad lifted his eyebrows, clearly expecting another one of her stories.

"She had to work at walking again. Her legs were injured the most. It nearly crippled her. There was a man who'd gotten in a climbing accident. He was seeing the same physical therapist. Once their appointments were back-to-back. My friend was finishing up and he arrived early for his session. They met and it was instant love."

"You're making this up."

She smiled, moving to stand in front of him and placing her hands on his chest. "She waited until he finished and they hobbled to a nearby café. They spent hours there just talking and then shared a cab when they left.

She took him to her house and he ended up moving in a week later. They were married six months after that."

"That's sweet," he said.

"It's a true story." She gave his chest a pat with one hand.

His mouth and eyes changed into an affectionate but derisive frown. "Sure it is."

"It is." This was one time she hadn't made it up. "I embellished a little."

"Which parts? All of it?"

"No, when I said they hobbled. I knew you didn't believe me so I told the story the way I would tell any other that wasn't true."

"Ah." He nodded, charmed.

"They both had a cane."

"A cane. Right."

"I went to college with the woman. Duke University. Her name is Annie Baker. His name is Max Timon. They live in Virginia. Look them up."

He just looked at her, sort of believing.

"Your friend Darcy reminds me a lot of them."

"Darcy was just divorced. Was your friend divorced?"

"No, but the man she'd been seeing broke up with her after the accident. The same happened with Max. His girlfriend left him. Some people find it that way." Sometimes she wondered if she'd found it that way. If Thad were open to the possibility, she'd think she had.

"Darcy isn't in love. He thinks he is but he isn't."

Lucy lowered her hands from him. "You're too stubborn to believe it."

"I'm stubborn?"

Did he think she was? "Yes. You refuse to take a chance on love. Even if you find it, you may pass it by be-

cause you're too stubborn to change the way you think."
A little frustration came into her tone. This weekend was
only missing that—Thad's flexibility on love.

"How do you know that?" he challenged.

"I…" What could she say? That after last night she
thought they had a real shot at forever? "I can tell. You
and I…"

When she didn't finish, he went white. "You're not
implying…" He pointed to her and himself a few times.
"You and I…"

"Have fallen in love?" She shook her head. "No."

"What are you saying, then?"

"You wouldn't give it a chance even if we are starting to fall for each other." There. She'd said it. "It isn't
casual enough for you."

He didn't deny that, and being right about him stung.

"Can you really say you don't feel anything for me?"
she asked.

She watched him go rigid and wanted to take the question back. Amazing, the chameleon change in him. Most
of the time he was Thad, the man who upheld the law,
the man of stealth and intelligence. And then he was
Thad, the man who shied away from love, the ideology
of marriage. Commitment? No problem. Marriage? Another story. What he didn't see was that commitment
required love, too, and he was holding back too much
to allow love to grow. He was doing that with her, right
now. If he allowed what had begun between them to
grow, he'd see that what Darcy had with Avery was possible for him, too.

There was something else that threatened his ability to love. And her name was Sophie Cambridge. Sophie melted every barrier he'd erected to protect himself

against anticipated failures. He based too much on the past and on what happened to other people, not himself. The temptation to break him of that tantalized Lucy. The cost to her heart was what stopped her. For now.

About two hours ago, Sophie came down in her pajamas and the birthday party had begun. Thad had brought down her presents, and she had just finished opening them. He and Lucy had picked up a few more before coming here. The living room was a mess, wrapping paper and boxes on the floor and cake plates on the ottoman. He forgot about why he shouldn't enjoy this. He just would, and when the weekend was over, he'd deal with the fallout then, if there was any.

The ugly thought came that there may not be any if Sophie was put into another foster home. If she stayed with Lucy, the entire situation changed, and he couldn't go there.

Sophie's eyes drooped, but she doggedly persevered in her play. Lucy laughed softly at the sight, adoration at its purest.

It was getting late. Thad went to the window to check the weather. The rain had turned to snow, slanting at an angle with the force of the wind. The beach house had been built solid, all out of stone and concrete. He could hear the wind every once in a while and that fact told him how powerful the storm was. No hurricane by any stretch, but enough to strand them here for a day or two.

"It's time for bed, Sophie," Lucy said. "We'll bring your presents up to your room."

Sophie didn't protest. She was practically falling asleep sitting up. It was after ten and it had been a big day—she'd sleep a long time.

"I'll bring her presents up," Thad said.

Lucy looked at him. "You want to stay up with me?"

Was she deliberately tempting him? "Yes." He didn't care about what would happen after they left Carova. He had a strong desire to spend time with Lucy alone. He wasn't going to deny himself that.

After bringing the presents up, paying special attention to the dollhouse and positioning it so that Sophie would see it if she woke, Thad went downstairs to get ready for Lucy.

He turned off the television and turned on the stereo, finding an easy listening station, idly wondering if they'd lose electricity. He'd done a check of all the systems here, as his mother had strategically sent him to do. He knew her real agenda—for him and Lucy to end up together. She didn't need him to come here and get the house ready. She could have sent servants to do that. Granted, a servant could be in disguise, but all of their servants had been employed by the Winston family for years. They had very low turnover because they were paid well and had benefits.

Going into the kitchen, he took a bottle of sauvignon from the wine holder and began to uncork it. All the while, conflicting motives churned in him. Seduce Lucy. Block Lucy from his heart. Seduce Lucy. Block Lucy.

He couldn't delude himself. Lucy did attract him and he wanted to be involved with her. Would she be willing? When he'd met her, she had been actively seeking husband and family. Would she forego that to be with him? At least put it off?

She had Sophie now. That changed the game, for her and for him. Sophie challenged his conviction. He vowed never to bring children into a dysfunctional family. But how could he look at Sophie and still call it dysfunction? That unsettled him.

He poured Lucy a glass of wine and then himself some eighteen-year-old Glenmorangie into a Scotch tumbler, followed by a splash of water. He rarely drank, but for some reason tonight felt like a celebration, and making it home through the storm had nothing to do with it. Lucy had everything to do with it. Last night. This morning. And, yes, even their conversation. Except, he couldn't pinpoint why. How could her challenging his beliefs feel good? Maybe it was the love she spoke of. Maybe it was the fairy tale. Was he beginning to believe in the fairy tale? No. He refused to do that.

He looked to his left when he heard Lucy come down the stairs. She appeared around the wall and his course was set. She wore jeans and a long-sleeved cream-colored knit shirt and socks. Not the nightgown that had captivated him before, but nothing could hide her beauty. Her dark hair fell over her shoulders and her trim hips swayed as she approached.

Seduce Lucy.

Passing the leather sectional, he met her in the open area between the entry and the great room. She took the glass of wine and looked down at his tumbler.

"A manly drink, huh?"

"One thing I got from my dad," he said. One of few.

Her light green eyes sparkled with appeal. "Did you get the art of seduction from him, too?"

She couldn't have asked a more digging question. How had she targeted him so accurately? His father had been a master with women. Did Lucy think he bore some similarities? He may not be unfaithful to the women he chose to develop relationships with, but he didn't settle for just one. It put him in check.

"I didn't mean…" Lucy began to apologize for implying he treated women the same as his father had.

"No." He stopped her. "You're right. We still haven't finished our conversation from this morning." He should never have considered continuing this with her without doing so.

Lucy sipped her wine, drilling him with her eyes. She was such a perceptive woman. Smart. With a funny streak.

"You want me to agree to a relationship with you for as long as you remain interested and then we go our separate ways."

She stated the fact, and not in a savory way.

"It may not be me who becomes disinterested," he said.

She strolled closer to the living room, looking through the window at the rain turning to snow.

He moved to face her. "And we may not go our separate ways."

Facing him, she sipped, her clever eyes making him feel as if she was way ahead of him. "You have it in your head that no relationship lasts, so one of us will initiate the separation. It will just be a question of time. Months. Years. But it will come."

He did believe that, but only because he didn't believe he'd find the real thing, the genuine article. True love. Plenty of people took chances on it, but very few found it. That was just reality. And he was very much a realist. He wouldn't be a crime scene investigator if he weren't. Having hope that everything would be all right in his line of work was dangerous. Everything was not all right if he was needed. If he was called to a scene, it meant someone had been gravely hurt or killed. Not all right. No fantasy there. Only reality.

"No marriage. No kids," he said. She had to understand that's the way he intended to live before any intimacy continued.

If that angered her, she covered it well. Putting her wineglass down on the credenza behind one side of the sectional, she went to him and slid her hands up his chest. With her body pressed to his, she tipped her head back.

"You can have this weekend," she murmured. "After that, you can't have me anymore unless you can be with me unconditionally."

With no conditions placed upon her that she could expect no marriage and no children with him. He inwardly went cold. *Unconditional* meant he had to be open to marriage and children with her—if their relationship progressed to that point. He could agree and still never marry her or have kids with her, but that would be dishonest and cruel. If he couldn't be open to giving her all she needed, then he shouldn't be with her at all.

Rising up onto her toes, she put her lips to his, eyes open and full of sultry shrewdness. "One weekend."

"Lucy…" She flipped on a sexual switch in him.

"After that, it ends unless there are no conditions," she insisted. "You don't have to decide now. You can decide when we get back to the estate. No conditions. You put aside your doomsday attitude and accept what we have, as is. No projections of the future, marriage or no marriage, children or no children."

He loved that she'd used the word *doomsday,* and then not. She had him figured out and that unnerved him. Why was she giving him the weekend? To cast a spell on him? She'd already begun to do that.

"And if the relationship progresses to something serious enough to move in together, what then?" he asked.

"You have to be open to marrying me. Someday. I require marriage. If not with you, then someone."

"You're asking me to change the way I view marriage."

"Yes. I am."

He wasn't sure he could do that. A haunting voice inside his head echoed, *Yet*. She eased away from him, and he thought she'd changed her mind. But instead, she lifted her shirt off and dropped it to the floor. "This weekend and then we decide what to do from there." She removed her bra and it fell on top of her shirt. "Agreed?"

Thad stared at her hard nipples, perched on round, creamy flesh that begged to be touched with his mouth. "Agreed."

Smiling her victory, Lucy removed her jeans in a striptease, slowly inching them down over her hips, lifting one slender leg out of one side, and then the other. Her underwear came next.

He put down his tumbler and went to her. Taking her against him, he kissed her. She lifted one leg beside his still fully clothed side. He ran his hands down her body, over her rear. Both of them kissed each other, seeking, hungry for more. She unbuttoned his thin flannel shirt and spread her hands on his chest. He shrugged out of the shirt.

Lucy planted wet kisses all over his chest. He watched her as he unbuttoned his jeans. She crouched and took over removing his pants, his erection jutting free. Both naked now, Thad held her against him for a long, deep kiss. All that mattered was her. This. Getting inside her.

Lifting her so that she wrapped her legs around him, he walked around the sectional, Lucy still kissing him, her hands on each side of his face. There were two leaf-yellow leather ottomans centered between the section and two multicolored striped chairs. Any flat surface would do.

He lowered her onto them, making sure her butt was on the edge. Then he braced himself by his hands on either side of her and his feet on the wood floor. She opened her legs. The sight made him groan and he couldn't prolong the penetration. Muscles straining, he sank deep into her. She held on to his biceps as he thrust back and forth. He sucked her breasts and then rose up to look at her, at their joining. It was strenuous work maintaining this position, but the angle was gripping.

Beneath him, Lucy arched and met his hips with hers. She was the most beautiful sight he'd ever seen. Wind spattered wet, heavy snow against the windows. Soft music played along with their breathing.

Putting his weight on her, he pumped into her, grabbing the end of the ottoman to leverage harder thrusts. He found her G-spot that way. She rasped ecstatic moans that escalated to a shout. He kissed her to keep her quieter, feeling her body tremble in orgasm.

With her limp and satisfied, he coaxed her up off the ottoman. She wrapped her arms around him, demanding a kiss. He gave her a deep one before turning her to face the ottoman.

"Get down onto it," he said gruffly.

Finally, she understood he wanted her on her hands and knees on the two big, square ottomans. Kneeling between her legs from behind, he held her hips and probed her opening, sliding in smooth and slick. Holding her hips still, he thrust deep and slow at first, until he heard her respond, aroused again. Then he thrust in hard. Pulled back. Thrust in hard again. Faster and faster. Skin slapped skin.

If he could get her out of his system, this would be the way. She grunted with the repeated impacts and put one hand on the sectional for balance.

Changing his angle just a bit, he continued the driving pace. He couldn't quiet her cries this time. She came with a sound that echoed in the room. A few more thrusts and an unending wave of pleasure engulfed him.

Lucy lay awake long after that bronco ride on the living-room ottoman. His hard pounding had sent her through the roof with a million rockets shooting off, but what had that been all about? Luckily, Sophie hadn't woken. The urgency with which he'd made love to her could have been due to his current certainty that he would never be able to be with her unconditionally. Well, if there was one goal she had this weekend, it was to teach him that love didn't end. After he left this beach house, he'd never be able to forget her.

That was the theory, anyway.

He lay beside her asleep. They were in his room now, farther away from Sophie's but close enough in case she needed them. She curled against him. It was still snowing outside. They'd be stranded for at least another day. While Sophie was engrossed in all her new presents, she planned on sneaking Thad into dark nooks and crannies of the house for quick reminders of how good it was between with them.

More and more, Lucy was convinced they had the makings of a lasting love, the kind Thad didn't believe in. Yet.

Pulling the covers all the way off him, she climbed onto him. He stirred, beginning to wake. This was how she wanted him, unsuspecting, waking slowly to her loving.

When his eyes fluttered open, she leaned over and kissed him softly.

He moaned and his hand came up, fingers sinking into her hair. He held her to his mouth, falling into the slowness just the way she planned.

Lucy didn't hold back. She kissed and touched to convey the way she felt. Unvarnished, unguarded. Genuine. She truly felt there was something real going on between them. Why didn't, or wouldn't, he accept that? She didn't know. But she did know that if her opening to him didn't reach him, nothing would.

She kissed him all over his body, slowly gliding her hands as she went. His neck, his chest, his stomach. She trailed her tongue up and down his hardness. When she finished, she stretched on top of him. His hands went to her back, her breasts mashed to his chest. Looking into his eyes, letting him see all, she kissed him purposefully.

When he could take no more, he rolled her onto her back.

She let him part her legs and push into her. When he stayed deep inside her without moving, she inwardly cheered. Taking her lead, he spent time kissing and touching her. Beginning with her mouth, he traveled downward, treating her to the same pleasure. Endless moments of sensation tickled her, full of meaning, more than they'd shared so far. She could feel it. He slid back and forth a few times, gentle and slow, and then slid completely out of her to kiss the lower regions of her body.

Back up to her mouth, he pushed into her with more force. When he began thrusting harder, she stopped him.

"I want it slow," she murmured.

A low groan rumbled from inside him, but he slowed his pace. Taking her hands in his, he gripped her and pinned her to the mattress while he moved with excruciating slowness. He watched their joining and then looked into her eyes.

Intense pleasure built up, circling in her groin and spreading. He thrust hard once and withdrew, thrust again.

It was too incredible to slow him down. She tried to stifle a cry, turning her head and shutting her eyes to the intense feeling.

Thad rammed into her without mercy. "Lucy," he groaned. "I…can't…"

"Do it." All that mattered was his hardness in her. "Do it."

With a low growl, he rose up onto his hands and let loose, pounding her hard and deep. Lifting her legs, she opened her knees, held them with her hands to keep them wide so that she could take all he had to give. From there it was a matter of seconds and the world flew away.

Lying flat with him collapsed on top of her, both of them recovering, she realized what had just happened.

"Damn it," she complained. "I wanted it slow."

He chuckled low and intimate into her ear. "No, you didn't."

She smiled with wicked appeal. Thad hadn't actively tried to purge her. They just couldn't get enough of each other.

Unconditional, Lucy reminded herself. After this weekend, he could not place any conditions on their relationship. In that, she could not compromise.

Chapter 17

All the way to Kate's estate, Thad withdrew more and more. Lucy watched it like a flower closing at the end of a hot day. Servants helped them unload the Jeep. Inside, Sophie ran to her room, excited about having two dollhouses to play with. She'd be busy for hours.

"There you are." Kate glided into the entry with a big smile and clever, observant eyes. She hugged Thad, leaning back for a close look, and then Lucy. "Well? How'd it go?"

"Great," she said.

"Sophie enjoyed it," Thad added.

"What about the two of you?" Kate hadn't missed how stiff they both sounded.

"The storm kept us in the house for a couple of days, but we managed," Lucy said when Thad's brow lowered as he looked at his mother.

"Hey, you're back," Darcy interrupted at just the right moment. He greeted Thad and Lucy, and then to Thad said, "I need to talk to you."

He must have found out more about the man who'd chased him.

"You're free to talk in front of all of us," Kate said.

Darcy's gaze passed over Lucy before he started in. He must have been surprised Thad had told her. Maybe he thought they'd grown closer.

"Andrew Lindeman is an ordinary guy. Shocked me when I got the background information. Mechanic at a small garage. Wife and two kids. Except he hasn't shown up for work in weeks and his wife left him recently. Apparently, he hasn't been home and she doesn't know where he's been going or staying. Acting very strange."

Mechanic-turned-henchman. Lucy agreed, that was strange.

"Why did he follow you and give you a warning?" Thad asked.

"Good question, and one I can't answer. Nothing in his background suggests he's a criminal. Has no record. Until he left his job and wife, he was a dependable worker and husband. The wife's pretty upset over it."

"When did you talk to her?" Thad asked.

"Yesterday."

"You're supposed to be watching my mother."

"Oh, Thad, I have countless agents swarming this place," Kate admonished. "I told him to go."

"Of course you did," Thad said cynically.

"I wasn't gone long. And I had to talk to some people to learn about this guy," Darcy said.

"And as you can see, I'm fine." Kate opened her arms to indicate her healing form.

"Why would an ordinary guy go after you in relation to Kate's shooting?" Lucy asked, more to herself. "Is he a political fanatic?"

"I found nothing in his background to indicate that," Darcy said.

"He's an average family man one day and an extremist the next," Kate said, voicing her thoughts much as Lucy had.

"Your theory about an organization behind all of this must be right, Thad," Lucy said.

While Darcy nodded his agreement, Kate looked off to the side as she pondered that. It was bad enough one shooter had gone after her, but a group?

"And they'll obviously go to any length to see that they succeed," Darcy said, and then murmured to Kate, "Sorry."

She held up a hand. "No, it's the truth. We have to find a way to stop them."

Thad's austere face revealed his determination to do just that.

"I have officers looking for Lindeman," Darcy said. "He seems to have disappeared. Found his car abandoned in a parking lot of an abandoned warehouse."

Another dead end.

"Do you think he was killed? It was so easy for you to find him," Lucy said.

"Yeah, all I had to do was run his plates."

"They know you looked in to him," Thad said.

"My guess is the chief is the one keeping them informed, whoever 'they' are. I assume he never got back to you on Sophie's kidnapping...?"

"No."

"I checked Layne's phone records on my own and isolated a number from Lindeman's mechanic shop."

That helped prove Lindeman had been the one to arrange the kidnapping, but Lindeman was now missing. And if Lindeman had been killed, they'd lost a solid lead. The only lead they had unless Jaden talked.

Thad sat with Darcy down in the media room at his mother's estate. His feet were up on the reclined theater chair, Darcy a mirror image beside him. They each had their own bowl of popcorn. The Carolina Hurricanes–Buffalo Sabres hockey game played, the giant screen and surround sound making it feel as though they were there live. For the first time in as long as he could remember, Thad wasn't in the mood for sports. He couldn't stop thinking about Lucy.

"What's going on with you?" Darcy asked from beside him. "The Sabres just scored and you didn't even notice."

"Nothing."

"You've been moping all week."

Thad ate a handful of popcorn. Moping. Brooding. Bothered. Yeah. He'd rather be excited about the game, but the nagging sense that he was making a big mistake wouldn't leave him alone.

"Did you and Lucy hit it off in Carova?"

Thad had to hand it to Darcy for letting this much time go by before asking that. Thad didn't have a reply. "Hit it off" didn't come close to what he felt.

"You'd be yourself if you didn't," Darcy continued. "But now you feel something and you're freaking out."

Thad sent him an unappreciative look. Like Lucy, Darcy knew him too well. Darcy, he'd expect. Lucy? How had she picked him apart so fast?

Some people find it that way. Had they hit it off so well that they knew each other already? Were they so much alike that it came naturally? Or had she simply focused on his commitment issue?

"Just because your parents screwed things up doesn't mean you will," Darcy said.

Thad sent him another look.

"Seriously, Thad. You're a good friend. I don't want to see you pass up something that's worth more than you're allowing. Let it go, man."

Thad didn't engage. He was too torn over the whole thing with Lucy. Making love at the Carova beach house. Sophie. All of it.

"Avery and I are getting married."

The shock of that announcement rippled through Thad as he turned to look at his best friend's profile. "When?"

"This May. It's going to be small. Just a few of our friends and family."

"Are you sure?"

"I've never been more sure about anything in my entire life."

Stunned, Thad believed him.

"I'd like you to be the best man."

Darcy was marrying a woman he'd just met. "Yeah. Of course."

"Don't you feel the same about Lucy?"

Yes, an inner voice responded. But Thad stopped it from going any further.

That's when he realized he did stop his feelings for Lucy. What would happen if he didn't? Wasn't that what Lucy had asked him to do? It was her ultimatum. She'd refuse any intimacy with him unless he stopped laying the law down with regard to marriage.

"You do," Darcy said for him. "I can tell." When Thad would have protested, Darcy cut him off. "I know you. You love her."

He didn't want to love her.

"If you throw it away, you'll never forget her, and you'll never find anyone like her. If you're really sure you'll never get married, you'll get exactly what you ask for if you let Lucy go."

The truth of that reverberated inside him. What if he was making a mistake letting Lucy go? Was he letting her go?

No. Something powerful inside him rebelled against that. And yet...

"It scares you," Darcy said. "You're afraid. I get that. But there comes a point when you have to leap forward and take a chance."

"I need time to think about it."

"Don't take too much time. Lucy won't wait for long." Putting his bowl of popcorn aside, Darcy stood. "I should get home to Avery. She's getting off work right now."

Thad stood, too, and then followed him upstairs. Seeing him out the door, he heard voices in the kitchen and went there. His mother and Lucy were still up and they were deep into a serious conversation.

"You're well enough to take care of yourself," Lucy said. "You don't need me anymore."

Was she going to leave? The swell of regret gripped Thad. No. She couldn't leave yet.

"Perhaps. And there couldn't have been anyone more capable than you, Lucy, but I'd like you to stay regardless. You're safer here."

"I was never in danger. Cam wasn't involved in the shooting."

"Lucy. We don't know what the shooter will do or who is working with him. You could be vulnerable."

"I don't see how."

"You mean something to Thad. You could be used against him."

"I don't mean enough. He's barely spoken to me over the past few days. I think it would be better for both of us if I just left. I need to get on with my life. Go back to work at Duke…"

Her voice trailed off, but what she would have said next hung in the air.

"Find a man," his mother said.

Lucy sighed.

"Give it a little more time," Kate said. "At least until after Trey's wedding."

His older brother's marriage was coming up next week, at the end of March.

"I don't know if I can." Lucy sounded sad, her voice low and without energy.

Thad turned away from the door and leaned his back against the wall, letting his head fall back. He had avoided her since they'd come back from the Outer Banks. So full of confusion, he didn't hear Lucy and his mother leave the kitchen. Lucy was the first to appear through the doorway. He lifted his head. His mother stopped behind Lucy, both surprised to find him there, both knowing he'd heard what had been said.

"I'm going to bed." His mother left them alone.

Thad straightened from the wall and faced Lucy, at a loss for what to say.

"I should go to bed, too." Lucy started to walk away.

Without knowing why, he took hold of her arm and stopped her, gently bringing her back to him.

"My mother's right. You should stay."

She eased out of his grasp. "Why?"

For him. But he couldn't say that, so he didn't say anything.

Disappointment dulled her usually bright green eyes. "Did it mean nothing to you?"

"No. It did." She had to know Carova had meant something. It meant too much. "I just…"

"Feel safer running away."

Many thoughts bombarded him, all of which he should verbalize so that she understood him. If only he could organize them all and start with one.

"Lucy…" He reached for her, wishing she wouldn't put so much pressure on him.

She stepped back. She'd made her requirements clear. She was asking him to be open to whatever the future brought. But he couldn't do that. Although she claimed not to expect marriage, he knew that she did. If not with him, then someone. The idea of her with another man gathered in a tight ball in the pit of his stomach. But then, so did the idea of getting married.

Watching him, Lucy's lips quivered subtly. He thought she would cry. She turned away before he could be sure. He didn't go after her. If he did, he'd comfort her, reassure her, and where would that lead? Down an unknown road with bends and curves he'd rather not travel.

Wiping the tear that tickled down her cheek, Lucy saw Kate peeking out her bedroom door. She waved Lucy to come inside. Wondering what she was up to, Lucy went into Kate's spacious master suite.

"You poor thing." Kate shut the door.

"I'm moving home in the morning."

"No. I was about to tell you something when we ran into Thad." She took Lucy's hand and led her to the sitting area before the windows, a lamp on the table between softly lighting the room.

Lucy sat down, tired and sad.

"I know he loves you, Lucy."

Love? "Oh, I don't—"

"I know my son. He's in love with you. Why do you think he's been avoiding you?"

"He's afraid I'll drag him to the altar."

"He's afraid that's exactly what he wants. He'll come to his senses eventually. But I have an idea that might speed up his decision process."

Lucy lifted her brow. Politicians could be wily, but what did Kate have in mind?

Chapter 18

Thad came down to grab some dinner before he met Darcy to work the investigation. That had kept him away the past few nights. He hadn't had many encounters with Lucy, and those he had were benign. In fact, she didn't seem to mind the distance between them, which had made him relax. He no longer felt cornered. His mother told him she'd gone to see her parents one night, and then met some friends another. He may have been apart from her, but he was still concerned for her whereabouts.

Lucy sat on the bench in the big window across the kitchen, cell phone in hand, a partial smile sneaking up her mouth. She was texting someone. And not one of her *friends*...

Thad kept his eye on her as he took out everything he needed to make a sandwich. Servants were busy cooking for the rest of the household, and he declined assistance in getting something to eat sooner.

Lucy stood from the bench and put her phone down on the kitchen island close to where he stood putting ham and cheese on some wheat bread. The screen was still illuminated, and he saw the texts.

See you at seven was the last one.

"Going somewhere tonight?" Was she back on her online dating site?

"Dinner."

When she turned her back to pour iced tea into a glass, he picked up her phone and opened her browser.

"With a girlfriend?" He froze as he looked down at the dating site, which was open to the last screen she'd used, one where she'd responded to a man who was interested. She'd given TakeYouToTheMoon@gettogether.com her cell number. That was who she'd just been texting.

Lucy snatched her phone from him.

"TakeYouToTheMoon?" What man would call himself that on an online dating site?

"His name is Matt."

Thad clamped down his rising ire. He had no right to be angry. He'd turned away from her. But how could she start dating again so soon?

"Didn't you learn from your last experience that online dating is dangerous?" he asked instead.

"That was one instance." Carrying her phone and the glass of tea, she left the kitchen and Thad standing there with everything male in him against her going out on a date. A date, for God's sake!

Yanking his phone out of its holder, he called Darcy.

"You're on your own tonight," he said.

"What? Why?"

"Lucy's going out on a date." He disconnected before

Darcy could comment and then went to wait for Lucy. She'd ensconced herself in her room with the door locked.

An hour and a half later, Thad paced outside Lucy's room. She sure was taking her time getting ready. He heard her on the other side. Finally, she opened the door.

"What are you—" He stopped short when he saw her. She wore a dark red dress that dipped low in front and exposed her knees. He'd never seen her in anything that sexy.

"I thought you were going on another stakeout with Darcy tonight," she said.

Was she hoping he wouldn't find out her plans for the evening? "You're not going anywhere in that." The thought of another man enjoying her dressed that way made him crazy.

"What gives you the right to tell me what I can and can't do?"

He didn't understand why her going out on a date bothered him so much. He couldn't give her what she was after, so why stop her?

She didn't wait for him to respond. Walking down the hall, she headed for the stairs. The dress hugged her curves, hips rocking, legs going on for a mile and arms swinging with a tiny purse in one hand.

He followed her. "Lucy, don't go."

"Don't go? Why not?" She stepped down the stairs, and he kept up with her.

What claim did he have on her? He'd turned away. He knew that. He felt foolish for trying to stop her, but something compelled him, something strong.

She left out the side entrance, where he saw his mother's driver waiting. At least Lucy wasn't going without protection. His mother's driver was a Secret Service agent.

Operating on an emotion he refused to name, Thad went to his Charger and began to follow the car. All the way to the restaurant where she must have agreed to meet her date, Thad questioned why he was doing this. He had no answer. He only knew nothing would stop him.

Inside the restaurant, he watched her meet a tall man with dark hair, and then a hostess led them to a table. He went there as they both sat down. The man smiled and kept glancing at Lucy's breasts.

Aware of how irrational he appeared, Thad forged ahead. Before he reached the table he wondered if Lucy was doing this on purpose. The way her date smiled suggested he knew her. Any man would look at her breasts in that dress. He saw Thad first, his smile flattening. Lucy turned with a slack jaw to gape at him. She hadn't expected him to follow her here.

"We need to talk," he said to her.

"Thad?"

"Let's go." He held out his hand.

She didn't move.

"I'm ready to talk," he added. And he was.

She faced her date, who grinned.

Why did he grin?

The man stood. "I'll call Kate." With a nod to Thad, he walked out of the restaurant.

"Well, now that you've ruined my date." She motioned to the seat the man had vacated, her hand palm up. "Why don't you join me?"

"He wasn't a real date." Thad moved to the seat across from her and she studied him without asking how he knew. "Why is he going to call my mother? Did she have anything to do with this?"

With a grunt, she picked up the menu. "How did you know?"

"It's okay. It worked." He couldn't believe how insanely jealous he'd gotten.

Looking at him over the menu, her eyes smiled.

But he didn't feel like smiling. This wasn't easy for him. "I need time to sort it all out, Lucy."

No longer smiling, she put the menu down. She understood what he was saying. He needed time to know whether he could come to her unconditionally, neither accepting nor rejecting the possibility of marriage.

"Okay," she murmured.

She'd give him time. Relief loosened his tension.

But Thad didn't delude himself. If he took too much time, she'd eventually give up on him, and rightfully so. If she ever went on another date, it would be for real.

"If I devote myself to this relationship, I have to be sure I come to you honestly," he told her.

Her face softened with what he could only call love. "I know."

She knew...

She was an incredible woman. And Thad would be a colossal fool if he let her go.

"Why don't we start with you coming with me to my brother's wedding," he said. "Sophie, too."

"Are you sure you can handle that?" she teased.

"Yeah, I'm very sure." And he was. Maybe this would be easier than he thought. If he just let go...

A crowd of Trey and Debra's closest friends and family filled the beautifully decorated ballroom at Kate's estate. Lighted curtain panels knotted in the middle lined two walls of windows. Yellow flower petals on white napkins and numbered glass candles adorned tabletops. Huge vases of flowers sat on several tall cocktail tables and waitstaff abounded to cater to the guests.

Lucy watched Thad dance with Sophie on the raised platform in the middle of the room. In a black tuxedo, he captured her gaze for lengthy periods of time. Every once in a while, he'd look over at her. The way he looked at her raised the temperature a few degrees. He'd noticed her in her long, black figure-hugging dress. Sophie was adorable in her white ball gown with bubble hem and flower in her hair. She'd had fun being girly at the hair salon with Lucy. They'd gotten their nails done, too. Lucy was going to have a hard time letting her go.

"I've never seen him like this."

She turned to see Kate, who'd just come up to stand beside her. "The date did the trick." Or, at the very least, stopped him from being so distant.

Thad lifted Sophie and held her as he danced in a circle. Her laughter rose above music and people talking.

"What are you going to do with Sophie?" Kate asked.

Keep her...

"I don't know."

"She's good for Thad."

Lucy glanced at her and then back to Thad and Sophie. His face did light up whenever he was with her. She didn't acknowledge Kate's comment. Turning her son into viable husband material was a big enough challenge.

The song finished, and Thad brought Sophie over to them. Sophie hopped up on a chair at the table where they'd sat for dinner and dug into the rest of her cake.

Thad extended his hand. "May I have this dance?"

Lucy gave him her hand and went with him to the dance platform with butterflies of delight tickling her. Could it be that he'd change his mind about marriage and family?

He brought her close, holding her hand and encircling her waist. She rested her hand on his shoulder and looked up at his face. His eyes had a happy light to them.

"What are you doing to me, Lucy?" he asked.

Smiling, she tipped her head up. "Stealing your heart." She kissed him once on his lips.

"You've already done that."

"Have I?"

His eyes answered for him, and then he showed her with his mouth, kissing her softly, lingering.

"Looks like you'll be next, little brother."

They drew apart as Trey and Debra danced beside them. To Lucy's delight, Thad didn't cringe or stiffen. He just smiled down at Lucy. Hope soared and she had to reel it in a bit.

Trey and Debra were so obviously happy, dancing close, eyes only for each other. Their wedding had been stunning in one of Raleigh's oldest churches. There were several other couples dancing. Lucy spotted Sophie with Sam, who bent over slightly as he held her hands and twirled her around.

As Thad danced her in a circle, she saw Sam's friend Mike was here, too. He sat at a table watching them.

The song ended and she and Thad went to their table.

"I'll be back." Lucy headed for the bathroom.

A few minutes later, she came out of the bathroom and headed toward the ballroom. The loud bang of gunfire made her freeze. Someone was shooting a gun at the wedding! Lucy ran through the formal entry toward the ballroom. All she could think about was Sophie. At the doorway, she bumped into Mike. He had a gun.

Oh, good. He could help.

But then he grabbed ahold of her and put the pistol against her head.

Seeing the Secret Service agents dive for his mother and that she hadn't been hit, Thad ran after Mike Harris. Mike Harris! He never would have guessed Sam's good friend would try to kill Kate Winston. Why?

The janitor at the building across from the hotel where his mother had been shot must have been mistaken when he said the man he'd seen had short hair. Mike was bald. The janitor had also said Mike had worn a hat, so maybe he had been mistaken about the hair. Every other descriptor matched.

Mike being the shooter explained so much. Jaden leaving the window and door open. The ease of access to the estate. Without Jaden's help, Trey's wedding offered the perfect opportunity. Mike was invited.

Thad emerged in the formal entry and came to an abrupt stop, aiming his pistol at Mike, who held Lucy around her torso with one arm and the gun at her head with the other. Her arms pinned, she stared at Thad with wild fear, but didn't fight Mike.

Thad stepped forward. As Mike backed across the entry, Thad moved to block an escape to the lower level of the house. Mike was forced to attempt his escape by going upstairs, where he'd be trapped, which was Thad's intention. All that consumed him was saving Lucy.

"Stay back or I'll kill her!" Mike shouted.

The shock of discovering Mike was the shooter began to wear off, and anger took its place. How could someone who was a friend of the family decide to kill their mother?

"You won't get away, Mike." Thad kept his aim steady and his temper under control. "Let Lucy go. She doesn't have anything to do with this."

"If you want her to live, you won't follow me."

Where did he plan to go? Would he jump out a window or off a balcony? What then? Did he think he'd get off the estate? By now the feds were gathering. Mike would be surrounded. Already he heard agents running into the entry. A glance back confirmed that, along with Sam in the lead.

"Mike," he said, breathless and still in shock. "What are you doing?"

At Sam's question, Mike's demeanor changed. His eyes grew panicked and his pistol unsteady.

Lucy managed to grip Mike's forearm as he climbed a stair at a time.

"Nobody follows or she's dead," Mike said.

Thad stopped at the foot of the stairs. "Don't do it, Mike."

"Stay where you are!"

Thad waited until Mike reached the top of the stairs before charging after him. On the second level, he caught sight of Mike forcing Lucy into an enclave down the left hallway.

What would he do? Would he actually kill Lucy? The idea gutted Thad. If he lost her…

There was still so much that needed to be said. So much that they still hadn't shared.

At the quaint sitting area in the enclave, Thad saw Lucy craning her neck. She saw him and some of her panic eased.

Mike saw him, too, his eyes round and crazed. He was not the Mike that Thad knew, not the Mike who'd helped save Lucy from Cam. What was wrong with him? What had made him go out of his mind like this?

"I told you not to follow me!" The pistol shook slightly in his grasp.

"Drop the gun, Mike."

"No! I told you to stay back!"

Lucy grimaced as Mike pressed the pistol harder against her head. Thad didn't have much time. He needed information from Mike, but if he let too much time go by while Mike lost his grip on sanity, there was no telling what he'd do.

Shoot Lucy. Thad could not allow that to happen. Every fraction of a second that passed felt like an eternity. Losing Lucy would take a piece of him too large to replace. He would not recover from it. She meant more to him than he'd realized. Real fear assaulted him, nearly stealing his concentration. His conviction over the odds of a failed marriage paled in comparison. He found it incredible that he'd ever placed so much importance on it, when losing Lucy would be so much more devastating.

"Mike...why are you doing this?" Thad tried once more. "Did someone pay you?"

Mike's breathing grew harsher in his altered state. He was going to kill Lucy. Thad felt it.

Thad didn't have a choice. He saw Lucy's fear, the certainty that she'd die, and fired.

Lucy screamed and crouched as Mike's body fell to the floor. Thad knew he hadn't missed. Lucy crawled away, toward Thad. She stumbled to her feet and launched herself against him.

He held her, still aiming his gun to make sure Mike

didn't move. Hearing agents rushing down the hall, he set Lucy aside.

"Stay here." He moved away from her and went to Mike's body, a pool of blood spreading by his head. He searched his pockets and inside his wallet, finding something there—a business card. He tucked it into his pocket just as the agents appeared in the enclave opening, weapons drawn.

Thad stood and backed away, allowing agents to do their own search. Seeing Lucy standing beside a stricken Sam, he went to her. Taking her into his arms, he met Sam's gaze. He hadn't known Mike was behind this, and would not recover for a while.

"Oh, Thad." Lucy kissed his cheek and then his mouth.

All of his attention shifted to her. "Lucy. If I had lost you…" He kissed her back.

"If you hadn't come when you did…"

He kissed her again. When he was assured she was all right and had calmed, he leaned back and kept her at his side. Love enveloped him. He knew the feeling on a deep, fundamental level. The beginning of it. He'd never known that before, never felt this way before. In love. Or falling into it…the real thing.

"Why did he do it?" Sam asked.

"I didn't have time to question him," Thad said.

"He was going to kill me," Lucy said.

Late that night, along with a few other law enforcement personnel, Thad finished examining Mike Harris's apartment. They were the first to arrive there. Thad fully expected the feds to be here soon, but by then he'd have gathered all he needed. Thad and his team found the sniper rifle used in his first attempt, and several printed articles on politics, heavy on radical viewpoints. The most interesting were the ones he found about various potential presidential candidates, his mother included. He instructed his team to leave everything where they found it. They took plenty of pictures and processed everything as they would any other crime scene, short of bagging the evidence.

"Thad."

Thad turned to the officer who'd called his name.

"You need to see this."

Thad followed the officer down the hall. In a spare bedroom, the officer joined another at an open closet door. He pushed it wider as Thad neared. Pictures of political figures covered the inside panel of the door, words and terms clipped out of newspapers over them. Senators and presidential candidates with their faces covered with terms like *Special Interest, Philanderer, Narcissist* and *Sinner.* There were red X marks over some of them. Most chilling of all was the photo of his mother. She had a red X and the word *Supremacist* taped over her mouth.

"Take lots of pictures," he said, not sharing his thoughts.

Clearly, more than his mother were a target. And whoever had convinced Mike to do the killing would find someone else...unless Thad could stop them. And he had an idea of where to start.

Carrying a file folder, Thad found Chief Wade Thomas in his office, busy at work like any other day. He had to have seen the news this morning. When he looked up, Thad noticed the subtle flinch of his head and his instant alertness.

"Thad. I heard what happened. Is your mother all right?"

The staged way he asked didn't get past Thad. "She's

fine. Mike Harris isn't a very good shot. Luckily, no one was hurt."

"Yeah. Mike Harris." He shook his head. "What a shock."

Thad moved farther into the office and stood behind one of the chairs in front of Wade's desk. "How did you find out?"

Wade's gaze moved up and down Thad. "It was all over the office this morning. On the news, too."

"Have you talked to anyone about it?" Thad asked.

Wade appeared taken aback by the question. "Like who?"

"Like whoever else is involved in the attempts on my mother's life."

Wade leaned back with a scoff. "How would I know that? And why do you think more than Mike Harris is after her?"

"You tell me." Thad dropped the business card onto the desk. "Was he supposed to call you after he shot her?"

Leaning forward, Wade picked up the card and then looked up at Thad. Some of his smugness faded. "I warned you not to interfere, Winston."

Many times. "And I'm glad I didn't listen. Who, other than you, is involved?"

"Now I'm involved?" Wade glanced at the folder Thad held. "Be careful, Winston. You're throwing some pretty serious allegations."

Dropping the folder onto the desk, Thad waited while Wade's hard gaze drilled into Thad's. An untold number of thoughts had to be racing through his head. He was beginning to worry.

Standing, Wade walked to his office door, closed it and turned back to Thad. "You better be sure about what you're doing. I'm in a position to crush you." He strode forward with staged bravado, stopping close to Thad. "Don't forget who you're talking to."

The chief of police. "Is that a threat? Like all the others you've sent?" He guessed at that. "I don't scare easily."

Wade didn't react.

Thad didn't back down from Wade's intimidation. He had to know Thad wasn't bluffing, that he *was* sure. He wouldn't have come here otherwise.

"What's in the folder?" Wade must have caught on to Thad's confidence. He began to falter.

"Have a look for yourself," Thad said.

With growing uneasiness, Wade returned to his desk. Without sitting down, he opened the folder. He picked up the photographs of the sniper rifle and Mike's closet door.

After a few moments, Wade looked up. "What is this?"

He knew damn well what it was, but Thad indulged him. "They're from Mike's apartment."

Wade fell into a long, grave contemplation. "I still don't understand why you're in my office giving me a song and dance about threats and involvement in Kate's shooting. Cut to the chase, Winston."

Thad sat down on the opposite side of the desk and steepled his fingers. "You knew about Sophie. You knew about Jaden. And you knew about Mike. You're involved. Do you think I can't prove it?"

At last, Wade reacted. He sat down on his office chair. The seriousness of his predicament finally began to sink in. His smugness faded. Mounting fear took its place... or was it resignation?

"What will I find when I look at your phone records?" Thad had no mercy for this man. He'd helped Mike try to kill his mother. He turned to face the desk. "Will I find proof that you talked to Jaden and Mike?"

Wade leaned back against his chair. He was caught.

"Why haven't you told me about the phone records in Sophie's kidnapping case?" Thad pressed.

Wade didn't reply.

"Darcy obtained them for me," Thad said. "Lindeman was talking to Layne, and now Lindeman is missing. Isn't that interesting?"

Still, Wade didn't respond, only his grim stare met Thad's.

"Why did you do it?" Thad asked.

"You have no idea what you're getting yourself into, Winston. You should have listened to me."

"Why did you do it?" he repeated. He had to know, not only for himself, but for the investigation.

"This is way over your head. Hell, it's over mine. You'd be smart to stop now. Get out while you still can."

"Get out of what?"

"It's too late for me," he said as though he hadn't heard Thad.

Thad lowered his hands, beginning to worry about how bleak the chief sounded. "If you won't tell me why Mike Harris tried to kill my mother, there are others who can."

"Like who? Layne Bridger?" Wade put his hands on the arms of his chair. "He doesn't know anything."

The police had questioned him and he hadn't revealed anything. Thad had wondered if he was afraid to talk or if he truly didn't know anything.

"Did you pay him or did someone else?" Thad asked.

"It wasn't me."

"Was it Andrew Lindeman?" Thad asked calmly.

That tripped the chief up for a second. "They don't tell me that."

"'They'? Who's 'they'?" Thad willed him to talk, meeting Chief Thomas's grim eyes.

Seconds passed and then Wade stared down at his desk. The degree of his gravity began to alarm Thad. Whatever haunted him, whatever trouble he'd gotten himself into, he saw no way out.

"My mother isn't the only political figure targeted for assassination," Thad said. "You can stop them."

Slowly, Wade's despondent eyes lifted. Thad didn't think Wade was actually seeing him, his thoughts were that heavy.

"It's bigger than you can imagine," Wade finally said, not sounding like the chief of police Thad knew.

"Is it some kind of extremist political organization?" Thad asked.

The desperation emanating from Wade slid behind a blank stare that chilled Thad. The chief opened one of the desk drawers. When he lifted a gun, Thad lost his breath. Would he shoot him?

He pulled his own gun from its holster. But Wade put the gun to his own head and, looking at Thad, fired.

Chapter 19

The chief had left Thad and Darcy with more unanswered questions than they'd had going into this. Wearing gloves, Thad carefully went through Wade's desk. His body had been removed and the police station cleared of unessential personnel. A place of law enforcement had become a crime scene.

"Something weird is going on," Darcy said from over at the two four-drawer file cabinets against the wall nearest to the desk.

He could say that again.

"Why are all these people involved in killing political figures? Why Mike Harris?"

Why Jaden? Why Andrew Lindeman? Why anyone? He'd talked to Sam already. His brother didn't know anything about Mike's plan to assassinate their mother. He was in deep shock over it. He couldn't believe his friend had done something so extreme. He hadn't seen the signs, hadn't recognized his friend had lost his mind.

Jaden had tried to leave the window and the side entrance door unlocked for Mike. He'd been helping both Cam and Mike. And now that Thad looked back on the night Lucy was kidnapped, he now realized why Mike had waited so long to call the police. Lucy's kidnapping had interrupted his attempt to get into the estate. If Thad hadn't seen Jaden unlock the door and disable the security system, he may have gotten in and killed Kate.

But he'd gone after Lucy instead. He had liked Lucy when he'd met her and had chosen to save her from Jaden rather than go to the side entrance door. That suggested he still had something of a heart, and whatever had driven him to try and kill Kate must have been bigger than he could manage.

"Might as well call it a night," Darcy said. "Avery is making dinner tonight. This isn't going anywhere anyway."

Darcy going home to his new love preparing dinner made Thad think of Lucy. Before he'd seen her held against her will with a pistol to her head, Darcy's romantic comment would have bothered him. Now he felt agreement.

The investigation wasn't going anywhere between now and tomorrow. Besides, there was something he wanted to do before going back to the estate…and Lucy.

"Is Lucy okay? She had quite a scare," Darcy said.

"She's doing fine. Staying at the estate to be safe. Mike was one shooter. There might be more." Thad went over some pages he'd found in Wade's desk drawer.

"Yeah." Darcy closed the file cabinet drawer and moved to the messy bookshelf. "I get nervous about living with Avery. I'm afraid for her safety, too. Wade isn't a threat anymore but that doesn't mean the threat is gone."

No. The opposite. The threat was greater than ever.

Darcy picked up a gaudy bear figurine that was left from Christmas, turning it in his hand for inspection.

"Have your feelings changed for Lucy?" Darcy put the bear back on the shelf and faced him.

Thad continued to study the pages he held, but a grin formed on his mouth.

Darcy chuckled. "I knew it."

"Excuse me, Agent Winston."

Thad looked toward the office door to see Gladys, the receptionist. She'd stayed to take care of the basic needs of the team and assisting in any office logistics that came up, like tracking down other officers or sending faxes or emails. A lot went into a crime scene investigation, and Gladys had the stomach for it.

"We just got a call from the Wake County Coroner's Office."

What now?

"Andrew Lindeman's body was found on the side of a country road. He was shot in the head."

Thad slapped down the stack of papers he'd been going through onto the desk. Great. Everyone who could tell him something about the political organization behind all this madness was either dead or not talking.

"They'll send over the autopsy report once it's completed."

"Thanks, Gladys. You might as well go home. We're wrapping this up for the night."

She hesitated in the doorway. "Are you sure? I'm glad to stay and help."

"I know. I've got to get back to my mother's estate."

He saw her ascertain that meaning. Apparently some-one had told her he was taken. Lucy was also staying at Kate's. Rumor did have its advantages. He didn't want Gladys having any false hopes for him. She always flirted with him, but he was no longer available.

Six weeks ago, he'd have cringed at that notion. Now it just felt…natural.

Lucy closed the book she and Sophie had read together. Sophie had started out with the reading, and Lucy had taken over when her eyes began to droop. Sophie's reading had improved by leaps and bounds over the past few weeks. Lucy had worked with her diligently and it had paid off.

Putting the book down, she turned off the light and bent to kiss Sophie on her forehead. While Thad had spent the day working, she'd been busy taking care of Sophie's future. With a smile on the inside, she left the room. Going downstairs for something to drink before she went to bed, she heard Thad talking to Kate and a spark of gladness hit her. They were in the informal sitting room, Kate with a book facedown on her lap and a steaming cup of tea on the dainty side table, Thad standing nearby, loosening his tie.

He saw her, and warmth for her smoothed the tension from his face.

"I was just asking Thad where he's been," Kate said. "I called the station at six and Gladys said you left."

It was after eight now.

"I had an errand to run." Thad turned to Lucy. "We need to talk."

Kate perked up. She stood from the chair. "I'll leave you two alone."

"No," Thad said. "You might as well hear this, too. You're as much invested in this as we are."

Lucy eyed him with a silent, *Invested in what?* He was acting strange. She hadn't had much opportunity to talk to him since Mike held her hostage, but his entire demeanor had changed. The way he looked at her, all warm and full of intimacy.

He took her hands. "Lucy, meeting you has taught me a few things."

Hope flew high as a kite and she had to hang on before it got away from her. What was this all about? She dared not speculate.

"The first and most important is that I should never say never. I never thought I'd fall in love with anyone. I didn't believe in love. But, Lucy, I do love you."

"Thad…"

"Shh." He lifted her hands and kissed the top of one. "I was afraid if I admit I could or did love you, that I'd be forced to marry you."

"Thad, wait." She had to tell him what she did today.

"Lucy, I was wrong. It's okay if I love you. In fact, it's a good thing."

Oh, dear God…

"Love isn't the problem. Love is what makes a relationship great. It—"

"Thad, I'm going to adopt Sophie," she said before he could go on.

That stopped him short. He stared at her, his hands squeezing hers briefly.

"What?" he finally said.

"Oh, this is getting good," Kate said, an avid audience. She picked up her tea and sipped with a delighted gleam to her eyes.

"I'm going to adopt her," Lucy said. "I know you don't want kids, but I can't abandon her. I just can't. She loves it here…with me…a-and you, but if all she has is me, she'll be all right. She'll be happy. She's already happy. And then when I find a man who can accept her, she'll be part of a family. My family."

Thad's jaw had dropped as he struggled to recover from her news.

"I'm sorry I didn't tell you before I started the process going," Lucy continued, fretting over his reaction. Was he taking this worse than she thought? "I didn't think it mattered. I'd made up my mind and what you wanted… well…so far hasn't been what I want, and—"

"Lucy." He finally found his voice. "It's okay."

That stunned her for a second. "It is?"

He chuckled, as amazed as her over his easy acceptance of adopting Sophie. "You surprised me with how soon you decided to adopt her, but it's something I was going to suggest anyway."

"You were?" both she and Kate said in unison.

Kate's cup clanked against the saucer as she put it down.

Thad let go of Lucy's hands and reached into his pocket. He brought out a small jewelry box.

All the blood drained from Lucy's face she was so taken aback. She searched Thad's face.

Kate drew in a startled breath. "Thad. Are you…?"

He looked at her. "This is why I wanted you to be here, Mother." Then he returned all his wonderful attention to Lucy.

He opened the box to reveal a simple but stunning round brilliant cut diamond. "This is my promise to you, Lucy. I'm not ready for marriage yet, but if there's going to be any woman who will give me the courage to stand on an altar, it's you."

Taking the ring out of the box, he let Kate take the box and then held Lucy's left hand and slipped on the ring.

She admired it for several seconds, still shocked by his gesture. Did he mean it?

She looked at him. "A promise ring?"

"A promise to marry you…someday."

She'd give him all the time he needed. "Oh, Thad." She flung herself at him, wrapping her arms around him and kissing his mouth.

He held her and kissed her back.

Then doubt raised its head. She leaned back. "Are you sure?"

"I've been sure ever since Mike put his gun to your head. Imagining life without you forced me to take a closer look at my attitude. I've been wasting a lot of time, Lucy. I'm glad I did, because maybe I'd have married the wrong woman. But I'm sure now."

"Sophie…"

"Will be part of this family."

"Our family?"

A family. Everything she'd always wanted. She wasn't getting it the conventional way. She wouldn't be married first and she was adopting her first child, but she couldn't be happier.

"Where do you want to live?" Thad asked her.

That hardly mattered. "Your house. Your mother told me about your house. It's bigger than mine but similar architecture. We'll need the space."

"My house it is. And when it comes time to have children of our own, you don't have to work."

Had he actually said "kids of their own"? "I want to

work." She needed to feel accomplished over something, and she genuinely liked nursing. And after working with Kate, she felt well on her way to making her own reputation, rather than on her father's white coattails.

"Whatever makes you happy," Thad said.

Lucy's smile beamed along with Thad's lopsided grin, each of them giddy with thoughts of a future together.

"A celebration is in order," Kate said, her eyes a bit misty. She put her hand on Thad's shoulder. "I'm so proud of you."

Lucy held her hand up to admire the ring over Thad's shoulder. "I can't wait to tell my parents!"

Thad stepped back and took her right hand. "Excuse us, Mother. We need some privacy now."

Kate laughed lightly. "You can have all the privacy you need. I'll make sure no one bothers you."

Lucy felt a little embarrassed as Thad winked back at his mother before leading her toward the stairs and the bed they'd occupy for however long it took to satisfy this new acceptance of their love.

They had a future now. Together. She, Thad and Sophie. A family. And a dream come true.

* * * * *

Available June 3, 2014

#1803 OPERATION UNLEASHED
Cutter's Code • by Justine Davis

Drew offers to marry his brother's widow and care for her son, though he never expects to fall for Alyssa. But when the child is kidnapped, Drew will do whatever it takes to make his family whole again.

#1804 SPECIAL OPS RENDEZVOUS
The Adair Legacy • by Karen Anders

After surviving torture, soldier Sam Winston sees threats everywhere. When his politician mother is almost killed, he teams up with his psychiatrist, the mysterious Olivia, to find the assassin. Except Olivia is keeping a secret....

#1805 PROTECTING HER ROYAL BABY
The Mansfield Brothers • by Beth Cornelison

As Brianna Coleman suffers amnesia, Hunter Mansfield vows to protect her...even when her baby proves to be royalty hunted by international assassins. But can he protect his heart?

#1806 LONE STAR REDEMPTION
by Colleen Thompson

When Jessie Layton arrives seeking her missing twin, rancher Zach Rayford defends his mother's lies. Together, they confront dangerous secrets, including the parentage of the "miracle child" holding Zach's family together.

YOU CAN FIND MORE INFORMATION ON UPCOMING HARLEQUIN® TITLES, FREE EXCERPTS AND MORE AT WWW.HARLEQUIN.COM.

HRSCNM0514

REQUEST YOUR FREE BOOKS!
2 FREE NOVELS PLUS 2 FREE GIFTS!

HARLEQUIN®

ROMANTIC suspense

Sparked by danger, fueled by passion

"We did this."

Her voice was soft, almost a whisper from behind him.
He spun around. She'd gone up with Luke to get him warm
and dry, and set him up with his current favorite book. He
was already reading well for his age, on to third-grade level
readers, and Drew knew that was thanks to Alyssa. "Yes," he
said, his voice nearly as quiet as hers. "We did."

"It has to stop, Drew."

"Yes."

"What can I do to make that easier?"

God, he hated this. She was being so reasonable, so
understanding. And he felt like a fool because the only answer
he had was "Stop loving my brother."

"I'm not Luke," he said, not quite snapping. "Don't treat
me like a six-year-old."

"Luke," she said sweetly, "is leaving temper tantrums
behind."

He drew back sharply. Opened his mouth, ready to truly snap this time. And stopped.

"Okay," he said after a moment, "I had that one coming."

"Yes."

In an odd way, her dig pleased him. Not because it was accurate, he sheepishly admitted, but because she felt confident enough to do it. She'd been so weak, sick and scared when he'd found her four years ago, going toe-to-toe with him like this would have been impossible. But she was strong now, poised and self-assured. And he took a tiny bit of credit for that.

"You've come a long way," he said quietly.

"Because I don't cower anymore?"

He frowned. "I never made you cower."

For an instant she looked startled. "I never said you did. You saved us, Drew, don't think I don't know that, or will ever forget it. I have come a long way, and it's in large part because you made it possible."

It was a pretty little speech, a sentiment she'd expressed more than once. And not so long ago it had been enough. More than enough. It had told him he'd done exactly what he'd intended. That he'd accomplished his goal. That she was stable now, strong, and he'd had a hand in that.

And it wasn't her fault that wasn't enough for him anymore.

**Don't miss
OPERATION UNLEASHED
by Justine Davis,
available June 2014 from
Harlequin® Romantic Suspense.**

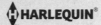
ROMANTIC suspense

SPECIAL OPS RENDEZVOUS
by Karen Anders

The Adair Legacy

Heartstopping danger, breathtaking
passion, conspiracy and intrigue.
The Adair Legacy has it all.

After surviving torture, soldier Sam Winston
sees threats everywhere. But when his politician
mother is almost killed, he teams up with his
psychiatrist, the mysterious Olivia, to find the
assassin. Except Olivia is keeping a secret....

Look for *SPECIAL OPS RENDEZVOUS* by
Karen Anders in June 2014. Available wherever
books and ebooks are sold.

Don't miss other titles from
The Adair Legacy miniseries:
HIS SECRET, HER DUTY by Carla Cassidy
EXECUTIVE PROTECTION by Jennifer Morey

Heart-racing romance, high-stakes suspense!

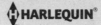

ROMANTIC suspense

PROTECTING HER ROYAL BABY
by Beth Cornelison

The Mansfield Brothers

A woman in labor. A man on a mission.
The Mansfield Brothers series continues...

As Brianna Coleman suffers amnesia, Hunter
Mansfield vows to protect her...even when her baby
proves to be royalty hunted by international assassins.
He'll do anything, pay the ultimate price if necessary,
for one chance to save the woman he loves and her
royal baby. But can he protect his heart?

Look for *PROTECTING HER ROYAL BABY* from
The Mansfield Brothers series by Beth Cornelison
in June 2014. Available wherever books and
ebooks are sold.

Also from *The Mansfield Brothers* miniseries by
Beth Cornelison: THE RETURN OF CONOR MANSFIELD

Available wherever ebooks are sold.

Heart-racing romance, high-stakes suspense!

www.Harlequin.com